THE PRICE OF PASSION

"Deliciously fun, naughty, and intriguing. . . . Palfrey effectively spins a tale of romance, red-hot sex, and mystery. . . . A thriller of a novel that will keep you turning the pages long past your appointed bedtime."

—*The Austin Chronicle*

"Well-developed . . . includes a few surprises, subtle humor and a mystery to be solved. . . . Evelyn Palfrey is carving out a niche with what she calls 'romantic suspense for the marvelously mature.'"

—*The Romance Reader*

"Every woman should read this . . . it is realistically done and pulls you into the story immediately."

—*Rendezvous*

"Engages with its attractive, sympathetic heroine."

—*Publishers Weekly*

"Palfrey always manages to spice her tales with murder, mystery and mayhem."

—Cox News Service (Austin, TX)

"Full of plot twists. . . . A thoughtful story about a woman finding the strength to reinvent herself. . . . Romance novels aren't always for everyone. But for those who can fully appreciate the genre, *The Price of Passion* is worth the read."

—*American-Statesman* (Austin, TX)

ALSO BY EVELYN PALFREY

The Price of Passion

dangerous DILemmas

EVELYN PALFREY

POCKET BOOKS

New York   London   Toronto   Sydney   Singapore

This book is a work of fiction. Names, characters, places and incidents are products of the author's imagination or are used fictitiously. Any resemblance to actual events or locales or persons, living or dead, is entirely coincidental.

 POCKET BOOKS, a division of Simon & Schuster, Inc.
1230 Avenue of the Americas, New York, NY 10020

ISBN: 0-671-04222-X

First Pocket Books trade paperback printing June 2001

10 9 8 7 6 5 4 3 2

POCKET and colophon are registered trademarks of Simon & Schuster, Inc.

Designed by Ruth Lee

Cover design by Anna Dorfman
Front cover illustration by Bryan Haynes

Printed in the U.S.A.

TREMENDOUS THANKS

To Delma Lopez, the lady who makes sure I put all the commas in, and who doesn't want me to lay at all.

To Tina Allen and Jeannye Polk, still the romance queens.

To Detective Pat Bailey, Casey Calhoun, Cecil Carter, Jr., Sue Coburn, Mosell Cofer, Peggy Evans, Irishman Frank Foerster, Joel Goldstein, Myra Green, Attorney Ken Houp, Sylvia Kenig, Judge Karrie Key, Judge Beverly Landers, Margarita Lee, Kim Pannachi, Gayle Posey, Velva Price, Lois Faye Randel, Judge Mitchell Solomon, Joyce Stanley, Detective Joel Thompson, Dawn Tisdale, Mimi Tran, Nancy Walls, and Barbara Williams for steering me in the right direction.

To Nigel Gusdorf, my electronic wizard, and the man I call on when my computer does weird things.

Long live the Beacho's. You know who you are.

To all the booksellers who work tirelessly, against great odds, to bring all of us the pleasure of reading. And to those brave souls who fought the good fight and still couldn't keep their stores open. It was a loss for all of us.

To the book clubs who selected my books for your discussions.

I hope you had fun. To those who invited me, I hope you had as good a time as I did.

To my readers. Your letters and e-mails saying that you enjoyed *Three Perfect Men* and *The Price of Passion* encouraged me in a way you can never know.

Thank you.

special
THanks

To Emma Rodgers, for your unrelenting support and advice.

To Judith Curr, Linda Marrow, Amy Pierpont, Christina Boys, and Jane Chelius for making the rocky places smooth.

To Lois Palfrey, my mother, for giving me a love of words. It was all those "thank-you" letters that you insisted I send, and crossword puzzles we shared, and word games we played that made me a writer. I hope I've made you proud.

To John Palfrey, my father, for instilling in me the certainty that I can do anything I put my mind to. Your spirit continues to guide me.

To my sister, Vanessa, for being the best friend a girl can have, and for reminding me that love comes in queen size, too.

To John and Meredith, for making me a stronger and better person than I would have been had I not been blessed with you.

Dangerous Dilemmas

THE DEATH

The gun felt hard. It felt strange. It even looked strange in his hand. Malcolm couldn't remember ever holding one before. His heart was pounding and beads of sweat were popping out on his forehead, even in the cool winter night. What to do with it now? He couldn't just walk down the street with it in his hand. If a cop saw him, he'd be dog meat. Put it in his pocket and calmly walk away? Yeah, he could figure out how to get rid of it later. But, with the silencer attached, it was too long to fit in his pocket. Should he tuck it in his waistband and pull his jacket around it?

The sound of bells jingling drew his eye from the gun to the store's partially opened door. A long, red arc smeared down the glass as the man stumbled through the opening, holding on to the door. Then he lost his grip and fell on the sidewalk close to Malcolm's feet.

Blood pumped out of his chest and formed a spreading pool on the sidewalk. Malcolm watched, horrified, as it spread under his expensive sneakers—the ones he'd bought from a crackhead for ten dollars.

The screams he heard couldn't have come from the mute face staring at him because the lips didn't move. When he looked up, he saw that the screams came from a trio of teen girls under the Houston's Finest Pawn Shop sign. One jumped up and down pointing from him to the man on the ground. Another held her hands over her ears, as if to protect them from her own screams. The third covered her eyes. None of them covered their screaming mouths.

A young woman rushed out of the store with a dazed look on her face. Her coal black hair fell in a blunt cut to her chin. Her jeans and T-shirt said all-American, but her eyes were of a place far away. She knelt on the sidewalk beside the old man and spoke softly to him in a language Malcolm didn't understand. Then, she looked up at Malcolm with big, sorrowful eyes.

Just then an ancient woman shuffled through the doorway, her arms wrapped around her waist, desperately clutching at her kimono. Standing behind the young one, she didn't utter a word, but her eyes spoke of the beauty of a faraway world. They spoke of having been wrenched from a dangerous and death-filled homeland, of being deposited in another that was supposed to be safe. A safe place where the future budded with endless possibilities. Only hard work was required to bring it to full bloom, and they were accustomed to hard work. Now the lifeblood of that beautiful flower was spread on the sidewalk.

Tears rolled down the young one's cheeks, then she bowed her head, and Malcolm could no longer see the pain in her eyes. He wanted to touch her, to console her, to tell her he was sorry. But he felt the hard, warm gun in his hand. And the teenagers were still screaming. A bag lady hurriedly gathered up her bundles and slinked away. Two men ran toward him. One shouted, "Police! Somebody call the police!" The other shouted "Somebody stop him."

Malcolm felt his feet moving. His hand opened and the gun made a clattering sound when it hit the pavement. He ran. Ran as fast as the expensive, ten-dollar sneakers would take him.

one

$\mathcal{A}$udrey held the motor home steady on the bumpy road. She expertly steered the big vehicle through the construction zone with no fear of hitting the concrete bunkers on both sides that formed the narrowed lanes. She smiled to herself with the thought that she was a better driver than Sam, even though he refused to let her drive him. Sam and all his macho bullshit. She was glad he wasn't with her on this trip—and glad RosaLee had agreed to come. After all that had happened, she felt the need to spend some time with her daughter. To try to draw closer to her first born. Or maybe she needed to give some of the mothering she felt she'd missed. It wasn't that she'd ignored her duty. It was just that this child hadn't needed as much mothering. In many ways had refused it. And Audrey hadn't insisted. Wouldn't have done any good with this child anyway. RosaLee had always had a mind of her own. Old folks say, when a child matures fast the way she had, they're getting out of the way for another. But Malcolm hadn't come for three years.

Malcolm had been different. Difficult birth, sickly baby, hyper-active kid. Although the art teacher had appreciated his talent, he was misunderstood at school, an underachiever. And now, at age twenty, this. She forced her mind away from it.

"While you're up, would you bring your ol' mama a soft drink?" Audrey called out in a teasing voice.

"Sure, Mom," RosaLee called back from the rear of the motor home.

Audrey crimped her mouth. Mom. She hated that. Too modern. Too White. What was wrong with "Mama"? When RosaLee set the two cans in the console, Audrey cast a disapproving glance her way.

"RosaLee, don't you think it's a little early?"

"Obviously, I don't. And stop calling me that."

"I mean, honey, wouldn't you rather have some juice?"

"No. Thanks anyway." She propped her feet on the dashboard, popped open the beer can, and put it to her mouth.

"RosaLee, I just don't think—"

"Get off the mother trip, okay? I'm twenty-three years old. I can decide what—and when—I drink. And please stop calling me RosaLee. I'm RL, now. Everybody calls me RL."

"But, baby, RosaLee is so dignified. So significant. When we named you after Mrs. Parks, I never dreamed—"

"It's old-fashioned. I hate it. It's burdensome. Like I have to live up to it. Ain't even any—"

"Aren't," Audrey corrected, in her schoolteacher voice.

"There aren't any buses anymore," RosaLee said, in resentful concession to the correction. "It's rapid transit now. Dallas Area Rapid Transit. It's a new day. And I'm RL."

Audrey didn't want it this way. They'd had this argument a hundred times. This trip wasn't for arguing. It was for healing.

"Alright, RL. I'll call you what you want, but I'm Mama. That's what I want. You hear?"

"I hear you," she said, with an indifferent shrug of one shoulder.

Just as the accord was reached, the construction zone ended and Audrey pulled onto the smooth slab of the interstate. The pine forest on both sides of the road welcomed Audrey home. Only thirty miles to Lake Texarkana. Lake Wright Patman, these days. She couldn't get used to that. Ol' Wright may have been a great guy, but the lake would always be Lake Texarkana to her.

"Why do you always have to drag me off to the country? I hate this. It's always too hot. Or too cold. And the mosquitoes, and the bugs. And no TV reception. And a bunch of old white people sitting around eyeing us like we don't belong. I hate this."

"But I thought we agreed—"

"You agreed, Mom. You agreed. I just didn't argue with you. You never listen, so what's the point."

Anger welled up in Audrey. "Bitch, bitch, bitch. Whine, whine, whine," she wanted to say. But she held her tongue. This was not turning out to be the idyllic mother-daughter trip she'd imagined. She didn't want to make it any worse.

Had she really expected to mother RosaLee? Maybe it was she who needed mothering. Maybe even expected it a little from her strong-willed daughter, who never seemed to need anything, or anybody. That's why she didn't have a husband, or even the prospect of one. Didn't need one. She made good money, even as she waited for her bar exam results. Had bought her own condo, cosigned by her parents, of course. She traveled when she felt like it. RosaLee didn't understand that men need to be needed—even if you have to pretend. And what's so wrong with a little pretending, if you get what you want, and it makes the other person happy? This brutal honesty that her daughter subscribed to was for the birds. In it, nobody got nothing they really wanted. Anything, Audrey corrected herself. She watched RosaLee come back with another beer and held the censure off her face. Held it tight behind the mask that she wore so often now.

The mask was hard as stone. Piece by piece, layer by layer, it had formed over the years. It started that night in college when she was turned away from the hospital. The botched, back-alley abortion had been the result of a dumb mistake on her part, but it shouldn't have been in their hands to let her bleed to death. Then, the day Sam got arrested during a protest march, she added another piece. Watching him ward off the blows from the nightsticks, praying he wouldn't hit them back, knowing they'd surely kill him if he did. Holding herself still to keep from running to block them. Not that they wouldn't have hit her, too, just not as hard. They would strike her out of duty, not out of the primeval hatred against her man that had been inherited, and nurtured, through generations. She could have stood the blows. But her intervention would have lessened him as a man. So she stood still and felt the hardness forming around her mouth.

Then, while he went to law school and she taught school, she was the sole breadwinner. In the face of the whispers, the hardness settled in, then migrated upward to her cheeks. "Ain't she the fool, minding them bad chil'ren all day while he just sitting around on his butt reading. Honey, he gon' divorce her for his first case."

When their babies came and she quit teaching to raise them, "Honey, she thank she big shit now." Watching their savings dwindle away with Sam's "investment" schemes brought it to her eyes. It had hardened into stone by the time she opened her front door to a howling pack of reporters, the bright lights of the TV cameras and the microphones stuck in her face.

"Mrs. Roberts, our viewers want to know how you feel about your son killing the convenience store clerk?"

RosaLee had a mask of her own. There was a certain defiance in the way she held the can of beer, but Audrey refused to be drawn into it. She took a calming breath and slowly expelled it.

"Alright, RL. Pick a place. It's our trip, not mine. We can go anywhere you want—as long as we're back before your father comes home from Chicago on Friday. You know he and I have that Urban League dinner Friday night."

"Why couldn't Daddy come with us? I can't see why he and

Paul both had to go for a deposition. It would have been cheaper to pay that witness's plane fare to Dallas."

"I don't know about that. I'll bet there's a golf course nearby that he and Paul wanted to try—and you know I only bet on a sure thing."

"Golf course? Hey! Why can't we go to the condo? It's not that far."

"Our condo? In Shreveport?" Audrey asked, thoughtfully, then shrugged away her vision of the trip. "We can go there, if you want."

"That's where I want to go," RosaLee said, perking up, snapping her finger, doing a little singsong. "We can go into town. Do a little gambling. Have some real fun."

"You gamble, I'll watch," Audrey said, laughing.

"Aw Mama. Loosen up some. Just make up your mind, you're gonna lose the first hundred."

"Hundred!"

"Scared money can't win, Mama. I'll just give you a hundred, okay? It'll be fun."

Audrey smiled, relaxed her spine against the chair back, and loosened her grip on the steering wheel.

*   *   *

At the gate, Audrey had to show her resident card to the security guard. He was new, and she hadn't been to the condo in how long? More than a year, maybe two. It would probably smell musty from being closed up for so long. She decided that when she got inside, she would open all the windows so it could air out while they were at the casinos. It would be safe with the guard and all, she thought, as she shut the motor off in front of their unit. She walked to the back of the RV and stood over the bed where RosaLee was fast asleep, with her fist pushed under her chin. She'd always slept that way ever since she was a baby.

"RosaLee? We're here."

No answer. Audrey'd forgotten. Wouldn't answer to that name. Audrey rolled her eyes.

"RL?" she grudgingly called to her.

Still no answer. Hard sleep, with that fist under her chin. All that beer, making her sleep hard like that, Audrey thought. Let her sleep 'til she took the food in, then.

Audrey turned and reached a plastic bag from under the sink. She opened the refrigerator and took out the steaks she'd planned to grill under the moonlit sky. Have to do it on the broiler inside now. That's okay. Then the shrimp that she'd planned to sauté in a generous skillet of garlic butter. Oh, and the rice. She filled two plastic grocery bags.

Audrey pulled on the brightly colored, abstract-print jacket to her silk jogging suit. If the designers hadn't taken so long to discover a market in queen sizes, she wouldn't despise plaids and tiny flower prints as she did now. Those were all that were available when she was a young girl, big for her age. Later, when she was a teenager, the dark colors her mother had insisted would make her look smaller made her feel matronly. Now, a confident and well-dressed woman stepped out of the RV.

Their condo sat on a cul-de-sac. Like the others, it appeared to be one story. But they were built on a slope down to the man-made lake, with the master bedroom downstairs from the main level. Sam had handled the legal work for the developer in exchange for clear title to the condo. He'd gotten a lot of used cars from criminal cases that way, too. Cars they hadn't needed. She remembered arguing with him about it. Then, they'd needed money more than a resort condo, but it had turned out to be a good deal. She had lots of memories of good times with the kids and with her friend, MaryBeth.

When she struggled the door open, she didn't hear the buzz of the security system. She could have sworn she left it on. She always did. Maybe Malcolm had been here since she had, she thought. Probably had brought some girl here to show off. Some silly girl with delusions of marrying into money. Some stupid girl, who didn't realize Malcolm had no money because Malcolm wouldn't work. Lord, now she'd have to change the linen.

The curtain was open to the sliding glass door that led to the deck and Audrey could see the big moon peeking through the tree branches. She set the bags on the kitchen table, thinking she could grill the steaks on the deck under the shadow of the tall pines that ringed the lake. She and RL could both have what they wanted. This was going to work out just fine. Maybe she should listen to her daughter more. She was grown now. About to be a lawyer, just like her dad. Audrey would have been thrilled for her to take up teaching, but RosaLee wouldn't even get a teaching certificate in college. She'd said there was no money in it. While Audrey conceded that point logically, she knew in her heart that RL's real motivation was to gain her father's approval.

The place didn't smell musty, as Audrey had expected. She opened the patio door and stood breathing in the clean, fresh smell of the damp night air. Nestled among the pines, the deck was such a romantic setting. Audrey remembered all the times she'd sat there alone, reading, while she waited for Sam to return from his golf game. When he did, he usually immersed himself in work he'd brought from the office. So, she was alone. The kids were usually gone—to the swimming pool, or movies at the clubhouse, or fishing in the lake with their newly made friends from around the resort. This was her place. Her quiet, alone place. She decided to wait until morning to uncover the patio furniture and arrange it just the way she liked it. Maybe RL would join her here for coffee in the morning. Right now she needed to wake her up.

When she started for the front door, she frowned at the pile of dirty dishes in the sink. Out of the corner of her eye, she saw a faint, flickering light. Downstairs. Couldn't be Malcolm—he was in jail. She walked to the top of the stairs. Could that be a candle in the bedroom below? Stupid Sam. Hardheaded Sam. She'd told him to take their condo off the rental list. She didn't like the thought of strangers in her house, sleeping on her sheets, using her dishes. They didn't need the money now—or the tax deduction. And who were these fools who left a candle burning while they partied at the casino?

Descending the stairs, she saw a piece of cloth. At the foot of the stairs, she bent over and picked it up, then realizing it was a pair of briefs, dropped them and shook her hand. Nasty people, too, she thought. The bedroom door was ajar. When she pushed it open, she knew she should turn and leave quietly. But she couldn't. She was mesmerized. She knew they hadn't heard her; they were too absorbed in their lovemaking. No, not lovemaking. Not the tender, rhythmic joining that she longed for. Fucking. Humping. The man humping.

The stark contrast of pale legs on either side of brown ones. Hairy legs, all four of them. Straight hair, curly hair. White toes, brown toes, white toes. Audrey had never seen anything like it. In the flickering candlelight, she couldn't see their faces, only the backs of their heads. Short, kinky hair, surrounding a bald spot. Short, straight hair, surrounding a bald spot. Then, she heard his groaning. A familiar sound. Familiar voice.

"Ou, that's it, Paul. Baby, that's it. Right there."

Audrey stood rooted to the spot, as a wave of nausea washed over her. She knew what would come next. How many times had she heard it?

"I'm coming. Daddy's com-ing!"

Then the shudder. The release. Then the collapse of his weight on her.

"Sam? Paul? What's going on here?" The sound of her voice was muffled, as though it reflected back to her through a wall of cotton.

What a stupid question, Audrey thought. Her mind was a ball of confusion. What should she do? Her first urge was to throw something at them. A biblical-like stoning. But she had no stones. Audrey watched Paul pulling the sheet around himself like a cocoon, and Sam scurrying around, almost comically, trying to put on his robe—the robe RosaLee had given him for Christmas. Sam rushed toward her and grabbed her by her upper arms.

"What are you doing here?" Sam demanded.

The answer was simple. RosaLee—RV—casino. But the words balled up in her mouth like a big wad of stale gum, sticking to each other and her mouth, unable to come out. So many thoughts were crashing into each other, she thought her head would explode. You. Paul. Partners. Chicago last month, San Francisco the month before. Austin. Bar conventions. Golf tournaments. How many years? How long? How could she not have known?

"Go upstairs!" he shouted, pushing her.

Audrey stumbled backward, then regained her footing. She returned his shove, then shoved him again harder, the heels of her fists crashing into his chest. With clenched teeth and an upswing of her arm, she slapped his face. A solid connection that felt good all the way from her hand, up her arm, to her heart. He grabbed for her arm, just as her other hand landed on the side of his head. She'd reached all the way back to East Texas—to the kids calling her "Fat Audrey"—for that one. Sam was stunned by the force of it. Before he could recover, she tore into him like a tornado through a trailer park. Pummeling his face, clawing at his eyes, snatching at his ears. Sam protected his face with his forearm and blindly grabbed at her flailing arms.

"Audrey! Audrey! Calm down!"

She couldn't tell which one was calling her back from that wild place. She felt Paul pulling her from behind, his arms clamped around her waist. "Don't touch me! Don't touch me! You bastard!" she shouted, wrestling in his grasp. She jerked her elbow backward, smashing it into his nose. Paul howled in pain as he fell back on the bed, holding his nose. In that instant, Sam uncovered his face and reached for her arms. He got hold of one, but with the other she continued pounding his head. He grabbed her in a bear hug, and in the jostling they fell on the bed on top of Paul. Audrey thrashed out of his grasp, mindless of Paul's painful yells underneath them.

RosaLee! What if she awoke and walked in on this scene? How would they explain it? What would RosaLee think? No child should witness something like this. Protecting her child was a stronger urge than killing Sam. Audrey had to get out. Now.

Her final blow knocked Sam away from her. She scrambled off the bed, stumbled up the stairs, and rushed out the door.

TWO

*A*udrey sat in her overstuffed chair in the den to catch a little breather. She had put in a full day already—and it wasn't even noon. Steam rose from the cup of strong, black coffee on the lamp table next to her. The first thing she had done when she got back from Shreveport last night was call a twenty-four-hour locksmith. There would be no need for Sam to ever cross her threshold again. If he did, she would kill him for sure. For deceiving her for years. For making her live a lie for so long. For not giving her a choice. She'd kill him. Dead. Dead as the place inside her.

The next thing she did, starting at dawn this morning, was methodically remove his presence. She stripped the bed and put on the really frilly sheets that she loved but that he hated. Then she stuffed his suits, shirts, socks, and underwear into big, black garbage bags. She unceremoniously raked all his paraphernalia off the top of the highboy into a box. In the bathroom, the masculine toiletries went into the box, too. Then, she sprayed the room with a suffocating dose of disinfectant to mask the aroma of his favorite cologne. It had permeated the room for years, and she wondered how many coats of paint it would take to eliminate it altogether. She carried it all, bag by bag, box by box, and dumped it in the driveway, blocking the path to the side of the garage where he usually parked his car. That last box took a little starch out of her collar. There had been a time she would have kept going until the job was done, but at this age she'd learned to pace herself. The office was all that was left. She'd tackle it when she finished this cup of coffee.

The little green parrot called to her from his cage on the hearth. "Audee! Polly wanna seed! Audee! Polly wanna seed!" Audrey knew Polly would keep it up until she gave in, so she walked to the fireplace and gave her a few sunflower seeds.

The four of them stared at Audrey from the portrait over the fireplace. She kept her eyes on RosaLee to keep from looking at him. If it wasn't for RosaLee, she would take that portrait down and razor-blade his ass right out of there. But how would she explain that? How would she explain any of it?

RosaLee had bought her story about the condo being rented. When they checked into the hotel next to the casino, Audrey faked illness and went straight to the room. She didn't really have to fake. The image of Sam and Paul stuck in her mind and made her sick. The next day she was so despondent she couldn't make herself get out of bed. When RosaLee had come back to the room around noon to check on her, Audrey told her it was only a stomach bug and that RosaLee should go back and have some fun.

Even flush with gambling fever, RosaLee insisted on staying with her mother. But under these circumstances, Audrey couldn't turn to RosaLee for comfort, and she couldn't mourn with her in the room. A couple of hours of the motherly attention she had longed for from her daughter before was all Audrey could stand. She called a travel agency and booked a four-day Las Vegas trip for two from Dallas. She insisted that RosaLee call a friend to go with her—even suggested that nice young fellow who had escorted her to the Law Day banquet. Reluctantly RosaLee had agreed and drove Audrey home. By the time RosaLee got back,

Audrey would figure out something to tell her about the breakup.

The marriage might have survived another woman. Fidelity was something she'd just assumed with Sam. And he'd never given any of the signs of another woman. No wonder, she thought in disgust. She'd put twenty-five years of her life into Sam, into this marriage. Everything that she was, everything that she had, was tied up in it. They could have talked about another woman. Surely, she would have ranted and raved about it, even threatened to break the woman's face. Sam would have backed down, she would have forgiven him, the marriage would have survived. She wouldn't allow another woman to destroy all she'd worked for for twenty-five years. But this? What was there to talk about? What was there to work through? It was too deep for her to even try.

Audrey refilled her cup, then went upstairs to the spare bedroom that Sam used as an office. She packed all the books into boxes and was pulling the drawer to the file cabinet open when she heard footfalls on the porch. She stood very still and listened to the sounds of the key in the lock. When she heard yanking on the door, Audrey set her coffee cup on the desk and braced herself. She didn't know exactly what to say. She only knew that he couldn't come in. She started downstairs. Relief rushed out in her sigh when she saw MaryBeth through the beveled glass panel to the side of the front door.

"MaryBeth. What are you doing here this time of day? And dressed like that? You didn't jog over here, did you?"

"You know I don't jog. There's not a sunscreen made that would keep me from burning. I came by to feed the damned bird, like you asked me to," she said, breezing into the foyer without stopping. "What are you doing here? You just left. I guess. Did you ever leave? Okay, okay, I didn't feed the damned bird yesterday. I meant to. Things got crazy at the store. It's still alive, right? Gimme some coffee. I know you have some coffee." MaryBeth kept up her monologue as she walked straight to the kitchen. "I'm telling you, they're making me crazy!"

"Come on in, MaryBeth. Would you like a cup of coffee?" Audrey said, quietly and politely, as if MaryBeth was still standing there. She closed the door and followed her friend to the kitchen.

"Those New Yorkers, I swear. They're gonna worry the color out my hair. You like this new color?" MaryBeth fluffed her pixie do, as she posed for Audrey.

"Better than the last one. The red looks better on you than that blonde. I like your natural color best, though. You better be careful with that stuff. Your hair is gonna all fall out one day."

"You could use a little color yourself," she said, settling herself on the bar stool. "You've just got to do something about that gray, Audrey."

Oh, God. Here we go again, Audrey thought, rolling her eyes.

"A little rinse or something. I'll do it for you. I've gotten quite good at it, don't you think," MaryBeth asked, shaking her head and fluffing her hair.

Audrey almost laughed at the thought of MaryBeth tangling up with her warrior woman hair. She knew who would win that one. "You've done fine, MaryBeth."

"You know I could afford a salon now. A real salon. And I could even get a discount in the salon at the store. But I've been doing it myself so long, ever since that bastard—"

"Have some coffee, MaryBeth," Audrey interrupted. "Hand me your cup." She knew what was coming next. She didn't want to hear his name.

"Paul left me for Pimbo," MaryBeth continued undeterred. "You know I call her Pimbo, because she probably still had pimples when he ditched me. Too young to be a bimbo, even. Maybe she's outgrown that. She must be thirty by now. She better be careful.

Getting to the ditching age. Five more years, max. Course, I bet he can't even get it up anymore. He turned fifty last year. Maybe she'll ditch him," MaryBeth laughed.

Audrey heard the bitterness in the laugh, saw it in her blue eyes. She wished MaryBeth would stop dwelling on the past. Sure, it had been a bad time, a hard time, being left with three children, kicked out of her beautiful home, having to take a job as a clerk at nearly forty. And Paul had acted like a real cad. Hiding assets, pretending to be broke, refusing to pay child support. While MaryBeth struggled with maternal responsibilities, Paul flaunted his masculine prerogatives. She paid for braces on the extended payment plan. He bought a powerboat.

But MaryBeth had survived. Triumphed, even. She'd pulled her rusty college degree off the shelf, added her natural organizational skills, and worked herself up from clerk in the department store to head buyer. The kids had survived it, too. Now Paula was a second-year med student and Jason had a good job doing "something important with computers," as MaryBeth put it. When the baby, Ryan, left for college last year, MaryBeth moved into the cutest condo. She was living large now, but it had been a real high-wire act for years.

It had been a tightrope for Audrey, too. She and MaryBeth had been through so much together. Helping their husbands with the fledgling law office—MaryBeth as secretary, Audrey as book-keeper. Having their babies together. Then, when the practice stabilized and the children were in school, doing volunteer work together. Audrey wouldn't think of turning her back on her friend, as some of the other Bar wives had. They'd remained fast friends through MaryBeth's sudden downward spiral. She couldn't divorce MaryBeth, just because Paul had. And their kids had remained friends. But Paul had been Sam's law partner, so they were all in her life. And although she'd been polite to Pimbo, she couldn't cozy up to her. It wasn't the girl's fault, but Audrey resented her having the advantages and comforts born of Mary-Beth's hard work and sacrifices. There had been some awkward moments, like Christmases, but somehow it had worked out, and with no blood shed.

"You know that son-of-a-bitch called me yesterday? Haven't heard from him in a year. Then out of the blue, he calls. Just like we're old friends," MaryBeth huffed.

Audrey's eyebrows raised slightly. "What did he want?" She steeled herself. She wasn't ready for anybody else to know just yet. This was stupid. Why did she feel a need to guard Sam's secret?

"That's the weird part. He was just too chatty. How'm I doing? How're the kids doing? Like he gives a damn."

"That's all?" Audrey asked warily.

"Well, he asked about you—before I hung up on him."

"Oh yeah? What did he say?" Audrey wore a worried look.

"To hell with him. I'm tellin' you, Audrey. You need to do something about that gray. You're lucky to have a man like Sam. I know he's been a good husband, but he's getting to that 'middle-age crazy' stage. His eye might begin to wander. He might decide he needs a younger woman, too."

"I doubt it," Audrey said, looking off.

"You never know," MaryBeth said with certainty.

"I know. For sure," Audrey answered with her own certainty.

She wanted to tell MaryBeth so bad she could taste it. Who else could she tell? Telling her would relieve some of the pain. And the knowledge would be healing for MaryBeth, too. But, knowing MaryBeth, she'd rent a billboard right in downtown Dallas for all the world to know. It would vindicate her. But, having a gay ex-husband was different from having a gay husband. It would be humiliating to Audrey to have people whispering behind her back and laughing at her. And what about the kids? Maybe MaryBeth would keep it under wraps for her kids' sake. No, she wouldn't.

They'd suffered at Paul's hands, too. Audrey thought of her own children, and how devastating it would be to them. No, she couldn't tell MaryBeth. She had to keep Sam's little secret for all their sakes. Audrey spied the cup in the sink.

"What are the Yankees doing to you now, MaryBeth?" Audrey asked, changing the subject as she picked the cup up and dropped it in the trash can under the sink.

"Why'd you do that?" MaryBeth asked, a wide-eyed, elfin look on her face.

"What?"

"Put that perfectly good cup in the trash. Sam's favorite cup."

"Oh, that? Well, he won't be needing it anymore."

"How can you be sure?"

Audrey picked up her own cup and took a sip, trying to buy time. She hadn't had time to think of what she would eventually tell MaryBeth. But MaryBeth was in and out of her house so often, Audrey knew she couldn't hide Sam's absence from MaryBeth for long. She set the cup on the counter.

"He doesn't live here anymore."

"What!"

"I've put him out." Audrey jutted up her chin, as though that would make MaryBeth drop it. But she knew better.

"Are you crazy? Are you okay, Audrey? It's that bleeding, Audrey. It's making you crazy. You need to do what the doctor says."

"Dammit!" Audrey shouted. "It's not the bleeding, MaryBeth!" She saw the look on MaryBeth's face and softened her voice for as much truth as she was willing to tell. "It's someone else."

MaryBeth slumped on the stool, defeated. "I should've known. The black ones aren't any different than the white ones. How young is she?"

"It's not . . . age doesn't have anything to do with it."

"She's his age? Oh, shit. This is serious. Can I do anything?"

"Bring your cup. I was packing his stuff. Come on up to the office."

★   ★   ★

"Wow-wee, you're really serious," MaryBeth exclaimed when she saw the boxes lining the upstairs hallway.

"As a heart attack. Tape the bottom of these boxes. I'll just dump these file drawers in them."

"Wait a minute, Audrey. You need to look at these files. There may be something you'll need. Income tax stuff. Car titles. Better for you to have it than have to pay a lawyer to make him turn it over later. That is, if this thing gets that far."

"I don't believe Sam would try to cheat me."

"Yeah, right. That's what I thought about Paul, too. Don't you remember how Paul hid all the records from me?"

Audrey remembered that debacle. How angry Sam had been at having the partnership records, his business records, subpoenaed. How anxious they both had been at the prospect of having to testify. Then MaryBeth ran out of money to pay her lawyer. Audrey wondered what lawyers charged these days.

"Sam won't give me any trouble."

"Whatever you say, Audrey. But I've been through this." MaryBeth took over, handing Audrey files to put in the box, laying others on the desk. "Stock portfolio stays here. Who is Amanda Goff?"

"Client."

"To the box."

When the file cabinet was empty, Audrey said, "You can unplug all this computer equipment, while I get the boxes it came in from the attic. I'll be right back."

"Don't be stupid, Audrey. He has computers at the office. You may need this equipment. If nothing else, for quick cash at the pawnshop."

★   ★   ★

After MaryBeth left, Audrey walked back to the office and opened the closet. None of Sam's clothes in there, just boxes. What was the computer box doing here? She pulled it out and opened it. She recognized the frames immediately. She'd bought them for Malcolm's drawings. The one on top was a portrait of Sam. A stick man with a big, brown head. Audrey remembered spelling the caption for him while he laboriously wrote the letters—"The Best Dad in the Wold." She hadn't corrected his spelling because he had been so proud of those letters. There was one for every Father's Day from first grade until he'd officially quit school. Eleven in all. Each year, the medium was less childlike, from crayons to ink; the style more proficient, from stick men to starkly realistic faces; the tone more angry, from smiling faces to defiant features. Since she rarely went in Sam's office she hadn't missed them, but she knew now when they were put in the box.

Audrey remembered the night of the first collect call from the Houston jail. Instead of Sam turning to her for consolation, or giving her consolation, instead of them discussing it, he'd made his pronouncement. I've done all I'm going to do for him. I told him the last time. Not another penny. We're washing our hands of him. Then he'd come into this room and closed the door. She had sat in her overstuffed chair in the living room. Alone, except for Polly.

Now, looking at the stick man picture, she did what she had wanted to do—what she should have done—that night. She picked up the phone and dialed Houston information.

"I need the listing for Sondra Ellis."

THree

Two days later, Audrey walked out of the jail visitation room, holding herself together the best she could. She didn't feel that she belonged there. But what was different about her, from any of the other mothers?

Thirty minutes before, seated across from her in his drab jail uniform and plastic slide shoes, Malcolm had repeated the same story he'd told her in those collect calls. If the story hadn't been so preposterous, she might have believed it.

He was just walking down the street, on his way by his homeboy's to score a little weed. A tall, pale white man backed out of a store and bumped into him. "Say! What's up, fool?" Malcolm had said in his most threatening tone, his street voice. The man turned around and put a gun to his head. Malcolm grabbed the barrel of the gun and pushed it away. He'd always had quick reflexes. Something had spooked the pale white man, because he turned loose the gun and ran off down the street. Then the little Vietnamese man stumbled to the door, blood covering the front of his shirt. He fell down in the doorway, blood oozing into a pool beneath him. Malcolm realized the man had been shot. He threw the gun down and ran. "I didn't know what else to do, Mama. I just panicked. You believe me, don't you, Mama?"

Looking into her child's eyes, she saw a liar. He'd lied to her so many times. Not about anything big, but lies just the same. Still, she couldn't see a killer. All she could see were the other times. The first time she'd seen him, a tiny, helpless creature squirming to find her breast. Him taking his first steps. His first day in kindergarten. His first school program—in the black pants, white shirt, and bow tie. His fifth-grade graduation. She didn't see a killer. She wanted to believe him.

"But what would a pale white man be doing in the heart of the ghetto?"

"I don't know, Mama. He was there. I swear."

"And why didn't any of the people who saw you see the man?"

"I don't know. Maybe they weren't paying any attention. In that kind of neighborhood, people mostly mind they own business."

"And why didn't he shoot you, since he shot the Vietnamese man?"

"I told you, something spooked him. I saw him turn his head, just before he ran off."

"And why did you run, Malcolm, if you had nothing to hide?"

"I got scared. I knew that little man was hurt real bad. There I was, holding the gun. Who would believe me? My own mama don't believe me. I knew my PO wouldn't."

"Your what?"

"My PO—probation officer. I caught a little evading case. I haven't had the money to pay the fees, so I just didn't go to the meetings. He's always sweating me, anyway."

"Probation officer?"

The slamming of the heavy doors behind Audrey—a metallic, clanking sound—made her every nerve stand on end. She wanted to grab her baby from the clutches of that sound. He didn't belong here. But it was beyond her power to rescue him. Her making a scene would make no difference. Tears burned just behind her eyes. The mask held firmly in place.

When it was her turn in the line of mothers, the deputy pushed her purse through the slot at the bottom of the barred window. The last of the exiting procedures. Where were the fathers? Hiding behind a wall of don't care enough? Too scared to care? Too ashamed? Where was his father? She walked out into the muggy Houston evening.

The teeny little economy car she'd rented sat lopsided. Flat tire. Fuck! It wasn't enough that the plane was late, that the rental car clerk had given her trouble about the credit card, that she'd had to suffer the indignity of the jail procedures. Now this. Damn. This was the kind of day that made her wish for a bad hair day. Well, she'd just have to fix it, she thought, with an angry sigh. Wasn't like she'd never changed a tire before.

She unlocked the car door and tossed her purse inside. She took off the expensive linen jacket and laid it over the seat back. Now what? The trunk. The jack would be in the trunk. She took the jack stand out of the trunk, fit it into the slot on the side of the car, and went back for the crank. She searched the trunk, then looked in the compartments inside the back of the car. No crank. Now what? She knelt down and looked under the car. No crank. She stood up, brushing off her knees and growling angrily, then hauled off and kicked the fool out of that tire.

Intense pain ripped through her foot and tears rushed to her eyes. She couldn't stop them—the tears she hadn't allowed to come for what Sam had done to her, the tears she hadn't allowed to come for her son. In this moment of weakness, they were stronger than she was. She couldn't hold them back now. They streamed down her face, melting the mask. She put her elbow on the roof of the car, the heel of her fist to her forehead, and just cried. She didn't know anyone in Houston, so she didn't care who saw her. The sight of the stark, barred building that held her child made the silent stream give way to great heaving sobs.

*   *   *

"Ma'am? Are you okay?"

It was a strong, deep voice. A caring voice. A Barry White kind of voice. Just the voice she needed to hear. It came from some place way in the back of her head. Surely she'd imagined it. Losing her damn mind, on top of everything else. Maybe that was for the best. "Oh, God," she wailed, shaking her head into more sobs. She couldn't help herself. Now that the dam had broken, no point trying to put a finger in it.

"I'll fix it for you. You don't have to cry."

"You can't fix it," she sobbed. "Nobody can fix it. Just go away. Leave me alone."

She imagined her body being turned and enveloped in strong arms. Just the comfort she needed. The comfort that she'd needed a long time and hadn't gotten. She relinquished herself into the hard mass of his chest. From so close, she could feel his heart beating, feel his body heat, smell the faint citrus aroma of his cologne. She wasn't losing her mind. He was real.

"There, there. It's going to be okay. Trust me. I really can fix it. I bet I've changed a hundred flat tires."

She felt his strong fingers kneading the back of her neck. It was so soothing, she gave in to it.

"But, you really can't fix this one," she said, shaking her head, burrowed against his chest.

"Yes, I can," he insisted, in that soft, deep voice.

She felt a little silly getting this stranger's shirt wet. She didn't want to face him. But he was getting on her other last nerve with his assumption that she was some helpless female, crying like the world had come to an end over a damned flat tire. Couldn't he see she'd put the jack in properly?

She drew away from him, and began wiping her eyes with the backs of her hands. He handed her his handkerchief and she wiped her face, then her hands.

"Okay, Mr. I Can Fix Anything—fix it," she demanded, looking up into his face. A smile danced around the blackest eyes she'd ever seen.

He walked to the trunk, bent over and searched around. "There's a crank in here somewhere," he mumbled.

"Not in there," she said emphatically, folding her arms across her breasts. "The crank's not anywhere in this stupid little toy car."

"Oh. Well, why didn't you say so?" He stood up straight, all six feet four inches, and looked down at her, a quizzical look on his face.

"That's what I was trying to tell you."

"Okay, I give," he said, with a conciliatory smile. "You were right. I can't fix the tire—Ms. I've Got a Secret."

"So, I'm back where I was before I got your shirt all wet. I'm sorry about that. I'll give you some money for the cleaners, and for the handkerchief, too," she said, looking helplessly at the lipstick and makeup smudges on it. As she stuffed it in the pocket of her skirt, she looked around the parking lot in exasperation. "Now I'll just have to call a cab. What's the name of a decent cab company here?"

"I take it you're not from here?"

"No."

"Where are you going? I'm just getting off work. I can give you a lift. Oh, I'm Kirk Maxwell," he said, extending his hand.

She looked up into his eyes, then looked him up and down as she shook his hand. Tweed sports coat, tie, khaki pants. A raping, robbing murderer wouldn't dress like that. Wouldn't have mesmerizing, black eyes like his. Wouldn't have those gray strands in his black mustache. Wouldn't have a voice like Barry White.

"I'd appreciate that. I'm Audrey. Audrey Rob—Williams." It sounded strange to her. Her maiden name again, after nearly twenty-five years. When she lifted her tapestry suitcase out of the trunk, he took it from her. She retrieved her purse and jacket from the car and locked the door.

"My car's just across the street in that other lot," he said. "I'll be glad to drop you off. And I'll call the rental company and tell them where to pick up their toy car."

Maxwell carried the tapestry bag in one hand and held the other up to stop traffic as they crossed the street. He opened the door to his white Lincoln Town Car, then closed it behind her— thinking she had nice legs.

"I appreciate this," Audrey said, as she settled in the luscious maroon leather. "I'm not usually this frazzled. I've had a rough day."

"Which part of town are you staying in?" he asked, as he pulled out of the parking lot.

"I'm not sure. It says here, take I-45 to the Melton exit," she said, reading from notes scribbled on an envelope torn in half.

"Where're you from?"

"Dallas."

"How 'bout them Cowboys! I was an Oilers fan myself, but now that they deserted us, guess I'll have to go with the Cowboys. I don't remember any hotels in this area."

"I'm staying with a friend," she said, as he took the exit. "Turn right, go about a mile and make a right on Rollingwood."

"How long will you be here?"

"I'm not sure," she answered vaguely. "A couple of days, maybe. Take a left on Oak Vista."

"I have a friend who lives on Oak Vista. Well, used to. She's put her house up for sale."

"My friend is selling her house, too. This is a really nice neighborhood," she said, looking out the window at the large houses set back on one-acre lots. "Is something going wrong with the neighborhood?"

"No. My friend got married and moved out of town."

"So did mine. Isn't that a coincidence? This is it. 2315. Turn in here."

Maxwell's mouth dropped open. "You know Sondra?"

"Yeah, do you?"

He nodded. "Isn't this a small world? How do you know Sondra?"

"We were roommates in college. What about you?"

"We go way back. Used to work together, sort of. Before she married and moved to some little place in East Texas. Well, actually it was more than that. We were really friends."

As he got out of the car, Maxwell thought about how close he'd felt to Sondra, when she'd been a judge and he'd been her protector. Now this one case had come between them. It wasn't the case. It was the principle of the thing. Why wouldn't she understand that he couldn't give her a copy of his report? Just because she'd quit her job didn't mean he'd quit his. Sure, he'd have done it without a second thought when she was a judge. But she was just another lawyer now. A good one, at that. She knew how to get it the right way, how to file the motion. There had been a time when he'd have thought her reaction to his refusal was decisive and judicially stern. Now he saw it as petulant, and even traitorous.

Maxwell set Audrey's bag on the porch while she worked the combination on the lockbox and retrieved the key. When she got the door open, she turned to him.

"Thanks so much for the ride. Can I give you something on the gas?"

"No, no. It was my pleasure," he said, a smile crinkling around his black eyes.

"Oh." Caught off guard, Audrey looked down at her bag. It was an awkward moment, as she pondered the thought of a man being pleasured by something about her. When she glanced back at him, he was still smiling at her. She hesitated, then asked anyway.

"Would you like to come in for some coffee?"

"I'd better not. Thanks anyway."

"Okay. Well, maybe another time."

Just as well, Audrey thought. She'd spotted the plain band of gold on his finger.

★   ★   ★

The living room was dark. The jangling of the telephone jolted Audrey from a hard sleep. She sat upright and saw her luggage still by the doorway. The magazine she'd been reading when she put her feet up had fallen on the floor. She checked her watch: 8:30. The phone rang again. No realtor would be calling this time of night. She didn't know whether to answer it or not. Since Sondra wasn't there, maybe it would be better to let the machine take the message. But maybe it was Sondra calling to check on her. She picked up the phone, wondering what Sondra's new last name was. She said the one she knew.

"Ellis residence."

"Ah, hello?" She recognized that deep voice.

"Yes?"

Just hearing her voice made him smile. "Maxwell, here. Just thinking about you. I mean, are you okay? Like, do you need anything? Sondra get there yet?"

"No. I'm not expecting her today. I'm just staying at her house for a while."

"How long a while?"

"I don't know. Maybe 'til tomorrow. Maybe a couple of days."

"Oh. You know anybody here? I mean, have you eaten? I just thought, maybe . . . well, seeing as how you don't have a car and all—" He felt like a babbling fool. He took a deep breath. "I could bring you something." His voice tilted up into a question mark.

She thought about Sam's betrayal and Maxwell's plain gold band. Anger bubbled inside her. No more being taken for a fool.

"Did your wife cook something?" she asked, sarcasm heavy in her voice.

There was silence on the line. And Audrey waited to hear what kind of lie he would tell.

"I lost my wife last year. She passed away."

"Oh. I'm sorry." Audrey didn't know what else to say.

"Yeah, me too," he sighed. "Would you like me to bring you a hamburger? Or would you like to go, ah, get something?"

"I'd like to get out of this house. It's so quiet. It's spooky."

"I'll be there in thirty minutes."

Maxwell put the receiver on the hook. He sat back in his big recliner and felt the rumble of excitement running through him. What was he doing? He was just being nice. That was it. Just helping a lady in distress. That was what he was good at. That was his job. He shook his head. He couldn't fool himself. He was feeling something he hadn't felt in . . . seemed like forever. Something he shouldn't be feeling. But why not? He was alone. She was alone. It was just a hamburger. But if it was just for a hamburger, why was he taking a second shower today?

He turned the faucets on for his usual hot-hot shower. As the water cascaded over him, he could see her eyes. Pretty brown eyes, the color of a rich bourbon. But there was something sad about them. Nothing sad about her body, though. Big, luscious melon breasts, full hips, a rounded butt just like he liked. And her legs. Really nice legs. She had what Danny called "well-turned ankles." Ankles he could grab and pull around behind him until those legs were wrapped around his waist. Suddenly, he turned the hot water faucet hard, and let cold water run over him.

*   *   *

Audrey pulled her knit pantsuit out of the suitcase. It seemed too casual. Maybe the dress would be better. She'd always worn a dress for a date, way back in the day. Date? Where did that come from? This was not a date. Jeans and a cotton sweater was what she settled on. He had said "hamburger."

As she hurriedly undressed for a quick shower, she checked for blood. Not today. She was lucky. She was so sick of it. Every day. Every other day. For how long now? A year? Two? She had quit marking her calendar months ago. She couldn't discern a pattern to it. She had resigned herself to always being prepared. Cotton, cotton, everywhere. In all of her purses, the glove compartment of her car. She thought of buying stock in a cotton company. That way, at least she could share in the wealth she was creating.

Her doctor kept telling her the solution, but she couldn't wrap her mind around that. Not that she wanted another baby—even if she could have one at her age. It was the scar. No. She knew it wasn't the prospect of scar tissue that bothered her. It just seemed like she wouldn't be a real woman after that, just like Mama said. No woman stuff in her except the pills they give you. All her girlfriends were taking them. They all said they make you feel better, but Audrey didn't want to take pills for the rest of her life. She wanted to believe this erratic, infernal bleeding was the onset of menopause. If she just waited long enough, it would stop for good. No surgery. Besides, who would take care of her if she had that kind of surgery? Sam was gone. Not that he would have been any good at it. RosaLee? Too busy. Malcolm? Oh well.

Audrey took her jeans, sweater, and her pretty panties, to the bathroom.

four

"Greasy's?" Audrey asked, when Maxwell parked the Lincoln in front of a building that must have been a McDonald's in its former life. "What kind of name is that for a restaurant?"

"Best burgers in town," he said with an assured smile, holding her door open. "Real burgers. Just like they used to be. Trust me on this."

"Sounds more like a mechanic shop to me," she said as she stepped from the car.

She ordered the oyster po' boy. He got the double meat burger, double cheese.

"Wow. You're not worried about cholesterol?" she asked.

"Nope," he said with a grin.

"Can you really eat all that?"

"Yep. Growing boy like me needs to eat," he said with a crooked smile and a wink.

"My daddy used to say that real tall men are hollow inside. Can't fill 'em up," she laughed, then sobered. "Listen. About what I said earlier. About your wife. I didn't mean it the way it sounded. I had no idea. I'm just not the kind of woman who would go out with a married man."

"That's okay. I could see how you might have thought that," he said, fingering his ring. "Does the fact that you wear a ring mean that you have a husband?" he asked, glancing at hers. Her eyes followed his to the diamond on her left hand.

"Not anymore." She put both her hands in her lap.

"Did he die, too?"

"Sometimes I . . . no. I'm . . . divorced." It was a flat-out lie, but it seemed like the simplest explanation. She certainly wasn't going into the details.

"How long?"

"Not long enough."

"Guess it's too soon to talk about, huh?"

"Yep. What about your wife? How did she die?"

"Cancer. Breast cancer."

"Oh, I'm sorry. I lost an aunt that way. How long were you together?"

"Would have been thirty years this year. We married right out of high school. We'd been sweethearts all along. Only regret I have is, we never had kids. We both loved them, but . . ." He shrugged, then sighed. "So I have nothing left, except a lot of good memories."

"Well, at least you have that. After nearly twenty-five years, turns out my husband took up with someone else." Audrey looked away so he couldn't see the anger and hurt in her eyes. "That pretty much wiped out my good memories."

"So what's wrong with him? Is he blind or something?"

When she looked into his eyes, a smile pulled at the corner of her mouth, then won. She didn't understand why she felt like a schoolgirl. Maybe because it had been so long since Sam had said anything to make her smile.

"Thanks for saying that." She looked away to hide her embarrassment. "I guess we'd better go. Looks like they're trying to close up," she said, nodding toward the young man stacking chairs in the path of his mopping.

"I meant it," he said, pulling her chair out for her. "A man would have to be out of his mind to risk losing a woman as attractive as you."

As he pushed the door open for her, a man shoved his way in. Audrey had to step back to keep from being bowled over.

"He's in a mighty big hurry," she said, frowning and collecting herself. Oh, damn! She hoped and hoped that the sensation she felt wasn't blood. Maybe it was just sweat—or her imagination. "Wait a minute. Gotta pay my water bill."

She saw Maxwell's confused frown.

"I need to make a potty stop," she said, winking at him. "I'll be right back."

Waiting in the vestibule between the glass doors, Maxwell's attention turned to the men at the counter. Something about the clerk's eyes didn't look right to him. Then he saw him nervously handing over stacks of money to the man—too much to be change for a burger order. He saw the glint of chrome in the man's hand. Maxwell glanced toward the hallway just in time to see Audrey push the bathroom door open. She was smiling. She looked happy. His eyes riveted back to the man, backing away from the counter. The man looked desperate. Maxwell could see his trajectory. They were going to collide. He pushed the glass door open, reaching inside his coat for his revolver, taking long strides. But he couldn't get there in time.

In a mad dash for the door, the man crashed into Audrey. She fell sideways over the mop bucket, hitting her head against a stack of chairs before sprawling on the floor.

Audrey's first reaction was anger, then confusion. She hadn't fallen in years. The sensation was strange and frightening as she tried to catch herself. It happened so fast. So slow. She saw the gun as she went down. She lay on the floor, stunned from the blow.

Maxwell stood his ground, blocking the man's exit. Before the man could raise his gun, Maxwell whipped the revolver out of his coat and stuck it right in the man's face.

"Brother, you don't really want to die today, do you?"

He disarmed the man and had cuffs on him before he knew what hit him. The sounds of approaching sirens outside told Maxwell that the clerk had hit the silent alarm when the robbery first started. When the uniforms took control of the robber, Maxwell rushed to Audrey and knelt beside her.

"Are you hurt?"

"My head . . ." she said, still dazed, sitting up and gingerly touching her forehead.

Maxwell put his arm around her and helped her to her feet. He felt the trembling in her body. He pulled her against him and held her until she stopped shaking. "It's okay. It's over," he said soothingly, rubbing her back.

"You have a gun? You're a cop?" she mumbled against his jacket.

He held her away from him, cupped her chin in his hand, and raised her face. "Look at me, Audrey."

She still appeared dazed, but he could see that her pupils were normal. Her eyes were the prettiest brown he'd seen. Her eyebrows were knitted into a frown. He rubbed his thumb over one, easing the frown away.

"I think you'll be okay. Here, sit down," he said, gently helping her into the nearest chair. "You want some water? Anything? Gilcrest!" he shouted over his shoulder. When the officer approached, Maxwell said, "Get her whatever she needs." Then to Audrey, "I'll only be a little while. Gilcrest will take care of you until I get back."

As the uniformed officers carried the man out, Maxwell barked orders to the others, and they obeyed.

When he strode back to her, he dismissed Gilcrest and held his hand out to her.

"We can go now. You ready?"

★   ★   ★

In the Lincoln, Maxwell saw Audrey wince when she touched her head. While he steered with his left hand, he released her seat belt with the other, reached around her shoulder, and gently pulled her against him. He didn't understand this need to protect her. It was more than just professional, almost territorial.

"You want to go to the emergency room? Maybe we should have a doctor look at that bump. Just in case." He felt her shake her head, as she settled against him.

Audrey melted into his strength, his warmth. She liked the feel of his hand resting on her shoulder, rubbing as he spoke, the feel of his caring. She needed that more than any kind of doctor. No doctor could cure her of the big lump of pain inside her. She'd have just as soon died, right there cushioned in the arm of this big man, than have a doctor save her, to face what had become of her life.

When Maxwell pulled into Sondra's circular driveway, he reached over with his left hand, pulled the gearshift into park, then relaxed against the seat back. He was in no hurry to do anything except hold her. He felt comfortable with her against his side. He liked the smell of her hair and the way it felt under his chin. As the Temptations crooned the classic tune "At Last," he closed his eyes and drifted into a world of his own. A world where there was no violence to clean up after, no victims to console, no mothers staring at him out of eyes filled with pain. An island of serenity where there was only peace.

After a while, Audrey stirred against him. "I guess I'd better go in, before you burn up all your gas."

Maxwell reluctantly withdrew from her, shut the motor off, and walked to the other side of the car. Audrey took his hand and

pulled herself out of the leather seat. He didn't release her hand until they got to the door.

While she unlocked the door, he asked, "Are you sure you'll be
okay? All by yourself? I don't want you to be alone. Maybe I should
come in."

Audrey looked up into his eyes and saw he wanted to. Why
should she be alone? In the few hours since she'd met him he'd
shown her more warmth and protection than she'd known in
years. Why should she deprive herself of the comfort she needed so
desperately? She'd almost forgotten what it felt like. All those years
she'd learned to live without it, to not expect it. All those years,
she'd made excuses—law school, the babies, his job, their age, her
bleeding. All those years she'd been missing it, Sam had been getting what he needed.

"Maybe you should."

★   ★   ★

Inside, Audrey set her purse on the coffee table and stepped out of
her shoes. "Would you like some coffee?"

"I've had a rough day. I'd rather have a shot of bourbon," he said,
walking to the bar. "Wine is Sondra's thing, but she usually keeps a
well-stocked bar. Ah, here we go," he said, holding up a crystal decanter.

"I'll have one, too."

"I don't know if you should. With that bump and all."

"It's okay. I feel fine. I've had a rough day, too," she said, dropping
on the sofa. "A rough week, in fact." A rough life, she thought.

"How would you like yours?" he asked, smiling at her sympa-
thetically. "On the rocks? Mixer?"

"Straight will be fine."

He poured the brown liquid into two glasses that matched the
decanter. As he handed her a glass, he said, "Here. Put your feet up
and tell me about it."

He placed two cocktail napkins on the glass table, held his glass toward her in a salute, then put it to his lips and took a swallow. He licked the liquid off his lips, set his glass down, then took his jacket off.

As she took a sip, Audrey watched him lay the jacket across the wingback chair. She'd always been afraid of guns, but the casual way he removed the shoulder holster gave her a feeling of security. Then he walked to the entertainment center and turned on the radio, the volume low on the "quiet storm." As he passed the bar, he picked up the decanter and set it on the coffee table.

"So, you were going to tell me about your rough day," he said, sitting on the couch. He picked up his glass.

Sam never wanted to know about her day. Maybe it was her being too chatty that drove him away. He always said she talked too much, and why couldn't they just have some comfortable silences. For her, the silences weren't comfortable—just empty. She knew he could be quite talkative with anybody else.

"I don't want to talk about it," she said, putting the glass to her lips.

"I know the feeling," he sighed, draping his arm across the back of the couch. He didn't want to talk about his day either.

Audrey put her feet up on the coffee table. With Frankie Beverly crooning softly in the background it wasn't silent, but it was comfortable.

"So, you and Sondra were roommates, huh?"

"Yeah. A long time ago. I was looking at some pictures of us yesterday. She was so skinny, she looked like Twiggy. Vivian, too. Our other roommate. Of course, I wasn't," she laughed. "Never have been. Used to want to be. I've always been a little on the heavy side. Big-boned, my daddy called me, like his sisters."

"You're just the right size," Maxwell said.

Audrey gave him a quick glance, then turned away so he couldn't see the little smile on her face. She was talking too much. Telling too much. She nervously sipped from the glass, then set it on the coffee table.

"You want to see the pictures? I brought them to show Sondra. I thought she'd get a kick out of them."

She pulled a stack of photos from her purse and handed it to him. He chuckled as he looked at each one.

"I'm not sure I would have recognized Sondra right off. She's not this skinny any more, and I've never seen her with long hair," he said smiling at the last picture. "You look just the same, though. So you finished UT?" he asked, handing the pictures back to her. He refilled their glasses.

"No, I didn't finish with them. I only had a semester and a half with them. I didn't even start with them. I transferred as a junior. You remember Bishop College in Dallas? Well, it's not there anymore. It's not anywhere. It's just gone. Damn shame. Folks only twenty years out of slavery, probably illiterate, start a college. A hundred years later, middle-class Negroes, driving Cadillacs and Mercedes, lose it."

"Yeah, damn shame," he said, shaking his head. "My daddy said the citified preachers were the cause. Damn shame."

"Anyway, I had to leave UT in the middle of the semester. I got real sick. Almost died. The next year, I went back to Bishop. That's where I met my husband. We married right after graduation. We had it all planned out. I taught school and sent him to law school. Then he was going to send me to graduate school. But that got put off while he set up his practice. Then I had my daughter. Somehow, the plan never got back on track. Things are so different now. Funny how life takes turns you never expect." All of the mirth had drained from her voice.

"I know how that happens," he said. Maxwell thought of all the things he and Shirley had put off until he retired. He put his arm around her shoulder and heaved a sigh.

"Maybe I should have just died, back then."

She had said it under her breath, but he heard the sadness in her voice.

"No," he whispered, shaking his head, and rubbing her shoulder. "Nothing can be that bad."

"Not even finding out your husband has a lover?"

"No. Not even that." He leaned her head against his shoulder. "There's a lot worse things can happen."

She took a sip, rolled it around with her tongue. Could she tell him? There was no one else she could tell, and she needed to tell somebody. Why not him? After tonight, she'd never see him again anyway.

"A lover named Paul?"

Maxwell's eyes opened wide, then a frown narrowed them. He took a sip before resting his glass on his thigh.

"Well, you got me there. That's pretty bad," he said, nodding matter-of-factly. "In fact, that's fucked up. But it's not worth your dying."

"I keep telling myself that. That it's not my fault. But I keep wondering what I did. What I didn't do. I tried to do everything right. It seems my whole life has been a sham. I feel so useless. No, that's not the right word for it. I don't know the right word for it. My friend MaryBeth kept telling me I should dye my hair. Get a facial. Go with her to the gym. Maybe if I'd been—"

"Hush. Don't say it," he said, rubbing his thumb along the ridge of her ear. He set the glass on the lamp table. "Don't even think it. There's nothing you could have done. The man has a problem. You couldn't solve it. He couldn't even solve it—else he wouldn't have married you at all. Of course, his real problem ain't being gay. It's being a liar. He shouldn't have married you. I don't understand guys like that. You deserve better. You're a very attractive woman, Audrey. You have beautiful eyes," he said, tracing her eyebrow with his finger. "A pretty nose," his finger slowly tracing down to the tip. "Pretty lips. Lips that should smile."

Just the words she needed to hear. Audrey looked up into his black eyes and felt herself drowning in his tenderness.

He took her chin in his hand and gently massaged her mouth upward into a reluctant smile. She closed her eyes and he felt her lean against his hand. "Lips that should be kissed." He bent his head and touched his lips to hers. It was a soft kiss. A kiss that said everything's going to be okay. Then, he leaned her head against his shoulder and held it there.

Just the feeling she needed to have.

Audrey felt his tongue tracing the place where her lips met, then his sweet invasion. Just what she needed. She lifted her face just enough to encourage him to do that again. And he did. Slowly and sweetly. While he held her tongue captive, he massaged her back. Places sparked alive inside her that had been long dead. She shouldn't allow a stranger to affect her this way. To touch her this way. She pushed her hands against him. But he was planting kisses on her neck. And the heel of his hand was massaging across her nipple. When his lips found hers again, his other hand was playing in her hair. He gripped a fistful of it, holding her lips against his. And his hand was still massaging her breast. And it felt so good. And his hand was under her sweater, touching her bare skin. And he was leaning over her, easing her down on the couch. And his hands were pushing her sweater up and freeing her of the bra. And his lips were on her nipple. And her arms were around his neck. And his hand was rubbing over the curve of her hip and across her abdomen. And she didn't even bother to suck in. And her fingers were massaging the back of his neck, pulling him to her. And his fingers were unbuttoning her jeans, then unzipping them. And his hand was inside them. And his finger was touching her in a place where he shouldn't—a place where she wanted him to. Then he was carrying her, like a child. And she felt weightless in his arms. And she loved the feel of his arm under her knees, and the feel of his lips on hers. And the sweet warmth of his tongue in her mouth as he lowered her on the bed, and lowered himself onto her.

*   *   *

The jangling of the telephone brought Audrey out of her beautiful dream. As she reached to touch her head, to soothe the dull ache inside it, she felt her arm brush by her bare breast. Strange. Where was her gown? She always slept in a gown. She looked around, trying to figure out where she was. The room and the white-washed pine furniture were strange. The bed, covered with white embroidered lace, was unfamiliar but comfortable. Maybe this was the dream. But the phone was ringing.

As she reached over to pick it up from the nightstand, she saw her clothes on the floor. Her jeans and sweater were folded like she would have done. Her bra strap peeked from beneath the pile. Maybe she'd knocked them off the bed in her sleep. But she wouldn't have put them on the bed. She ran her other hand down her hip and across her pelvis. Something sweet throbbed inside her. Surely, he didn't. But she didn't remember getting herself to the bed.

"Hello?"

FIVE

"Ellis residence," Audrey mumbled into the receiver.

"Good morning."

A sweet shiver snaked through her at the sound of his deep voice. She glanced at her watch. She couldn't believe she'd slept so late.

"Did I wake you up? How do you feel this morning?"

"I'm fine," she answered quietly. She glanced at her clothes on the floor, and wondered again. She knew better than to drink bourbon. A glance to the other side of the bed didn't tell her if he'd slept there. She couldn't ask him, and she couldn't remember. All she could remember was telling him about Sam. Embarrassment heated her cheeks. Bourbon always made her talk too much. So that was why he was calling? He felt sorry for her because of what she'd told him last night? She didn't want his pity.

"Your head hurt?" he was asking.

"A little," she answered, touching it. She couldn't tell if the hurt was from her fall at the restaurant or the hangover.

"I feel so bad about what happened last night, Audrey. I'd like to take you to lunch."

What did he feel bad about? Had he taken advantage of her

when she'd had too much to drink? She sat bolt upright. The sheet fell away from her breasts. All she had on were her pretty panties.

"I was just leaving," she said hurriedly, swinging her feet over the side of the bed. "I've got a plane to catch, so—"

"Well, could I take you to the airport? I can be there in ten minutes."

"No. The cab just pulled up. I've got to go. Thanks anyway."

*   *   *

When the line went dead, Maxwell held the receiver out and stared at it in disbelief. Then he put it back to his ear and pressed the switchhook on the pay phone a couple of times. He'd expected her to be happy to hear from him. He was caught off guard by the sudden coldness in her voice, as though last night hadn't happened. As though she hadn't clung to him like her life depended on it. As though he hadn't held her like his did, too. As though he hadn't spent the night, thinking about caressing her face, her breasts, her hips. Thinking about touching her deepest recess, that place that would make her cry out in joy.

His next thought was to hop in his police cruiser and race to Hobby airport, sirens blasting, to be there when she arrived. But what if her flight was from Intercontinental? He couldn't get there in time. He didn't even know how to reach her in Dallas. He jerked the receiver off the hook, put another quarter in and hurriedly punched in Sondra's number. The line was dead. Then, he remembered. It costs thirty-five cents now. He desperately fished in his pocket for a dime. The phone rang and rang and rang. Then the machine answered.

*   *   *

Audrey ignored the phone, tying the belt on her robe as she made her way to the kitchen. Maybe she should go back today. There were flights to Dallas every hour. She could make half a pot of coffee, dress and pack, then call a cab.

Audrey was surprised to find the coffee pot full . . . and hot. She didn't remember making coffee last night. She hoped it wouldn't be stiff and acid-tasking from sitting so long. Eyeing it suspiciously, she poured a cup, then sipped it. It tasted surprisingly fresh. She decided against making another pot and took the cup to the table.

A blood-red rose torn from the bush by Sondra's front door sat in a water glass in the middle of the table. Next to it was a McDonald's sack, and the newspaper. She opened the sack and touched her hand to the cold package. Maybe he didn't think too ill of her, since he went to all this trouble. Maybe she should have answered the phone. Or maybe he just felt sorry for her. Or maybe he really liked her. When the phone rang again, she answered it.

"Ellis residence."

"Girl, quit answering my phone like that. I'm Mrs. Evans, now."

Audrey felt relief—and disappointment. "Evans. That's right. I forgot. Well, I won't be answering your phone anymore. I was just about to pack."

"Can't you stay until tomorrow?" Sondra asked. "I'm planning to drive down to Houston today, so I can get an early start on the case in the morning. I want to see you. Can't you stay?"

"I want to see you, too. If you're coming to town today, I'll stay until you get here. See you then."

Audrey hung up the phone, then sat at the table and picked up the cold sandwich. As she savored the salty cheese and sausage wrapped in the crumbly biscuit, she opened the newspaper and read the headline: AIDS GROWING FASTEST AMONG HETEROSEXUAL WOMEN.

Alarm spread through her as she read the article. The statistics on African-American women were frightening. There was so much she didn't know. She realized that she didn't know the difference between HIV and AIDS. She hadn't paid much attention to the issue before, always having thought of AIDS as a gay man's disease.

Why hadn't she thought about it in the three days since she'd found Sam and Paul together? It should have been her first thought. Anger and hurt had kept her from thinking logically. Now she had to.

Audrey tried to remember the last time she and Sam had had sex. She vaguely remembered hearing that the incubation period for AIDS is ten years. Although their sex life had waned over the years, she was certain it hadn't been that long. In fact, it had been maybe a month or two. They hadn't used protection. She'd quit taking birth control pills, believing she couldn't get pregnant at her age. Sam refused to wear a condom. He always said he didn't like the way it felt. And she'd foolishly trusted him. Now she would have to take a test. But would the test reveal anything during the incubation period? Or only if the incubation period was over. Had Sam been this way ten years ago? Did it mean she couldn't have sex for the next ten years? She didn't even know where to take the test. Certainly not her family physician. Damn Sam!

When the doorbell rang, Audrey started into the living room before thinking that it couldn't be for her. Maxwell's outline through the beveled glass was unmistakable, and she knew he saw her, too. She stood there, not knowing what to do.

"Police. Open the door."

Audrey slowly opened the door. Caught in a lie, she couldn't bring herself to look in his eyes.

"I brought you some ribs for lunch," he said, holding up two bags. "I didn't know if you had a thing about pork, so I got beef."

Audrey didn't move. "How did you know I would be here?" she asked in a quiet voice. She pulled the robe about her tighter in a guilty gesture.

"A cop's intuition. No ring of truth in your voice. You're not a good liar." He gave her a crooked, half-smile. "Not much of a drinker, either, are you?" When she averted her eyes, his smile turned sympathetic. "There's a bottle of Bloody Mary mix in the other bag. Can we eat now?"

Audrey backed away from the door and followed him into the kitchen. She sat at the table and saw he'd moved the newspaper aside to spread open the package of ribs. The headline stared back at her. She looked from it to him at the refrigerator. Could she have given him a deadly disease? How could she have been so careless?

Maxwell set two glasses filled with ice on the table and took a seat. He poured the Bloody Mary mix in one and a soda in another.

"I got these at Harlon's. The best in town. Whatdya' think?"

She picked up one and gingerly bit into it. "It's good," she said, nodding her head. On her next bite, the succulent meat fell from the bone. She tried to catch it and her fingers got covered with grease and barbecue sauce. He laughed at her failed attempt and handed her a napkin. The moment eased the tension in Audrey just a little. She laughed at herself, as she wiped her fingers on the napkin. She picked the meat up and savored it. She noticed Maxwell had no trouble managing the ribs.

"About last night . . . Did I . . . I mean if I . . . I'm embarrassed to say I don't remember much." She looked up at him.

"Not much to remember," he said, sitting back with the satisfied look of a man with a full stomach. "We talked a while. You leaned your head against my shoulder, then you were out like a light. That's how I know you aren't accustomed to drinking. You only had two drinks. If I'd been the kind of man to take advantage . . ." He gave her a wicked smile.

She didn't know how else to ask. "Are you that kind of man?"

Maxwell saw her discomfort. He enjoyed it for a minute, before shaking his head. He saw Audrey's sigh of relief. He didn't have the heart to tell her that he'd put her to bed. Maybe he would tell her later. Maybe he never would.

"I've got to be going," he said, rolling up the bones in the butcher paper. "Duty calls. What are you doing later? Maybe we could go somewhere. Somewhere nice and quiet. No robberies, I promise. I'll call you when I get off. Is that okay?" he asked, at the door.

"Sondra's coming sometime this evening. Maybe we could all do something." Audrey saw his expression change, but couldn't read it.

"Maybe. Thanks for lunch. I'll call you," he said, as he strode to the big cruiser.

*　　　*　　　*

Audrey heard the car in the driveway. She'd spent the afternoon since Maxwell left being torn between unsettling thoughts about him and excitement and apprehension about seeing Sondra. She had such good memories. But she hadn't seen Sondra in thirty years. Had she changed? Over the years she had read the articles in Sam's bar journals chronicling Sondra's legal career, her rise to a judgeship, and her leaving the bench. Would she now be a stuck-up, society bitch bragging about her successes and possessions? She hadn't been like that back then.

Audrey remembered her as a studious girl, with a sharp mind and a sharper tongue. Always judging, even then. Audrey wondered how she would judge her now? Would Sondra think she was a failure, having chosen to stay home for her family rather than wrestle her way through the school politics to principal or administrator?

She walked to the back door and held it open. A broad grin crossed her face as she watched Sondra climb down from the big, black truck. She would have recognized her anywhere. Even though Sondra had picked up a little weight in thirty years, it looked good on her.

Sondra held her arms open, and they walked into a hug that had been a long, long time coming.

"You look good, Audrey," Sondra said, when they could separate themselves. "I'm so glad to see you. Ou-u, wouldn't it be great if Vivian was here!"

Audrey wished Vivian were here, too. The three of them had been inseparable back when they'd all been young. Before she'd separated herself from them. She still had every letter Vivian had written wrapped in a rubber band in her bottom drawer. After her parents died she'd had the mail forwarded from their farm in East Texas. Each time one came—always on her birthday—she got them all out and reread each one. The first two or three had been long, rambling, and full of details. As the years wore on they became more terse, but still reaching out to her. The last few could have fit on a postcard. They were resigned, but still reaching. "Happy Birthday, Audrey. I still miss you."

Audrey could never bring herself to answer them. What would she have said? The first year, she might have said, "I'm sorry I cut out on y'all that way. Shame makes a person do strange things." The third year, "I married a lawyer just like you did." The seventh year, "Sorry you couldn't have a baby. You'd have made a fine little mother. A baby might have given you the backbone you needed to get that 'can't quite figure it out' look off your face." The tenth year, "I had two more babies . . . and I kept them." This year, "One has never needed me, and the one who did is in jail. You might have been spared a lot of heartache."

Sondra was pulling her by her hand into the house. "Was everything okay? I'm sorry there wasn't much food here. I took as much of my stuff out as I could. I was hoping for a quick sale. Hah! No such luck. I don't know what I would have done if I had a house note to make."

"Everything was fine. Really," Audrey assured her.

"You made coffee. You remembered," Sondra said, with a crooked smile on her face, then hugged Audrey again.

"I figured you'd still be a caffeine addict. I am. Sit down." Audrey poured coffee into the two cups she'd left on the counter and took them to the kitchen table.

"You're still taking care of everybody. You got to stop that, girl. Who takes care of Audrey?"

"Audrey takes care of herself."

They started with the day they met at the dorm at UT, so glad to see another black face in the sea of white. Before they could decide whether to protest that all the black girls were housed together, they decided they needed each other. So there they were, three in a suite meant for four. The overnighters they'd pulled, studying for exams. Coaching each other. Understanding the only help they would get would be from each other. The Friday nights they'd spent at Scholtz's. "Vivian told me they'd sold it or something." The night they'd climbed the ninety-nine steps to the top of Mt. Bonnell. "We were lucky those policemen didn't arrest us for violating the park curfew. If we hadn't had those UT ID cards, they'd have taken us to jail."

Along the way they moved to the living room. Sondra filled two crystal goblets with wine and handed one to Audrey. Then she put on Natalie Cole's *Greatest Hits* and they would periodically break out with the background singers. They ended up sitting on the floor, leaning back comfortably against the sofa. Sondra laughed when she noticed Audrey playing with her toes. "You still do that."

They skipped over the night they'd taken Audrey to the hospital. That was something neither of them was brave enough to talk about. Skimming over the rest of the college years after Audrey left, Sondra took her through the years of her marriage to Michael. Audrey remembered Michael, but she didn't remember him quite the way Sondra did—so saintlike. Still, it was hard to believe he was dead. Dead was so final.

Audrey told her about her life with Sam. And how it ended. Well, not all of it. She wanted to tell her, but she just couldn't find a way to fix her mouth to say "My husband of twenty-five years would rather fuck another man than me." So she just said they'd grown apart, that he'd found someone else. Not the whole truth, but the truth.

"I'm sort of drifting now. I was anchored to Sam. With Sam, I knew everything I was supposed to do. Now, I don't know . . . my world has been turned upside down. This is the lowest I've ever been."

"Sometimes lowest is where you have to be before you can get up," Sondra said, matter-of-factly. "I felt that same way when Michael died. The twins were ten. I thought my world had come to an end. But I had to go on for them. I poured myself into my girls, and my job. There was nothing else. Good mother. Good judge. But something was missing in my life. I was dead inside. When Natalie and Tiffany left for college, I really went into a tailspin. I was depressed. What did you say—drifting?"

Audrey nodded, then took a slow sip from her glass.

"Then I met Ike, and under the strangest circumstances. You wouldn't even believe it if I told you. Sometimes, I don't even believe it myself." Sondra stopped, then smiled shyly. "He's a country boy. Raises cattle. At first, I didn't think we had anything in common. I fought it—hard. Looking back on it, I think I had just grown comfortable with that zombielike existence I was living. Everybody thought I'd lost my mind when I refused to run for reelection. Instead, I took a big chance. I married him and moved to Pine Branch. And I've never been happier."

"I can see that," Audrey said, with a smile not as broad as Sondra's.

"And look at Vivian. You never met Walter, did you? Pretty boy. First-class jerk. Twenty years, her wanting a baby so bad. Then he brings home his baby by another woman. Vivian was pretty low. She was almost finished with law school when . . ."

"Wait! Vivian went to law school?" Audrey broke in. "Good for her."

"Yep," Sondra said, proudly. "She's working with another woman lawyer now. The one who handled her divorce. Anyway, she was in her last semester when that bastard brought this baby to her. But she fair fell in love with that baby. Even took it with her when she left him. Can you imagine?"

"You can't be serious!"

"Serious. Well anyway, she started dating a professor. But Lord, then she got pregnant—right in the middle of the divorce. You know how naive she was? Well, she still is. Walter started giving her shit about the baby. I'm telling you, he's a first-class jerk. Told her if she wanted to keep the baby, she'd have to quit the professor and come back home. I keep telling her it would make a good novel." Sondra laughed. "Anyway, it's way too much conframa for me."

"Conframa?"

"You know, confusion, drama—conframa. So anyway, I think the lowest Vivian ever got was when she went to have the abor—" Sondra stopped abruptly. Her eyes met Audrey's. All night, they had been avoiding it. It fell to Audrey to relieve the awkwardness.

"Did it work out?" she asked quietly. "Is she happy?"

Sondra smiled and nodded. "After a lot more drama. She couldn't go through with the abortion, so now she has two beautiful little girls. She's doing great. Life's going to be great for you too, Audrey. Soon as the smoke clears. Time always brings about a change. Sometimes it brings heartache, but it brings happiness, too."

Audrey nodded an acquiescence that didn't have the force of belief behind it. She felt Sondra's eyes on her.

"Look Audrey, I can't keep watching every word I say. I need to know. Why did you cut us off? You just disappeared. Why did you do that? I've missed you. It's like there's a big piece missing from my life."

Audrey wouldn't look at her. "Shame makes a person do strange things."

"But we were your friends, Audrey. You hurt us—me—leaving that way. We knew what had happened. It didn't make us any difference."

Audrey shook her head. They didn't know. Nobody knew. Even now, Audrey couldn't bring herself to tell Sondra about those nights she'd lied to them about going to the library. He'd asked her to meet him here and there. Later she'd realized it was always a place where they wouldn't be seen together. She'd been so thrilled to have the attention of a football player, and a star player at that. What a fool she'd been. She winced when she thought of that night he'd sneaked her into his room in the athlete's dorm to listen to his new Isley Brothers album. It had been so exciting, breaking the rules.

In his room he'd coaxed her to sit on the bed next to him. Then he kissed her. And kissed her some more. She liked it, the feelings she'd never had before. When his hands began to stray, she'd protested. But he wouldn't quit. As she struggled with him, he accused her of being a tease. Even as big as she was, he was stronger. He pushed her down on the bed, ripped her clothes, and just took it. It hurt, but not nearly as much as the ugly words he'd said. She didn't cry out for help because she was wrong for being there. Then there had been strict rules against girls being in the boys' dorm. All she could think about was getting put out of school, how that would hurt and embarrass her parents. She was the first in her family to go to college, and they were so proud of her. All of their hopes and dreams rested on her shoulders.

When he finished, he didn't even walk her to the door. She'd walked across the dark campus alone, clutching her clothes around her, mindless to any danger that may have lurked there. What worse could happen to her? She sat under a tree across from her dorm and waited until the light went out in their room. No way she'd let Sondra and Vivian see her this way. No way they would know what a fool she'd been.

For a week she brooded over it, tried to get up the nerve to report him. But to whom? And who would believe her? When she saw him again, he looked right through her. She knew he would deny it. Her name would be muddied. She would be the one they would whisper about and point at. She decided to let it go, to let it be a lesson learned the hard way. She had no idea how hard a lesson it would be, until she missed her period.

"I'm sorry I hurt you. I just didn't know what else to do. I was young. Scared. I've thought about this for all these years. But the more time went by, the harder it was to explain. Right now, my son's in trouble. His life's on the line. I don't have anybody else to turn to. Maybe the only good thing that will come of this is that it got us back together."

"I'm really glad about that." Sondra reached over and squeezed Audrey's hand.

"Me too, Sondra. Me, too," Audrey said, patting the back of Sondra's hand.

"Let's talk about Malcolm," Sondra said. "Did you get to see him? What did he say?"

Audrey launched into the tale Malcolm had told her.

"Do you believe that?" Sondra asked, her expression intent.

Audrey drew her lips tight. "No. I really don't. But I know he didn't kill that man, Sondra. I know my child. He's not that kind of person."

"What kind of person is he?" Sondra asked, reaching for a tablet and pen from the coffee table, and began writing.

"He's a sweet child. Thoughtful. He never forgets my birthday. Or RosaLee's. He always draws a special card for us. He's an artist, you know."

"No. I didn't know." Sondra saw Audrey peering over at the paper. "I'm just taking notes. You never know what could be important. It's just a habit," she said, shrugging. "Why was Malcolm living in Houston?"

Audrey leaned back against the couch and sipped her wine. Somehow, Sondra's writing it all down made her uneasy, made her choose her words carefully. She felt like she was being interrogated.

"I don't know. I think living in Dallas was too much pressure for him."

"Pressure?"

"Well, his father is a lawyer. And his sister was in law school. He had no interest in that. He's more of a creative person. I think he felt like he could be his own person, be judged on his own merits, in another place."

"I can see that. What was he doing here? Where was he working?"

"I don't know. He never said anything about a job." Audrey could tell from the expression on Sondra's face that that didn't sound good. She rushed to his defense. "He was probably selling his art. Maybe caricatures. He used to go down to West End or Dealy Plaza and do that for the tourists sometimes in Dallas. He's really good."

"Does he have a wife?"

Audrey gave her an annoyed look. "He's only twenty, Sondra."

Sondra returned the look. "Okay, does he have a mybaby-mama?"

"A what?"

"Mybabymama. You know. Are you a grandma?"

"Oh. I don't think so. I don't know. I think he would have told me. Well, maybe not. I don't know."

"What about drugs?"

"What about drugs? I mean, I told you he smokes marijuana."

"Other drugs. Does he do drugs? Has he ever stolen from you?"

"No, of course not!"

"Several of my friends have deadbolts on their bedroom doors."

"A couple of my friends do, too, but I don't. Malcolm would never do anything like that. I'd kill him myself."

"What about church?"

"I raised him in the church. I doubt he goes now, though."

"When I was on the bench, the guys whose mamas wouldn't come to court—I mean if your own mama won't speak for you, you're a goner. Will you go to court and testify for Malcolm?"

"Of course."

"What about his daddy?"

"Sam? I don't . . . I need to talk to him. RosaLee will, that's for sure. And my friend MaryBeth will too. She's known Malcolm all his life. Have you found out anything?"

"Not much. The district attorney's office is playing this close to the chest. They're going to put me through my paces. Pissed me off. I used to be able to get all the information I wanted in a phone call," Sondra said, laying the tablet back on the coffee table.

"Well, I guess since you're not a judge anymore—"

"Fuck that! Those people were supposed to be my friends. That's okay," she pouted. "I'm not going through my paces without taking them through theirs. No question about that. Tomorrow I'll start with a visit to Malcolm. Then the DA. If he thinks I've forgotten how to be a lawyer, he's mighty wrong. Then I'll talk to the judge on the case and try to get a bond set."

"Malcolm doesn't belong in jail. Can you get him out?"

"I don't know. That would be better. Very few people who come from jail to trial escape prison. Even if I can get a bond set, it's going to be high."

"How high? How much does it have to be?"

"Well, the judge can set the bond in any amount he thinks is enough to make sure the person comes to court, and to protect the community. It could be one dollar or a million dollars. More, even. Just depends."

"A million dollars!"

"A man is dead. This is a serious case. Has the potential for stirring up racial tensions. If it were in my court, I would set the bond around $100,000. That would mean you'd need to have property worth that much to sign over to the bondsman, but you'd only have to pay ten thousand dollars in cash. The cash is his fee. If Malcolm shows up for all his court appearances, you'll get the property back. If he misses even one you could lose it all."

Audrey didn't say anything, but her brow held deep furrows. She supposed she'd rather get "just the facts, ma'am" from someone she trusted. Sondra hadn't changed after all. She'd always been a straight shooter. More than once, Vivian had accused her of being too logical, of having no feelings. But in this situation Audrey had enough feelings for the both of them. As much as she hated to hear it, she needed to know the real deal.

Sondra yawned and stretched. "Girl, let's go to bed. I've got to get up early tomorrow. Got a long row to hoe."

"You go on. I'm a little wired," Audrey said, with a weak smile.

After Sondra left, Audrey sipped the wine and laid her head back on the couch, eyes closed, trying to sort through it all. She rubbed her forehead to ease the pounding in her head. The house was worth more than $100,000. That part would be easy. Sondra had made $10,000 sound like $59.95. Audrey tried to imagine ten $1,000 bills. Ten didn't seem like so many, but she didn't know if there even was such a bill. She'd never seen one. To her, a hundred dollar bill was a big one. A hundred of them made a pretty big stack in her mind. Did they have that kind of money? Sam handled all their finances, but she felt free to buy the things she wanted. She always let him know if she spent more than a couple of hundred dollars. She strained to remember the balances on the bank statements she'd put back in the drawer the day she packed his things. Mary-Beth had been so right to make her keep them, and the stock portfolios. As soon as she got home she'd check them.

But what if Malcolm skipped out? She'd lose her home, her security. She shook her head. He'd go to court. Sure he'd go. But what if he didn't? She shuddered at the thought and wished this would all just go away. After a while, she decided she could toss and turn as well in bed.

When she stood up, she saw Sondra's tablet. There was a horizontal line under the heading "Malcolm Roberts," then two columns. Audrey had no trouble figuring out their meaning. Each entry was preceded by a crisp hyphen. On the left side "unemployed," "drugs," "no wife, no babies," "no church," "father—no." The right column contained only one entry: "mother will testify."

*   *   *

"A fella takes a couple of days off and all hell breaks loose," Danny said, striding into the office. He dropped his backpack on his desk, pushed the earphones off his ears, and raked his fingers through his hair where it was long on top. Then he pulled the case of CDs and the portable CD player out of the backpack. He gave Maxwell an expectant look.

"You didn't miss much," Maxwell said nonchalantly. "Just some joker in a fit of desperation."

"Unlucky bastard, wouldn't you say? Trying to take down the restaurant where the lieutenant of robbery was dining. And with a lady, at that," Danny said, his eyebrows raised in a question, a big grin on his face.

Maxwell looked down at the file on his desk and pretended to read it, so Danny wouldn't see the gleam in his eyes. After two years he and Danny were close—in a way. Danny didn't fit well in the cop culture, and he didn't care enough to try to gain acceptance from them. Peculiar, some of them called him. But Maxwell had come to like the kid—in a way. He liked Danny's quick wit, and even grudgingly admired his independent streak. He didn't think of Danny as a son, or even a little brother. They were friends—in a way. Still, not in a way that allowed him to share his inner thoughts and feelings. Danny didn't need to know that he'd foil a thousand robbers for another night with her.

"Yeah, I'd say unlucky," Maxwell said as nonchalantly as he could.

"And the lady? Anybody I know?"

"Nah." Maxwell quickly picked up the phone and called the victim on the case in front of him. He had interviewed the man already, but he had to do something to deflect Danny's attention. Danny hadn't moved from his perch on his desk across the room, and his eyebrows were bouncing up and down like Groucho Marx. Maxwell finally couldn't think of anything else to ask the man, so he concluded the conversation and hung up the phone.

"Nah?!" Danny charged right in. "Nah? Is that it? Just nah?"

"Yeah, that's it. Just nah."

"So, it's 'nah' that brings a smile to the usually somber lieutenant's face?"

Just then the door burst open, and a small-framed Vietnamese man charged in, the sergeant on his heels.

"You people should protect! You do nothing!" he shouted.

"I'm sorry, Lieutenant. I told him you were busy. I couldn't stop him, short of shooting him."

"It's okay, Ockletree. Have a seat, Mr. . . . ?"

"Pham. I'm Pham."

"Well, sit down, Mr. Pham. I'm Lieutenant Maxwell. What can I do for you? What's the problem?"

The man shook his head, refusing to sit.

"Dung Nguyen was my friend. We come here together. Now he dead. You do nothing," he spat out. "You tell us, don't have gun in store. The nice policeman come to our meeting. He tell us 'don't have gun in store.' The blacks steal our goods. The whites take our money. No more. I have gun. Gonna shoot. I not afraid. If I die, they die, too!"

"Calm down, Mr. Pham," Maxwell said, softly. "I'm sorry about your friend. Sergeant O'Connor and I are assigned to that case. Where is your store?"

"Dowling Street. 7537 Dowling."

"Have you had any trouble recently?"

"Have trouble every day. Every night. Police do nothing." Pham's hands shook with rage.

"I'll assign a unit on close patrol, starting tonight," Maxwell said. "The units in that area will pay particular attention to your store. They'll park in front of your store to fill out reports. Things like that. Here's my card. Call me anytime."

"I don't know 'close patrol.' I know shoot! I warned you." He stormed out the door.

Danny released an indignant sigh. "Boy, that little chink sure has his nose out of joint. He opens a store in the worst part of town. What does he expect us to do, be his own personal bodyguard?" He flipped through the canvas case looking for the right CD to begin his day.

Maxwell's eyes narrowed, and he took measured breaths. "Danny, there ain't no chinks."

"What?" Danny asked absently, as he thumbed through his phone messages.

"I said, there ain't no chinks. Ain't no spics. No wetbacks. And there damned sho' ain't no niggers. There are only taxpaying citizens—citizens we've sworn to protect. Now, if I ever have to explain this to you again, it'll be while I'm kicking your peckerwood ass. Sabe?"

Maxwell stared at Danny a long minute, then jerked around to face the computer and put out a close patrol order for 7537 Dowling Street. While the minutes ticked by, his anger hung heavy in the air, filling the space between their desks.

"Say, boss," Danny called out, glaring indignantly at Maxwell. "I'll have you know, I am not a peckerwood!"

Maxwell turned and glared back at him.

"I'll have you know, I am proudly descended from a long line of hard-drinking, potato-eating micks, who came to this great land of opportunity to escape the tyranny and prejudice of the mother country." Danny rolled his R's in a perfect imitation of a cartoon leprechaun.

Maxwell reared back in his chair, stared at Danny's quirky grin, then shook his head. His anger dissipated through the chuckle he hid with a contrived cough. Danny's grin was disarming, but Maxwell knew they had come to an understanding.

SIX

Sam paced from the window to his desk and back. He'd left messages on their answering machine every day for nearly a week, but Audrey hadn't called him back. Now she'd be here any minute, and he still didn't know exactly how to approach this. For years he'd dreaded this day. He'd always known it would come. In a way, it was amazing that he'd gotten away with it for so long. There had been times when he'd wondered if she knew. Wondered whether she had made a pact with herself, like the one he'd made with himself.

He loved Audrey. After twenty-five years, how could he not love her? But he wasn't *in* love with her. Never had been. He always had had another desire. He didn't know it at first. He only knew that his feelings hadn't mirrored what the other boys talked about in the locker room. There was only one girl at Carver High who wouldn't be lying if she said she'd slept with the all-star football player and straight-A student. For him, it hadn't been anything like what the other boys described.

After that, he'd dated only one girl—the one who made as good grades as he had. Doris was sweet, deeply religious, and took pride in her virginity. It was in no danger from him. He didn't desire it.

He enjoyed her company, the assurance that he could depend on her as an escort . . . and cover. Just like with Audrey.

In the sixties, when he'd come of age, gay wasn't even a word for what he was. Then there were only two choices for a black man: stud and sissy. He only knew he couldn't stand the kind of vicious ridicule and abuse they heaped on Lester, their classmate who they all knew was a sissy. So he chose stud. He hadn't understood what was so threatening about Lester that the other boys beat him up on a regular basis. Even now he was ashamed of his cowardice, his failure to come to Lester's defense. Not because they were different in the same way, but because Lester was a human being and what the other boys did was wrong.

It wasn't until he was in college that he came to grips with it. Finally accepted it. Made a decision. He'd always intended to be a lawyer. He didn't know any sissy lawyers. So what he needed was a wife and family. Cover. He could live with the frustration—or so he had thought.

Sam stopped his pacing and sat at his desk. Here he was, a fifty-year-old man, respected in his profession, a leader in his community. After hiding it all this time, he certainly couldn't afford to come out now. He had a solution.

*   *   *

"You can sit down, you know," Sam said, trying to sound casual, trying to hide the wariness he felt. "Can I get you some coffee?"

"Yes. You know how I take it," Audrey answered.

Sam pressed the intercom and gave instructions to the receptionist. Audrey could tell that her looking around the room was making him nervous, so she looked around some more, touching things here and there. At least he could be as nervous as she was. She walked over to the window and fingered the rich fabric of the drapes as she looked down at the street below.

Sam's office was on the top floor of the three-story building he and Paul had bought when the area was developing. They leased out the other two floors to help pay for it. Good investment, Sam had said. She had wanted a house in a newer neighborhood.

When she looked back at him, he looked away quickly, as though he hadn't been watching her. The receptionist came in, set the tray on his ornate, glass-topped desk, and left quietly.

Audrey sat down and fixed her coffee. And out of habit, his, too. It was just like any morning in their kitchen, except now his attention was acutely focused on her—not the newspaper, not a brief, not a stack of pleadings. Audrey placed the spoon on the tray, sipped the coffee, then set the cup on the table beside her.

"You can relax, Sam. I didn't come to talk about our little . . . difficulty. We can deal with that later. Right now, our son needs us. We've got to help him. I've hired him a lawyer."

"There you go again. Always coddling him. Always cleaning up behind his messes."

"You've got to testify for him, Sam. The lawyer said that's important."

"Testify about what? You know how much I've invested in him. What did that come to? Nothing but disappointment."

Audrey took another sip of coffee and took a deep breath.

"We need ten thousand dollars."

"Ten thousand dollars? For what?"

"A bail bondsman."

Sam shook his head. "I'm not doing that."

"We'd have spent more than that sending him to college," Audrey said.

"Yeah, but he wouldn't go to college. Remember?"

"And we need to put up the house." She strained to remain calm.

"The house? Our house? We can't put up the house, Audrey," he said, shaking his head. "It's almost paid for."

"We'll get it back when all this is over. He's our child, Sam. He's been in that jail over a month now." The tears she swore she wouldn't cry wrestled with the voices that told her that big girls don't cry. But why couldn't big girls cry? Big girls hurt, too. She snatched a tissue from the box on the table and dabbed at the corners of her eyes.

"I've been to that jail, Sam. You should see that place. He doesn't belong there. We've got to do it, Sam." She saw the panicked look on his face. He always looked like that when she cried.

"Don't cry, Audrey. I'll think about it. It doesn't make any sense, but I will think about it." Sam relaxed a little when Audrey folded the tissue in her lap. "I've been doing a lot of thinking lately. In fact, I've been thinking of moving back in the house."

Audrey looked up at him. "What? In the house? Why?"

"Because I'm tired of staying in a hotel. Because I'm too old to start over. Anyway, what's different now? Other than that you know. I'm the same person I've always been. It may be hard for you to believe, but I've always cared for you, Audrey. Loved you in the only way I could."

Sam looked out the window. "We can go on just like before. I'll keep providing for you, just as I always have. You have a nice, comfortable life, Audrey. You've never wanted for anything. Not really. I could even take the downstairs bedroom, if that would make you more comfortable. No one would have to know. I can't change the way I am. I will continue to be as discreet as I've been. At this stage in our lives, it doesn't make any sense to destroy what it's taken us all these years to build. I know you'll agree with me, once you've had a chance to think it through."

*   *   *

Audrey pushed the vacuum cleaner back and forth in the same spot, staring vacantly at the fireplace. Not a particle of dirt was left in the two feet of carpet in front of her. Normally, throwing herself into some heavy-duty house cleaning would take her mind off any problem. But today it wasn't working to keep her mind off of Sam. Her visit to his office this morning hadn't turned out exactly as she'd hoped. Dressed in a suit, he looked so masculine, so normal. But no matter how hard she tried, she couldn't get the image of him and Paul out of her mind.

She wondered for the hundredth time what she had done to make him that way. She had to believe that it was something about her that had changed Sam. It was just too painful to believe that he always had been that way. She could reckon with fault, but she couldn't accept that he could have deceived her so deeply.

Audrey caught a glimpse of herself in the tall mirror across the foyer. Aunt Jemima. She snatched the scarf off her head. She always wore it when she cleaned. It kept the dust out of her hair. No, it was just habit, learned long ago from her mama when they used to beat the rugs outside on a clothesline. Then she saw the gray in her hair. Maybe he had turned because she'd gotten old. Maybe she should have taken MaryBeth's advice and chemicalized away the signs of her age. But Paul was older than she was—and they all knew he had his hair dyed. That slimy weasel. She thought for an instant of dying her own, fixing herself up, and taking her man back. That's what she would have done if it had been a Pauletta. But what could she do to take him from Paul?

Maybe he'd changed because she was fat. No, she wasn't fat. She hadn't been fat since elementary school. She was big. She couldn't help that. Took after her daddy's people. And that was nothing new. She didn't weigh ten pounds more now than the day they'd married. So, why?

Audrey cocked her head, listening. Yes, it was the doorbell. She turned the vacuum off and walked into the foyer. Through the beveled panel she could see the pissed look on RosaLee's face.

"Hey, baby." Audrey hugged her daughter. "I wasn't expecting you until tomorrow. When did you get back?"

"I got in early this morning. My key didn't doesn't work. See?" RosaLee said, trying the key again to show Audrey.

"Yeah, I know, baby. I had the locks changed. I've got a new key for you."

"Oh." RosaLee looked puzzled a moment, then said, "I'm on my way to the office to pick up a couple of briefs. Thought I'd come by and check on you. How're you feeling?"

"I'm much better. Come on in. Did you have a good time in Las Vegas?" Audrey asked as she shut the door behind RosaLee.

"It was aw-ite."

"Alright?" Audrey thought of the airfare and hotel she'd charged on their credit card. She wanted to say, "For nearly a thousand dollars, I would have had a stone ball." Instead, she asked, "Lost money, huh?"

"A little. Don't ask how much."

"Okay. Would you like some juice?"

"No thanks. You gotta beer?"

Audrey felt RosaLee was baiting her, but she wouldn't go for it. "There may be one in the fridge."

RosaLee headed to the kitchen, and Audrey walked to the den. She slowly wrapped the cord of the vacuum, thinking. She still didn't have a plan for what to tell RosaLee. She had thought she'd have until tomorrow to come up with one. She certainly wasn't going to tell her the truth. But she couldn't think of anything else that would make sense. She pushed the vacuum into the foyer closet and drew a deep breath.

When she returned, RosaLee was seated on the couch, one shin crossed over her other knee. Audrey resisted the urge to tell her to sit more like a lady. She was struck as she always was at how RosaLee had her father's mannerisms, his hair, and his coloring, but otherwise she was Audrey made over.

When Audrey sat on the couch next to her, RosaLee looked at the overstuffed chair as if she wondered why Audrey hadn't sat in it, like usual.

"RosaLee, you know I love you. And I'm real proud of you and all you've accomplished."

"Okay, what's going on here?"

"Your father and I have separated." She waited for RosaLee's reaction. RosaLee looked away, twisted her mouth to the side, then took another sip from the beer can. She rested the can on her knee, and turned to Audrey.

"What brought this on?"

Audrey wasn't sure what she'd expected. She knew RosaLee wasn't prone to histrionics. But she had expected her reaction to be a little more emotional.

"Well, we just agreed it was for the best."

"You agreed, huh?"

"Yes. We agreed. But you don't have to worry, it shouldn't change your life in any way. We both love you."

RosaLee rolled her eyes, then smiled sheepishly. "I know that, Mom."

"Well, I just wanted to say it. To make sure you knew."

After a couple of minutes of awkward silence, RosaLee cleared her throat.

"So, is this a menopause thing?" She paused. "Or something else?"

"Something else like what?"

"I don't know. Just wondered," RosaLee said, looking away and shrugging her shoulders nonchalantly.

Audrey watched RosaLee turn the beer can up and drain it.

"Mama, I'd better get on to the office. I'll check on you later." She stood up, so Audrey did too.

"Are you gonna be okay, Mama?"

Audrey nodded.

"What about the key?"

*   *   *

A week later, Audrey straightened her suit jacket and steeled herself as she pulled open the door to the courthouse. On the long drive from Dallas she'd thought about nothing else, except how she would handle this. She would rather be almost any place on earth, but she had to be here. She was his mother. She wanted the judge to know that someone cared. She wanted Malcolm to know.

The day after her little talk with Sam, Sondra had called with the news of today's hearing. Sondra had told her how bad the case was, how the DA opposed a bond for Malcolm, and how the judge was not inclined to grant one. She'd discouraged her from coming. But no matter what happened, he was her child. Sam could sit up there in Dallas behind his big desk pretending this wasn't happening. But she was here laying her purse on the conveyor belt into the X-ray machine.

Inside, the hallways were crowded. It was easy to tell the lawyers. They wore expensive suits and shiny shoes. Even the cowboy boots were shiny. She imagined that they all had stopped at the shoe-shine stand she had passed on the first floor, right outside the door to the sheriff's department. The two men working the stand wore orange uniforms, Harris County Jail stamped in large black letters on their backs. The clients were easy to tell too, dressed in their Sunday-go-to-meeting clothes, some fairly smart, most not so smart.

Audrey stepped into the courtroom and looked around for Sondra. The high-ceilinged, mahogany-paneled room was filled with all the official trappings. The raised bench, flanked by the state and national flags and a large replica of the state seal, dominated the room. The official players were in attendance: prosecutors, defense lawyers, various clerk types. The court reporter sat just in front of the judge's bench, to the right of the witness stand. Her long legs were crossed provocatively beneath her short skirt. She kept tossing her blonde mane and smiling coyly at one particular lawyer—the young one, who appeared uncertain where he fit in.

The raised enclosure on the other side was not as high as the judge's bench and several clerks sat behind stacks of files. The other lawyers were engaged in congenial conversations with each other and the court clerks, but Sondra was not among them. Audrey wondered if she was in the wrong courtroom. But she'd checked the docket posted outside and Malcolm's name was on it. Two deputies lounged by a side door, near the judge's bench. She wondered if Malcolm was behind that door.

Audrey was making her way to the front of the spectator section when she saw him. Maxwell walked through the side doorway, shaking the deputies' hands as he passed. She'd thought about him more than once since that night two weeks ago. He was just as handsome as she remembered. The sprinkling of gray in his mustache and at his temple contrasted against his coal black hair and the rich color of his skin. The players interrupted their conversations to greet him. Towering over them, he basked in their respect. She wondered how he would react when he saw her. He hadn't even bothered to call. He could have gotten her number from Sondra. All those sweet words meant nothing. Would he even recognize her? She'd just pretend she didn't know him, either.

When he saw her, Maxwell broke mid-sentence and walked straight toward her. Pressing his lips together as tightly as he could didn't keep the smile off his face. By the time he stopped at the rail, the smile had won.

"Hi, Audrey Rob Williams. This is my lucky day. I thought I'd never see you again." He wanted to grab her up in his arms, but this wasn't the place. "I'm so glad to see you."

"It's good to see you, too." Audrey suppressed her own smile.

She would have blushed, but she was way past the blushing age. Her intention to ignore him flew right out the window. She was so glad to see a familiar face in this unfamiliar arena. She was so glad to see *him*.

"I would have sent a thank you note for the dinner, but I didn't have your address," she said.

He reached for her hand and held it in both of his. "I would have called you, but I couldn't get your number. You're not listed in Dallas."

"I know," she said, looking down.

"When I called the number Sondra gave me, it was a law office. And they said there was no Ms. Williams there."

"I have a cell phone now." Even as she said it, she wondered about that. She'd let Sam have their old number, since he got a lot more calls than she did. Maybe he'd had the phone forwarded to his office. But Sondra had her new number. She'd called it to tell her about this hearing.

"How long will you be here?" he asked, barely able to contain the excitement in his voice. "Let's go to lunch. I'm working now, but this shouldn't take long. Then I'll be free."

"I'd like that. But I don't know how long I'll have to be here." Audrey reluctantly withdrew her hand from his.

"What are you doing here anyway? Come to observe your girl in action?"

"All rise!" the bailiff called, as the judge strode in and took the bench. "Four hundred and twentieth district court is now in session. Judge David Goldstein presiding. Be seated." A momentary hush fell over the courtroom and all the players took their positions.

"I'll wait for you outside," he whispered, then turned and walked back through the side doorway. The deputies were now standing at attention. Everyone else took their seats. Audrey anxiously looked around for Sondra.

A young man, clad in an orange uniform with black letters on the back, walked through the door between the deputies and stood before the bench. Audrey noticed that he clasped his hands behind his back. She thought the pose conflicted with the look on the man's face—not quite disrespectful, but not exactly respectful either. She saw the young lawyer wink at the court reporter, before he turned to stand beside the defendant. She listened intently to the hushed conversation, trying to glean some clue as to how this game was played. She was too far away to hear much, in the muffled din of the courtroom.

The next man through the door was in street clothes, but Audrey noticed he held the same pose—hands behind his back. She wondered if Malcolm would be able to assume that posture of apparent submission. The third man didn't, until one of the deputies approached him menacingly, and tapped his arm with the baton. "Assume the position." She was offended by that, but her thoughts were interrupted by Sondra's appearance. Just her presence allowed Audrey a huge sigh of relief. Sondra took her hand in hers.

Just then, the judge announced the end of the plea docket, and took a recess.

"We're next," Sondra said, sitting next to Audrey. "Are you sure you want to stay for this? It's not going to be pleasant for you. You may hear some things said that you will wish you hadn't. Maybe you should wait in the hall."

Audrey shook her head. "I'll be okay."

"Okay, then. Just hang in there."

Sondra walked through the swinging gate to the table in front of Audrey and sat down. One of the deputies came over and shook her hand. As other players migrated over and spoke to her, Audrey felt a little more comfortable. Sondra appeared to be in her element. She opened her briefcase and began setting up, spreading books, folders, and papers on the table. Audrey saw the two women at the other table get busy, acting like they were getting ready, too. But she could tell they weren't nearly as confident as Sondra was. Maybe it was the difference in their ages.

She didn't think of Sondra as old. After all, she and Sondra were about the same age. But she was struck by how young the other women looked, not much older than RosaLee. She could see the tension, maybe fear, in their body language. She understood that. She had seen it in the young teachers that time when she'd taken a long-term substitute position for a teacher on maternity leave. In two days, she had more control of her classroom than they did after several months. Age and experience brought certain advantages.

"All rise," the bailiff announced, as the judge took the bench again.

"State versus Malcolm Roberts," the bailiff called out, as though the whole courtroom cared.

When Audrey first saw Malcolm in the doorway she almost fainted. Manacles held his wrists, and shackles were clasped around his ankles, with a length of chain running between them. The image in her mind was "slave." She fought the urge to run to him, to rip them off. She wanted to tell the judge that all that wasn't necessary. Malcolm was not a threat. He was an artist. But she knew there was no use, so she held herself still as Malcolm shuffled over to the table and sat down next to Sondra.

The judge riffled through the file, reading for a while, displeasure building on his face.

"All right, counselor. I've read your motion. Anything to say? Beyond what's in your form motion?"

Audrey heard the obvious sarcasm in the judge's voice and wondered why he was treating Sondra that way.

Sondra stood. "I'll proceed with the testimony." She pointed to the deputy by the door, brushed her skirt under her, and sat back down.

"Call your witness," the judge demanded in a haughty voice.

"I've already called my witness," she said snippily.

As the deputy opened the door, Audrey heard the impertinent tone in Sondra's voice and wondered why she would risk pissing the judge off. Hadn't her mama told her you catch more flies with honey than vinegar? Maybe it was some lawyer strategy that she didn't understand. But from the looks on both of their faces, Audrey decided it was something personal, something real personal. Could Sondra actually have—the thought was chased from her mind when she saw Maxwell coming through the side door the deputy held open.

He walked to the witness stand, and Audrey wondered what he had to do with this. As he took the oath, then settled his large frame into the chair, she remembered that he was Sondra's friend. She relaxed a little.

"What is your name, sir?" Sondra's voice was so cold and business-like, it didn't seem to Audrey that they were friends at all.

"Kirk Maxwell," he answered curtly, giving Sondra a blank look.

"What is your occupation?"

"Detective. Houston Police Department." A faint smile came to his lips, as he looked past Sondra, to Audrey.

"What do you do for the Houston Police Department?"

"I am responsible for investigating robberies."

Audrey breathed a sigh of relief. Surely he'd met a lot of robbers, and he was Sondra's friend. That's why Sondra had called him as a witness. To help Malcolm.

"Are you acquainted with Malcolm Roberts?"

"Yes."

"How did you come to know Mr. Roberts?"

"I was called to the scene of the store where he had robbed and killed the clerk."

Audrey jerked forward, as though if she could see him better, her ears would hear something different.

"Did you happen to see Mr. Roberts commit this robbery and murder?"

Maxwell didn't answer, his attention focused on Audrey. He had seen her reaction. He looked from her to Malcolm and back. A pained expression crossed his face as he saw the resemblance.

"Detective Maxwell! Answer the question, if you don't mind," Sondra demanded.

"No, but—"

"Then you can save the commentary and opinions. Just answer my questions. Truthfully. Did you prepare a report on this incident?"

"Yes." A deep frown furrowed his brow as he turned to her, and anger was clear on his face.

Referring to his report, he robotically answered her questions about Malcolm's fingerprints on the gun, the eyewitnesses, and taking Malcolm's statement.

Audrey didn't hear the questions or answers for the anger and hurt that washed over her. Why hadn't he told her? But why would he? He hadn't told her anything about his work. And since she'd given him her maiden name, there was no reason for him to connect her with Malcolm. But she knew he was a cop. Why hadn't she mentioned it to him? She'd told him about Sam. Why not about Malcolm?

"Now, you testified that when you arrived on the scene of the incident, two men were holding Mr. Roberts. Is that correct?"

"Yes."

"Who were these men? Did you know them?"

"No, I didn't know them." Maxwell riffled through the pages of his report. "One was Manor Jackson, 4720 Lyons. The other was . . ." He turned another page, then looked up at Sondra. "I don't seem to have that information."

"And you arrested my client on the word of these two strangers, right?"

"That's correct."

"A man died in this incident. From a gunshot wound. Isn't that correct?" As she spoke, Sondra walked around the table and leaned back against it.

"Yes."

"At close range?"

"Yes."

"Did you observe blood on Mr. Roberts?"

"There wouldn't necessarily be—"

"Did you observe any blood on my client?"

"No."

"Thank you. Did you search Mr. Roberts, incident to that arrest?"

"Yes."

"Did he have any money in his possession?"

"Yes," Maxwell answered, riffling through his report again. "Six dollars and thirty-seven cents."

"Hardly the booty from a robbery. And when you questioned Mr. Roberts, did you read him his rights?"

"I believe the other—"

"Did you read him his rights?"

"He wanted to—"

"Did you read him his rights?" Sondra demanded, jabbing her finger in the air toward Maxwell.

"He was talking when I walked up."

"That's all, Lieutenant Maxwell. You may step down." Sondra walked back around the table and sat down in a huff.

"I'll excuse the witnesses in my courtroom, Mrs. Evans," Judge

Goldstein admonished, then turned to the young prosecutor. "Any questions?"

She hurriedly stood. "Lieutenant Maxwell, does the fact that only a small amount of money was found on the defendant mean there was no intention to commit robbery?"

"Objection," Sondra interrupted. "Calls for speculation."

"Your Honor," the young prosecutor almost whined. "Lieutenant Maxwell is a twenty-year veteran of the force and has handled countless robberies."

"Objection sustained," Judge Goldstein barked.

"No further questions." The young prosecutor looked crestfallen as she sat down.

"Any other witnesses?" Goldstein asked toward Sondra.

"No, your honor. The testimony presented establishes my point, and supports my form motion. Our constitution and code of criminal procedure provide that a defendant in a criminal case has a right to a reasonable bail except in very limited circumstances. It is only in the case of capital murder where the proof is evident that bail may, not must, but *may* be denied. Even in a case of a heinous crime, say intentional murder, the defendant would be entitled to bail. And you would have a duty to set an amount of bail.

"My client has been held in Harris County Jail on a charge of capital murder for a month and a half with no bail. Capital murder is defined as murder in the course of another felony—in this case, robbery. While it is clear that a death occurred, there is no evidence of a robbery. My client denies killing the victim. For all we know, the two men who held him and turned him over to the police may be the murderers. Now, considering the weakness of the state's case, but also the seriousness of the accusation, I'd suggest a bond of thirty-five thousand dollars. Thank you." Sondra sat down and clasped her hands together on the table. No one could see that her fingers were crossed inside her hand.

"Well, Mrs. Evans, the court is ever appreciative of suggestions from learned counsel, and particularly a former judge. I'll take this case under advisement. Both sides will be notified of my decision in writing within ten days." Goldstein noticed the young prosecutor standing at her table. "Did you want to say something?" The annoyance was still in his voice.

"The state requests that bond be denied. We're sure the court will make the right decision."

★   ★   ★

By the time it was over, Audrey's face was ashen. The mask was in place, but she could feel it cracking. Right there around her mouth. Not now, she thought desperately. Not here. As Sondra gathered her papers, Malcolm shuffled back toward the door. He turned and looked at Audrey. His eyes pleaded with her.

"I'm sorry, Mama," he mouthed.

No sooner than the door closed behind him, Audrey fought her escape through the people entering the courtroom. Mercifully there were few people about when she stumbled into the hall, frantically searching for the ladies room. In the stall, she broke down. She saw shoes in the stall next to hers, and so she was careful not to make any noise. Racking sobs shook her body as she thought of her son being strapped to a gurney in the recesses of Huntsville Prison waiting for a needle. Silent, scalding tears flooded her face.

Now she understood why Sondra had been evasive when she'd asked about Maxwell. And why Sondra hadn't given him her phone number. Sondra could have saved her all those thoughts about how nice he was, how protective he had been, how he had said the things she needed to hear. How he had loved his wife in a way that Sam couldn't have loved her. How he would have been a good father if he'd had children. How in her dream he had touched her in the right places, had given her satisfaction before he took his. How they might have had a comfortable relationship when she got settled down. Sondra could have just saved her all that by telling her the truth. A lot of hard truth, Audrey could stand. Preferred it to those soft, cottony lies and evasions. They always hurt worse in the end, she thought, as she pressed a wet paper towel against her eyes.

seven

When Audrey pushed open the courthouse door, the bright sunlight hurt her swollen eyes. She was at the top of the wide, concrete steps when she saw him. Maxwell stood on the sidewalk below, impatiently checking his watch. It was obvious he was waiting for her, but she was too overwrought to talk to him now. Just as he looked up, she turned and walked back toward the courthouse, hoping he hadn't seen her. She stood in the crowd of people waiting to go through the metal detector, looking at her watch, and waiting for him to leave. Six minutes. Ten minutes. Then it was her turn. Maybe he would be gone. She turned to leave.

"Say you! Come back here," an officer shouted.

She glanced over her shoulder at the sound, and kept walking. Whatever it was wasn't her business. She heard the bleep of a momentary alarm. Just as she reached sunlight again, she felt a hard grip on her arm.

"Ma'am! You have to come in."

Audrey frowned at him and jerked her arm from his grip. "But I don't want to go in. I changed my mind."

"You mind if I look in your purse?"

Audrey's frown deepened. "Of course I mind. Why would you want to look in my purse?!"

"Drugs. Guns. Things you wouldn't want to go through the detector."

"I assure you, sir, I don't have drugs or a gun. I just came out of there."

"You have to come with me," he said sternly, snatching the purse.

"I don't have to go in if I don't want to. Turn loose," she commanded through gritted teeth, as she held on to her purse. When he wouldn't let the purse go, she tried to jerk it from him. He held it tighter and Audrey leaned back on one leg for leverage. If he succeeded in wresting the purse from her, he was sure going to be sore in the morning.

Suddenly, the officer quit the struggle and looked up, over her shoulder. Audrey heard the soft, deep voice.

"Let me handle this for you, Bruce. I'll take the purse," Maxwell said firmly. "Come on, Miss. You have to go with me."

Even blind with anger and spoiling for a fight, Audrey could see the better course was to go with him. She allowed him to lead her by her elbow, out of the courthouse vestibule, down the wide steps. When they reached the sidewalk, she flinched away from his grasp.

"Can I have my purse now?"

"We have a lunch date, remember?"

"You must be crazy. I am not about to go anywhere with you."

"Would you rather get yourself a room in our hotel? Bruce will be happy to accommodate you. Or you can give him the satisfaction of going through your purse," he said, a twinkle in his eye. He knew he had her, and she knew it too.

"He has no right," she huffed. "Just let me have my purse."

"Only if you agree to have lunch with me. We need to talk, Audrey."

"There's nothing for us to talk about."

"I'm not going to let you go until we do."

Audrey saw the determined look on his face. It matched his voice. "Well, if I'm under arrest, I suppose you can just do whatever you want," she huffed. "Don't you want to handcuff me?"

"That's not what I had in mind," he said, searching her eyes. "But I will, if that's what it'll take."

She didn't feel intimidated by his threat. At her size and in her state of mind, Audrey knew she could have whipped that Bruce before the others subdued her. She felt like whipping somebody. But she knew it wouldn't be Maxwell. Not this big bear of a man. Maybe that was why she had never been attracted to big men. She preferred men she knew wouldn't be able to push her around. Not physically, anyway.

"Well, talk, then," she said, an angry challenge on her lips.

"Not here. Come on." He held the purse out to her as a peace offering.

He led her through the same parking lot where they'd met. In the car, she crossed her arms over her breasts, and refused to say a word.

"I'm sorry, Audrey," he said softly. "I really am. I didn't know he was your son."

"Would it have made you any difference?" She looked sideways at him, out of angry eyes. "And 'he' has a name."

Maxwell thought about her question a minute. He had thought about her so many times. About how good she'd looked in those jeans. He liked a woman with some meat on her. A woman who could fill his hands up—and he had big hands. About how calm she'd been through the robbery at the restaurant. He couldn't stand a skittish, screaming kind of woman. He remembered the way she'd clung to him that night. The expression on her face when she said, "Thanks for saving me, Mr. I Can Fix Anything" just before she drifted into a deep sleep. Would his thoughts have been different if he had known she was the boy's mother? He knew the answer.

"I'm a cop, Audrey," he said matter-of-factly. "A good cop."

"Malcolm's my son." Her tone matched his.

"It's not personal for me. I'm just doing my job."

"It's very personal for me. I'm a mother. Malcolm's mother."

Maxwell's face softened. "Mr. Nguyen had a mother, too. She's eighty-four years old. He just brought her over here three months ago. She doesn't speak any English. She doesn't understand any of this any better than you do. Or than I do."

They rode in silence, until he pulled into the parking lot at Tino's Casa Mexicana. He opened the car door for her.

"I hope you like Mexican food. But they have other stuff, too. This is my favorite place. I come every Monday."

When she stepped inside, Audrey knew from the decor that the food would be real, not the pallid gringo kind. The piñatas hanging from the ceiling were not the newfangled, cartoon-character kind. There were the traditional donkeys, stars, cacti. Portraits of Mayan princesses painted on black velvet graced the walls. There were fig-urines of saints and a large crucifix with a bleeding Jesus. A large bowl of plastic-wrapped, homemade pralines sat on the counter. A thin, middle-aged man with a head full of black hair sat on a tall stool behind the cash register. A broad grin spread on his face when Maxwell said, "Tino! My man!"

"Ah, Señor Maxwell! Es Lunes. I knew you would come." He grabbed a couple of plastic-laminated menus and, casting an appre-ciative eye at Audrey, led them to a table by the gurgling fountain.

"I saved your usual table for you. Tu señorita es mas bella que Señor Danny," Tino said under his breath. He winked at Maxwell as he held a chair out for Audrey.

"Gracias, pero soy la prisionera del Señor Maxwell," Audrey said, in perfect Spanish, as she took her seat.

Tino raised his eyebrows at Audrey, "Ah, pero, creo que la señorita may find herself a prisionera del amor."

Maxwell was nonplussed at their banter. What little Spanish he knew all had to do with jail and crime. But he did know "amor" and he didn't think Tino should be talking to her about that.

"I'll have my usual," he said. "What would you like, Audrey?"

Audrey turned to Tino. "Quisiera enchiladas de camarón. Tiene?"

"Bueno," he said, nodding.

As soon as Tino retreated, Audrey lit into Maxwell.

"My boy isn't a killer. Why—"

"Let's eat first." The quiet demand in his deep voice made her crimp her mouth. Minutes passed with neither of them saying anything.

A young man who Audrey guessed was Tino's son set two tall glasses of iced tea on the table. Maxwell grabbed three packets of sweetener, tore them open, and dribbled the grains into his glass. As Audrey poured sugar into her glass, she let out a harrumph.

"What?" he asked quizzically.

"I guess you think you can sin without suffering."

"Huh?"

"You want the sweetness, but not the calories."

Maxwell took a sip and let it pass. He didn't want to argue with her.

"So, do you still teach school?" he asked, when the silence grew too heavy for him.

"No," she answered curtly.

"Retired?"

"No."

More minutes ticked by in silence.

"I've been to Dallas a couple of times. For the police Olympics."

"Is that right?" Audrey's voice showed as little interest as she could manage.

Maxwell could tell she was still spoiling for a fight. He knew they had a big mountain to climb, but he didn't intend to do it on an empty stomach. He hoped a good meal would mellow her out, too. Tino brought their steaming plates just in time. He gave Maxwell a sly smile as he backed away.

"That looks good." He waited for her to take the first bite, then dug into his plate of carne guisado.

Audrey wouldn't give him the satisfaction of a response, but the cheesy enchiladas were so good it was a hard fight. She was certain Tino had put extra shrimp in them.

When he finished, Maxwell pushed his empty plate aside with an air of satisfaction and sat back to wait for her to finish. Audrey pushed her half-eaten plate aside too and folded her arms across her breasts. He saw the challenge on her face.

"All right, Audrey. Let's talk."

"You talk," she said, testily.

Maxwell blew out a sigh, then leaned forward, elbows on the table. It was get-to-the-point time.

"Okay, Audrey. From the first moment that I saw you in that parking lot, I haven't thought about much of anything else. I can't explain it, even to myself. I felt alive again. I enjoyed being with you—even with all that happened. I tried every way I know how to find you. You don't have a drivers license or car title in the name of Audrey Williams. And you've never been in trouble with the law. Not even a parking ticket. I checked with a friend on the force in Dallas. I even checked the FBI files. I may have even broken the law trying to find you. It was almost like you didn't exist. Like you were a figment of my imagination."

Audrey's arms were still folded across her chest. "You don't have to be Sherlock Holmes to find me. You could have just asked Sondra."

"I did. You don't know how hard it was for me to have to go to her and ask for your number. Sondra and I had already had some heated words over this case. She asked me to do something I considered unethical. She didn't see it that way, but that's the only way I can see it. I only went to her as a last resort. I told you she gave me the wrong number. When I saw you today, I knew she had done it on purpose. She knew all along this involved us both. Maybe she called herself protecting you. Or maybe me."

A frown creased his forehead as he thought about that for the first time. That would explain it all. They had been friends for so long. Maybe the whole misunderstanding had been his fault, his not trusting her. She'd even said something about trust. How could he have been so wrong? It was his mistake. He'd just have to fix it.

Maybe he was wrong about this, too. Another mistake. Even a fool could see that the course he was on was fraught with danger. He would have told any junior officer, even Danny, to leave her alone. Maybe loneliness was strong enough to throw his moral compass off. But even so, when he looked down into Audrey's face, he knew what he was going to do.

"It wasn't the wrong number," Audrey said, quietly. "It was my old number. Maybe she just forgot."

He shook his head. "She didn't forget. She was trying to warn me. To make me stop and think. And I've been thinking about it ever since we were in the courtroom. I don't think we should let this come between us."

"How can this not come between us? You're a cop. You're trying to put my child in prison. How can there be an 'us'? What kind of mother do you think I am?"

"This isn't about Audrey, the mother. This is about Audrey, the woman."

"I know my child. My son has done some things that I'm not proud of. He has disappointed me. But he's no killer."

"He made a choice of what to do with his life. Now you have a choice about your life. You're not the only person who ever had a child who didn't turn out. Don't let denial and guilt deprive you of living. You could die next week."

"I don't want to hear this. I gotta go." Audrey pushed her chair back, grabbed her purse and started for the door.

*   *   *

They were heading back toward the courthouse when Maxwell felt the vibration from his pager.

"I'm not going to have to fix a flat today, am I?" he said, trying to lighten the mood as he pulled the pager off his belt. When he looked at the display, he immediately put the blinker on and turned the car. "I'm sorry. I've got to do this now."

"Duty calls for the good cop?" she asked, sarcasm heavy in her voice.

"Sort of. It's Cedric."

"Your partner?"

"Danny's my partner. Cedric is my little boy."

Audrey noticed that Maxwell now drove with a sense of urgency. "You told me you didn't have any children."

Maxwell glanced at her. "Me and Shirley never had any children of our own. Cedric's a kid I'm sort of raising. His mama's a crack-head—and a prostitute. I don't know anything about his daddy. Probably a crackhead, too. Or in prison. Cedric doesn't know anything about him. Or won't tell. He's streetwise. The mama had him selling drugs. He's only nine. But then, she's only twenty-two. One night a couple of years ago, she OD'd and he called nine-one-one. I was working third shift. Traded with one of my guys whose daughter was getting married that night. I was close by, so I answered the call. You can't imagine the filth in that apartment. Child Protective Services couldn't find a placement for him that night, so I took him home with me. Me and Shirley sort of adopted him.

Not legally. We would have. But then Shirley got sick. And the mama won't let him go, anyway. I've tried. She'll straighten up just enough to persuade the judge not to terminate her rights. Not that Cedric lives with her. He's in a good foster home. I told him that if he ever needs me, I'll come. No matter what. I can't let him down. He has all my numbers. He wouldn't page me if it wasn't something serious. I'll get you back across town as soon as I can, but I've got to do this first."

As Maxwell parked the car in front of Hilltop Academy, he noticed the surprised look on Audrey's face.

"I pay for him to go here," Maxwell explained. "He's real smart. He needed a different . . . environment. He's handling the academics fine. But there are some adjustments. I don't think this will take long."

As she waited in the car, Audrey was surprised at the peaceful atmosphere on the quiet, tree-shaded avenue. She'd expected a graffiti-covered building like those where she'd subbed in Dallas. After a while, it got stuffy in the car. She grew impatient. What was taking so long? She got out and walked into the school, into the office. No one was there, so to pass the time, she read the notices on the bulletin board. The posting for an educational consultant with the Broadnax Foundation caught her attention. She read through it while she waited, then took it down and put it in her purse.

She walked back to the car and leaned against it. Before long, she saw them heading her way, hand in hand. Maxwell's face was taut with anger. Cedric looked indignant and scared at the same time. When they were close, she got a better look at the child's face.

Maxwell turned loose his hand. "This is Ms. Williams, Cedric. Say hello."

"Hello," Cedric said sullenly, looking away from her.

"Okay, get in the car," Maxwell said sternly, as he walked around to the driver's side.

Audrey squatted down, so that her face was even with Cedric's. She turned him to face her.

"Let me take a look at that." She cupped his face in her hand and turned it at an angle. "Who hit you in your eye?"

"Matthew," he answered, even more sullenly.

"Why did Matthew do that?"

"Cause I called him a peckerwood."

"Well, you shouldn't have done that. You mustn't call people names. Where did you hear a name like that?"

Angry tears welled up in Cedric's eyes, and his bottom lip trembled.

"But . . . he started it. He called me a nigger."

Audrey frowned as she pondered the burden of that for a nine-year-old child. Even growing up in East Texas, she'd been shielded from that kind of hurt—at least until she enrolled at UT.

"Then, you should have beat the tar out of Matthew."

"I did." The look on his face was one of sheepish pride.

A slow smile broke through Audrey's face and she held up her palm. Cedric eyed her warily, then slapped her palm.

All the way, Maxwell kept up a steady beat-beat about how Cedric should have handled the situation differently, how fighting doesn't solve a problem, how he should have reported the incident to the principal, how he should have called him. When he stopped in front of a neat frame house, he opened the door for Cedric.

"Say good-bye to Ms. Williams."

Audrey turned around to face him. He gave her a little grin and said, "See ya." Then his face turned somber again as he got out of the car.

Maxwell and Cedric walked to the door and rang the bell. Audrey saw him squat down, talking to Cedric, his hands on his shoulders. Before he relinquished Cedric to the stern-faced woman who opened the door, he hugged the boy to him. Cedric hugged him back, but his arms weren't long enough to stretch around Maxwell's broad shoulders.

When Maxwell got back in the car, his lips were tight, his breathing shallow. He didn't speak for a couple of blocks.

"I don't think that what you said was appropriate," he said. "Cedric has to learn to hold his temper in check. To roll with the punches."

"What exactly do you think is 'appropriate' when somebody calls you a nigger?"

"I've been called a nigger a bunch of times and—"

"Well, I'll bet Matthew won't call anybody else one. Not out loud, anyway," she chuckled. Then she sobered. "Did they put Cedric out of school?"

"Just for today," he said, nodding.

"Did they put Matthew out—just for today?" she asked sarcastically.

"Of course. It's a good school. They have rules against fighting."

"Do they have rules against using racist names?"

"It wasn't that clear who started it, Audrey. I'm satisfied with the way it was handled."

"Well, somebody's got to stand up for our boys."

"I can't stand for all of them. I'm standing up for Cedric."

"Your job is to put them all in prison."

"Only the ones who hurt people, Audrey. Ain't nothing holy about being black."

At her car, Audrey beat him out of the Lincoln. "Thanks for the ride."

"Can I call you?"

"I'm leaving."

"You're really leaving this time?"

Audrey turned and got in her car.

*   *   *

Here she was at the jail again. The family visiting hours were damned near like those at an ICU ward, but since she had a long drive ahead of her back to Dallas, the morning one-hour period fit her schedule. This time she'd locked her purse in the trunk of the car in hopes of speeding up the process. It didn't. By the time she got to the big, noisy room, Malcolm was there waiting for her. He looked thin and gaunt.

"What are they feeding you in here?" she asked.

"Stuff. Nasty stuff. I don't eat much of it."

"You need to eat, Malcolm."

"I know, Mama. I'm doing the best I can. Since I don't have any money on my books, a lot of time I use the slop they feed us for coin. In here, you do what you gotta do."

Audrey looked off, feeling like it was her fault.

"How much do you need . . . on your book?"

"Don't worry about it. I don't want nothing from y'all you ain't willing to give. I'm a man. I can make it."

Anger jerked the guilt out of Audrey.

"Don't you give me this shit, Malcolm. I got you a lawyer. She says I may have to put up my house to get you out of here."

Repentant and hopeful, Malcolm turned to face her. "Would you do that, Mama?"

"Well, I'm not sure, Malcolm. I'm not even sure the judge will give you a bond. But if he does, it's going to be a whole lot of money. More money than I have. A bondsman will take a lien on the house. But if you don't show up for court, they'll take my house. Do you understand that, Malcolm? I'd have no place to live."

"I'd go to court, Mama," he said anxiously. "I'll do anything to get out of here. I'm going crazy. You know I wouldn't let you lose your house."

Audrey looked at him and thought of the times he hadn't shown up. For Sam's birthday party, for RosaLee's graduation, for his probation officer.

"If you could get out, where would you live?" she asked.

His eyes lit up. "I still have my place, I guess. The rent's a month behind, but it's only four hundred dollars. I'm sure if I gave the dude last month's rent and this month's, he'd let me stay."

"Do you have a job? The lawyer said you have to have a job."

Malcolm looked down. "I can get a job. My homeboy knows a place that hires people on paper."

"People on paper?"

"Probation. Yeah, I could get a job. And I been in here long enough, I could pass the pee test."

Audrey put her hand to her forehead and massaged it with her thumb. Then, she looked up at Malcolm.

"Tell me the truth, Malcolm. Did you do this thing?"

"Mama, you know I couldn't do nothing like that. I swear. You believe me, don't you?"

Audrey searched his eyes. She still didn't see a killer.

"Are you gonna get me outta here, Mama?"

*   *   *

As she walked across the parking lot, Audrey wondered what she had done to bring all this on herself. Nothing she did seemed to work out. She had left the purse in the car to save time. Now it would take twice as long to go back to leave money on Malcolm's books.

EIGHT

On the drive to Sam's office, Audrey thought of Sondra's call. She was relieved that the judge had set a bond amount for Malcolm. At least that gave her something to work toward. The bond was $100,000—just like Sondra had said. Plus electronic monitoring—whatever that meant.

As she rode the little elevator to the top floor, she thought about Sam's calls that she hadn't returned. Did he really think she would let him move back in her house? That she would willingly live a lie? His life would be back on course. Hers would be in shambles. She thought about the things she'd moved to fill up the places where Sam's stuff used to be. There was no place for him now. She liked the way the house was now. The house she'd cleaned and lovingly cared for all these years was all hers now. No more tension. No more having to be quiet. She could play her music all into the night. It was her house. Why should she let him move back in her house? Was there any good reason? Hell no. In exchange for her son's freedom? Well. . . .

*   *   *

"Hello, Audrey."

"Sam," she said, nodding as she sat in the armchair across from his desk.

"Well? Did you decide?"

"Yep, I sure did. I've talked to Malcolm, the lawyer, and the bondsman. All we have to do is sign a lien against the house. As soon as the case is over, he'll release the lien. It's pretty simple."

Sam looked surprised. "I wasn't talking about that. I'm not about to give my house to a damned bondsman. I deal with those sharks all the time. And what if he runs? That boy has been running away from problems all his life. What if he runs, Audrey?"

Audrey gritted her teeth and took deep breaths. She felt the tears fighting their way, again. These were angry tears, but she was angrier. This time, she was stronger.

"Alright. I'll tell you what, Sam. It's one thing to do what you've done to me. It's another thing altogether to turn your back on your own flesh and blood." Audrey stood and leaned over the desk, right in his face. "Now, you listen to me, and you listen good. I've decided to cash in as much of that stock as it'll take to pay the bondsman. You are going to sign a paper that says I can handle the house, and I'm going to sign the house over to the bondsman. Then, I'm going to file for divorce."

"Audrey, I don't think you should make a rash decision," he said in his soothing, lawyer voice. "You're just being all emotional. Do you realize how much it will cost us to get a divorce? Why, just splitting the—"

"It ain't gonna cost me shit, Sam. This is your fault. It's gonna cost you. Everything. I'm unemployed. I have no retirement. No nothing. I'm going to get the most expensive lawyer in town—that woman you and Paul are always bad-mouthing. And yo' ass is gonna have to pay her."

"Okay, okay, Audrey. Just calm down. What if I file all the papers?"

"That's fine with me. I don't care, as long as you put it in those papers that I get the house, all the furniture, all the bank accounts, the RV, the condo—"

"Wait a minute. Wait just one minute. Why should you get everything!"

"Because I'm going to have to start my life over—from scratch—at forty-nine years old. And if I'm going to have to do that, then you ought to, too. At least you have the law degree I paid for. I have nothing. You will make some more money tomorrow. Oh, and don't forget this building."

"Now, hold on, Audrey. You know I only own half."

"That's not what MaryBeth's divorce decree says. And that's a public record. You know, Sam, it's funny. I was willing to accept anything from you, I mean anything, even letting you move back in and living the charade you want. Anything, for you to help my son." Audrey slung her purse over her shoulder and turned a cold eye to Sam.

"You have the paper about the house delivered to me tomorrow by noon, and the rest of the papers by Friday, Sam. Otherwise, you can just get yourself ready, 'cause I'll drag yo' ass out of the closet, kicking and screaming. And that asshole Paul, too. You got that?"

★ ★ ★

Maxwell had left for the day a little early. He'd been doing that all week. Danny found it more than a little curious. Usually he left Maxwell sitting at his desk, sometimes piddling, sometimes immersed in a case, but always avoiding going home to an empty house. The gym bag he carried all this week made Danny wonder. Even though the lieutenant was in great shape for a man his age, Danny couldn't imagine Max working the weights.

Danny fingered through the piles of papers on Maxwell's desk until he found the file. He felt an urgency to get the Roberts case wrapped up and sent to the district attorney now that a bond had been set. He couldn't believe the judge had set a bond, and especially one so low.

Danny read the ballistics report again. Where would a boy like that get a silencer, he wondered. The curious thing to him was that there were no fingerprints on the trigger. Why would the boy be careless enough to leave prints all over the barrel, the handgrip, but not even a partial on the trigger? He'd even had Ballistics do the test over, just to be sure. Still no prints on the trigger. The second technician had been more thorough, even found prints on the bullets still in the gun. Curious that they weren't Roberts's. ID hadn't gotten back to him yet with a match. But the most curious thing was the gun itself. When he ran the serial number, trying to trace an owner, he found it had been confiscated in another case. So why wasn't it in the property room?

*   *   *

The next afternoon Audrey overnighted a package to Sondra with a cashier's check for ten thousand dollars, the paper Sam had sent for the house, and two four-hundred-dollar money orders made out to Malcolm. Two weeks later she had leased the house to a nice couple and, with MaryBeth's and RosaLee's help, had put her furniture and her memories in storage. What she needed for right now, including Polly, she put in the motor home. It actually would be a relief for her to be out of the house, maybe out of Dallas, away from so many memories. Then she could really put some closure on this thing with Sam.

She had searched for an apartment, but her heart wasn't in it. They were all adequate, but she wasn't looking for a home just yet. She had in mind taking a long trip in the RV. She'd always wanted to see the leaves change in New England except this wasn't the season. So, she decided she would meander out west. See all of the canyons, starting with the Palo Duro out by Amarillo. Then the Grand Canyon. Then, the Canyonlands of Utah. Zion Canyon was the one she especially wanted to see. Then maybe on to California. Just with herself—and Polly. She'd never done that. Always had the kids, or Sam. It could be sort of like a honeymoon. The start of her new life.

The day the letter came from the Broadnax Foundation Board of Directors requesting that she come to Houston for an interview for the consultant position, she was poised to sign a lease. She had found an apartment complex where she could park the RV when she got back from her honeymoon. But the letter put a different light on things. She folded the lease and put it in her purse, then called Sondra.

Sondra insisted that she stay in her house, but Audrey liked having a place of her own. And she didn't know how long she'd be in Houston. There was nothing in Dallas for her to come back to—no job, no house, no husband. Besides, Malcolm was in Houston. And there was a westward highway out of Houston, too. She hooked the car up behind it and drove the motor home down to Houston. She parked the RV around back of Sondra's house, behind the swimming pool, and unhooked the car. The extension of the driveway was the perfect place, like it had been laid just for an RV.

The next morning, Audrey sat in the reception area on the sixteenth floor of the Broadnax Foundation Building while the board met behind the conference room doors. She wasn't sure she really wanted this job—any job, just yet. She wasn't rich by any means, but she and Sam had accumulated a little something over the years, according to the statements she'd studied. And besides, he was making money every day. She could just keep living like she had, charging what she needed on their cards and writing checks for cash. So far he'd cooperated, but she didn't know how long that would last. Still, it would be nice to have a certain income. And especially in work that she'd been trained in, and that evoked her passion.

Right now, she dreaded being looked up and down by these strangers. Would they think she was too old? Or too big? Or too black? When the chairman of the board opened the door and beckoned her, Audrey already had decided that she'd wow them so hard, the job would be hers to accept or reject.

The board probably thought the interview was grueling. It was definitely more grueling for them than for her. They were just well-meaning people who had a good idea and a lot of money. She knew the subject at ground zero. By the time she walked out of the interview, she knew she had the consultant position.

When she took the letter out of Sondra's mailbox three days later, she didn't even have to open it to know. But she opened it anyway, and a big smile spread across her face. She wanted to celebrate. But with whom? Sondra wasn't due in until the weekend. She didn't know another soul in Houston. Except Malcolm. Maybe they could have a quiet dinner.

When she called him, the phone rang and rang. He should have been home. Maybe he had found a job. Or maybe that electronic monitoring thing messed up the phone. That setup had cost her a pretty penny. This whole ordeal was nickeling and diming her to death—except in hundreds. She dialed the phone she'd paid for, again. When there was still no answer she thought she should get him an answering machine. The only other person she knew was Maxwell. She pursed her lips. Did she dare? Of course not. Why not?

It took a while for her to work through the automated answering system: Press 1 if you have this kind of problem. Press 2 if you have another kind of problem. Blah, blah, blah. In a moment of bold impatience, she thought about dialing 911, but finally pressed "0" instead. RosaLee had told her that would get you to a real person on any of those stupid time-saving systems. Whose time did they save, anyway? Certainly not hers.

"Detective Maxwell, please," she said, to the real person on the other end of the line.

When she first heard his deep voice, her nerve faltered, and she almost hung up.

"Hi. This is Audrey. Remember me?"

"Audrey who?"

Her nerve failed completely. "Never mind. Wrong number." She took the receiver from her ear.

"Audrey! Wait! Don't hang up! Audrey? You there?"

"Yes," she answered hesitantly.

"Of course I remember you. How could I forget a lady who takes shrimp in her enchiladas and speaks of love to a stranger? And in Spanish at that?"

Audrey smiled. "I've got something to celebrate. Sondra's not here. I don't know anyone else in Houston. I wondered, I mean, would you like to go to dinner?"

"What time should I pick you up?"

*   *   *

They'd agreed on 6:30, and at exactly 6:30, the doorbell rang. Audrey looked at her watch, then finished putting on her lipstick. Right on time. She liked a timely man. She caught one last glance in the mirror and liked what she saw. The silk pantsuit was her favorite color, and the coral looked good against her skin. The top was cinched at her waist with a wide silver belt, a rhinestone serpent on the clasp. Most women her size gave in to the muumuu dresses. No muumuus for this chick, she thought, smiling as she smoothed the silk over her hips. Audrey grabbed her purse and hurried to the door. For a moment, they stood there looking at each other, neither knowing what to say. Both wondering if they were doing the wrong thing. Then she smiled.

"Is there some place in particular you'd like to go?" he asked, as he opened the car door.

"I don't know anything about Houston. Tino's would be fine with me. The food was good."

"No way, José. I can't have you and Tino talking about amor. He'll tell Danny. And that boy will never let me live it down. I know just the place. A couple of brothers just opened a seafood franchise out of New Orleans."

*   *   *

"What are we celebrating?" Maxwell asked, when they were seated in the quiet elegance of the restaurant.

"Let me show you," Audrey answered. She took the letter from her purse and set it on the polished mahogany table in front of him.

He scanned the letter, then looked up at her. "Hey, this is great. When do you start?"

"Well, I haven't exactly decided to take it. It's just a good feeling, knowing that they want me. I've been out of the job market for a long time. I've kept my finger in the pie, doing a lot of volunteer work. And lately I've been doing substitute teaching. I've seen what's happening in the schools. Kids running wild. Not learning nearly enough. Teachers blaming parents, parents blaming teachers. Everybody finger-pointing. None of it's making the schools better for the kids. A lot of them are being left behind on the information highway. Some of them, just left behind period."

"I see them every day. A lot of them end up with us."

She nodded. "The folk at this foundation have good hearts—and a lot of money. So much good can come of that, if it's used the right way. And I've got some ideas about how to use it. They have a particular interest in inner-city schools. They assured me I would have a pretty free hand."

The waiter set down a plate of blackened salmon and wild rice for her and one with steak and a baked potato for him.

"Does this mean you'll be moving to Houston?" he asked. Pleasure danced around his eyes at the prospect.

"I wouldn't have to. What with faxes and e-mail and all, I could manage from anywhere."

"Why do that? Why stay in Dallas, if your job is here?"

"I didn't say I'd be in Dallas. But, I do have a child there. A daughter. She's grown, of course. A lawyer. She's doing real good."

"You have a child here."

Audrey looked down at her plate.

"I'm sorry," he said. "I know we agreed not to talk about that. And this is your celebration. Let's order champagne," he said, brightly, then summoned the waiter.

When the waiter brought the champagne, Maxwell offered a toast. "To your new job."

After the second glass he asked, "What kind of music do you like?"

"I like music, period. Except opera. All that hollering and screaming just gets on my nerves. Love shouldn't hurt like that."

He laughed out loud, then smiled wryly. "I guess love hurts different people in different ways. Come on. I know just the place."

When Maxwell took the exit and stopped for the red light, Audrey looked out the window at the bright lights from a carnival set up in the parking lot of a shopping center.

"Look at that! When was the last time you went to a carnival?"

"About a hundred years ago," he laughed. "When I was a kid, we used to go, once a year, when it came to town."

"We went to the state fair in Dallas once a year, on Colored Day. I haven't been in years. Let's go to that one."

"Are you serious?"

"Yeah. Why not? Let's stop by, just for a minute. Wonder if they have cotton candy?"

Maxwell turned the car into the parking lot. "It's your celebration. We can do whatever you'd like."

They walked through the brightly lit arch and joined the noisy crowd.

"Oh look! A ferris wheel!" Audrey said, excitement ringing in her voice. "Where do you get the tickets? I want to ride it."

Maxwell looked uncertain. "I don't think that's such a good idea. We just ate."

"Do I look like a woman with a weak stomach?" she said, laughing, her hands on her hips. "You must have one."

"No. I was just thinking about you."

When they were seated and the wheel rose to load the next car, Audrey saw the way his fingers gripped the bar. With a mischievous smile, she began rocking the car.

"Stop it! Don't do that!"

"You scared?" she asked, with a twinkle in her eye.

"Not at all. I just don't want this thing to get unbalanced or something."

When the wheel rose again to board the next car, Audrey rocked theirs again. Maxwell put one arm around her, took her hands off the bar and held them on top of his thigh. "You're making these other people nervous."

She gave him a sly smile. She knew who was nervous. Maxwell relaxed just a little when all the cars had been loaded and the ride smoothed out, but Audrey saw his eyes squeeze shut and felt his grip tighten on her shoulder each time they crested the top and started the descent.

"What don't you like about this?" Audrey teased. "It's slow and easy."

"I like it. I like it," he lied.

"You're not in control. That's it, isn't it? You like to be in control."

"Naw, I just like to keep at least one foot on the ground at all times," he said with a nervous laugh.

Audrey liked the feel of his hand enclosing hers and his arm around her shoulder. It reminded her of the night they'd met.

"Now, wasn't that fun?" she asked as he helped her down from the ride.

"Never had so much fun in my life," he said breathlessly, wiping the film of perspiration into the hair at his temple.

They walked down the midway, eating cotton candy. Applause and yelling rose just as they passed the basketball stand. A tall, lanky kid had just won a big teddy bear.

"Oh, I want one of those," Audrey said. She pulled him against the crowd that was dissipating. Before she could get her purse open, Maxwell had paid the barker for the five balls. He bounced the first ball a couple of times to get the feel of it, then shot it straight through the hoop. He missed the next two. Audrey grabbed the next ball.

"Move, move," she said, urging him aside with her hip. "Watch this." She took her time, made a couple of fakes, then pushed the ball up. It fell straight through the goal. She turned to Maxwell with a proud smile. "It's all in the wrist." She pitched the last ball. It rolled around on the rim until it fell in.

The barker disinterestedly handed her a miniature stuffed bear, and immediately began calling out to the passersby. Audrey waved dollar bills in his face to get his attention.

"Five more." She made the first three, then he took the next ball from her. He made that one, but missed the last one.

"Football was my game," he said apologetically.

Maxwell saw the disappointment on her face, as she looked at the two little bears.

"You really wanted that big one, didn't you?"

"These are okay. Nice souvenirs," she said, trying to hide the letdown. "You 'bout ready to go?"

"Come on." Determined to bring the excitement back to her face, he took her hand and pulled her to another booth. "How many shots for the big bear?" he asked the barker.

"Six straight. Dollar a shot."

Maxwell handed him a ten-dollar bill and picked up the gun. "Hand her the change," he said, as he crossed his forearm in front of him as a brace. He placed his other hand across it and took aim. He let the first duck pass. The next six were his. On the last one, Audrey let out a gleeful shriek, jumped up and down, then threw her arms around his neck.

"I'll swap you," Maxwell said. He handed her the huge teddy bear with a big red bow around its neck, and took the little bears from her. Cedric would like them, he thought.

"Name him Mighty Max. That's what they call me—behind my back."

★   ★   ★

Audrey looked skeptical when Maxwell opened the door to the Grand Royal Lodge for her.

"Somehow you don't impress me as a 'lodge' kind of fellow."

"I'm not," he said, knocking on the glass window.

"But that sign said PRIVATE CLUB. MEMBERS ONLY," she said, as they waited in the tiny entranceway lit by a dim bulb. A man peeked through the curtain behind the glass ticket window. Then she heard the snapping of the deadbolt being turned. When Maxwell pushed the heavy door open, the sound of music rushed out to greet them. Audrey stepped through the door to the appraising leer of a man seated at the bar to her left.

"Don't even think about it, Jake. She's already spoken for," Maxwell grinned as he stepped in, too. He grabbed Jake's hand and shook it.

"Haven't seen you 'round here in a while, Max. Guess you been busy." Jake looked Audrey over from head to toe and back, stopping a second at her hips. Maxwell put his arm around Audrey's shoulder possessively, urging her on.

"Get your own woman, Jake, or go home to your wife," he tossed over his shoulder with a laugh. "See ya, man."

He found a table and pulled the chair out for Audrey.

"This crowd may be a little geriatric for you, but they have the best music in town. Tonight is oldies night. One of the civilian employees in the property room is the DJ."

While he ordered drinks from the gum-smacking waitress, Audrey surveyed the crowd. She wouldn't have described the dancers on the small wooden floor as exactly geriatric, but she and Maxwell were on the younger end of this spectrum.

When "My Girl" came on, he pulled her out of her chair and led her to the dance floor. The tempo was just right for a slow swing-out. Maxwell held out his left hand. Audrey put her right hand in it and her arm around his broad shoulder. After a couple of swings, Maxwell felt comfortable that she could follow him, so he broke out in a fancy step. It was the same version they did in East Texas when she was in high school. Audrey didn't miss a beat, twirling around under his arm, behind his back, then around into his arms. "Hello Stranger" was next. He caught her hand to keep her on the dance floor, put his palms against hers and led her into the cha-cha. She was good at that too, and they moved together to the beat. While the mood was going strong, the DJ slid into the electric slide. Not only couples, but most of the women without escorts poured onto the floor for the dance that didn't require a partner. So many people crowded onto the little dance floor that those seated around the edge had to move their chairs back.

When Max turned to leave the dance floor, Audrey held him back and insisted that he join in. He protested that he didn't know this dance, but she wouldn't take no for an answer. She laughed at his stumbling around and bumping into the other dancers. He took her teasing good-naturedly, and by the end of the cut had gotten the hang of the thing. He gave her a confident "See there?" smile.

A slow song was next, "One in a Million, You," and most of the sliders returned to their seats. This was more Maxwell's beat, so he put his arm around Audrey's waist and held her on the dance floor. Holding her in his arms, remembering their first night, Maxwell felt like he was in heaven. She fit so perfectly against him, he couldn't let her go on "Baby, I'm For Real."

Audrey loved being ensconced in the arms of this big man. She felt safe from all the cares of the world. She didn't want this night to ever end—until she felt the bleeding start.

*   *   *

Maxwell wore his new suit. Well, it wasn't exactly new any more, but it was his best one. The one Shirley had given him on his birthday the year before she died. Every Sunday at exactly two o'clock, he turned the Lincoln into the tall wrought-iron gates of the perpetual-care cemetery. For nearly two years now, he'd done this. In the rearview mirror, he straightened his tie.

"Come on, Mitts. It's time," he said to the big, black cat with the white paws lounging on the seat next to him. He'd never liked cats, especially black ones. Shirley was the only person he'd ever heard say that black cats were good luck. A German shepherd was the kind of animal he would have kept. Maybe a rottweiler. But Shirley had a fear of dogs. So he'd tolerated the stray cat she adopted—and Mitts tolerated him. At least it was a tom.

He'd thought Mitts would leave when Shirley did. But he'd stayed, so Maxwell fed him. That was the only interaction they had, except for their Sunday ritual. He got out of the car and held the door for Mitts. The cat raced ahead of him on the familiar path up the hill to Shirley's grave.

Uniform, flat bronze headstones were a requirement at the perpetual-care cemetery. They made it easier for the mowers to perpetually care. Flowers were only allowed at certain times—

and for only a week. And of course, only those purchased from the perpetual-care florist were permitted. Shirley had picked this place and bought the plots. Maxwell would have preferred for them to go home to Louisiana to the cemetery where their parents were buried.

The perpetual-care administrator hadn't been happy when Maxwell brought the park bench and chained it to the pine tree, but in the face of Maxwell's stern glare and stubborn refusal to "cooperate with the uniformity policy," the administrator conceded. During their long-running dispute, Maxwell had never admitted to casting the seeds of the Johnny jump-ups that bloomed in a precise rectangle over her grave. Their tiny blue and yellow blooms lay so close to the ground that the mowers couldn't cut their heads off. He was a man who played by the rules, but . . .

Mitts stretched out on the grave, lazily spreading his claws, scratching at the earth. Maxwell took his seat on the bench. Hoping to relieve the heaviness on his heart, he began.

"Hi, Shirley. It's me. Kirk. Well, it's been another week without you. But this week was a little different. We need to talk about that. Shirley, you know that I'll always love you. You know there's never been another woman for me. I thought I'd have you forever. I just don't understand it. You were the one who believed, but you were the one who died. I guess God needed you more than I did. Seemed it would only be fitting if it had been me. When you first left me, I prayed to join you, and you know I ain't a praying kind of man. But it don't seem like the Lord—or the devil—want me just yet. Everywhere I look there are reminders of you. But you're not here. I can't touch you." Maxwell sighed.

"I've been to the clubs. You know I like a drink every now and then. But it seems everybody's got somebody to go home to, except me. Plus, I'm too old for that kind of life. Not that I've taken to going to church, or anything like that. I have been giving a check to your church every month. I thought you'd like that. But you know, Shirley, I can't see no good come from that, except the preacher bought a new car."

He sighed and tightened his lips. Mitts sat up, on alert, watching him. Maxwell imagined a look of disapproval on Mitts's face.

"I planted your garden again. Enjoyed it, too. Now I wish I had done it with you all those times you asked me. No one can replace you in my heart. But I'm lonesome. I need to touch somebody. Can you understand that, Shirley?"

Mitts sauntered over to Maxwell and began rubbing against his leg.

"That brings me to my point. I don't know how you're gonna take this. I've met a lady. Reminds me of you. I feel comfortable around her. She likes children. And she doesn't bake me pies. I told you about all the pies all those ladies brought to console the grieving widower. For a while, seems like every time the bell rang, it was some lady with a lemon meringue pie. I don't even like lemon meringue pie. I didn't want to hurt their feelings. I sneaked and gave them to this old homeless guy who hangs around by the station. He was in tall cotton there for a while," Maxwell chuckled, then resumed his serious pose. "I didn't tell you about a couple of ladies from your church. Even your friend, Loreen. Guess they're looking for a man with benefits."

Maxwell absentmindedly picked the big cat up and set him in his lap. He rubbed Mitts behind his ear as he continued.

"This lady's not like that. I'd like to spend some time with her. But I need to know that it's okay with you. You and me, we been together so long. You're a part of me. I need to be at peace about it. I mean, I'm not thinking about marrying her or anything like that. I just want to spend a little time with her, and I don't want to feel like I'm sneaking around behind your back. I never did that before, when you were here with me. And it's not like I didn't have plenty of opportunities. Women like the uniform, I guess. But I was never unfaithful to you, Shirley. Never. Even if this thing is okay with you, I'll still come every Sunday. Me and Mitts here."

Mitts sat up, drew himself up tall, and stared intently into Maxwell's eyes. When the cat cocked his head to the side, Maxwell thought his expression was just like the one Shirley used to give him. Funny, he'd never noticed the cat looking so much like Shirley before. He mused about how, over time, animals came to look like their owners. Then he thought, surely it must be simply that people chose animals that looked like them. Mitts rubbed his head against Maxwell's chest.

Suddenly, Mitts leaped down out of his lap and sauntered to the top of the hill. Maxwell called out to him.

"Come on, Mitts. Time to go."

When Mitts didn't come, Maxwell looked over his shoulder just in time to see him walk over the hill.

Every time Maxwell thought about leaving him, he'd think that Mitts was the only part of her he still had. So he called his name and waited. Maxwell waited until nearly dark. Mitts never came back.

NINE

*A*udrey had spent the morning setting up her new office. The board had spared no expense in making available everything she needed, including a laptop and printer. Even as excited as she was about the job, she was exhausted by two o'clock. She decided to take the laptop home and spend the afternoon familiarizing herself with it. When Maxwell had called with the invitation to dinner, all he said was he had something to celebrate too, and he wanted to share it with her, but he wouldn't tell her what. Now she'd find out what all the mystery was about. She could tell from his voice, it was something happy. When the bell rang, she was ready for the celebrating to begin.

The big smile fell from her face when she opened the door and saw the young white man standing on the porch.

"Yes?" she asked in the off-putting tone she reserved for vacuum-cleaner salesmen.

He looked her up and down with steely gray eyes. "Are you Audrey Williams?"

"Who wants to know?" she asked, drawing her chin in, a frown on her face.

He put a chauffeur's cap on his head and a sardonic smile on his face. "You must be her. I heard you were a woman with an attitude. Give me your arm."

"What?"

From behind his back he produced a clear box filled with shredded iridescent plastic. He held it up for her to see by the light of the chandelier hanging over the porch. Then he untied the gold ribbon from around it and opened the box. Three perfect lily buds surrounded with tiny white daisies and baby's breath lay nestled inside.

"Just stick your arm out," he said impatiently. He took the corsage out, set the box down, and awkwardly slipped the elastic around her wrist.

"Your coach awaits, madam." He bowed at the waist, and made a grand flourish that ended with his hand pointing toward the cruiser. Audrey burst out laughing.

"You must be Danny."

"Sergeant Daniel O'Connor—reduced to coachman. At your service, madam. Lieutenant Maxwell got held up at the station."

At the car, he held the back door open for her. Audrey looked at the mesh screen separating back and front seats, noticed there were no handles on the doors, and shook her head. "I'll sit up front with you."

"But—"

"Forget it. I'm not sitting back there like a prisoner." She opened the front door, surveyed the mess, then gave him that mama's "you better clean this room up right this minute" look.

He leaned inside and quickly gathered up the empty fast-food boxes and gum wrappers and stuffed them into a Popeye's sack. He looked at her sheepishly, and met her "You're not finished, young man" glare. Crimping his mouth, he turned back to the car and brushed the crumbs out of the seat. He closed the door behind her, then tossed the sack in the backseat before hurrying around to the other side.

Danny stared straight ahead as he drove. He didn't say a word, but his fingers tapped a rhythmic beat on the steering wheel, and his head bobbed a little as though he heard the music in his head. She was nothing like he'd expected. Maxwell hadn't said much about her, but he knew the man. Ever since that night of the robbery at Greasy's, he'd been different, but Danny was reluctant to pry. Sometimes he'd catch him just staring into space, a little smile on his face. He'd only gotten in Maxwell's business once, and he'd vowed he'd never do that again.

From the beginning, Max had treated him like a little brother, patiently showing him the ropes, protecting him from his blunders, urging him to fit in. After Shirley died, Max started missing little clues, clues he'd taught Danny to look for. Danny suggested that he take a little vacation.

"Trying to get my job, huh? Just be patient, Danny Boy. I'll be leaving soon enough."

As time went on, Danny found himself becoming the protector, checking behind Maxwell. He thought Maxwell was grieving too hard, too long. When Maxwell really dropped the ball on one case, he'd suggested Max make an appointment with Dr. Baum. Maxwell had such a fit, he thought the man was going to hit him.

"The shrink! I'm not crazy! I lost the only woman I've ever loved. You can't understand that. You've never loved anyone, but yourself!"

Lately Max had been his old self, and Danny had relaxed, grateful to the woman, whoever she was. That is, until today, when he found out who she was.

Monday, Maxwell had come in the office, grinning like a Cheshire cat, pumped up and energized. He'd plowed through files on his desk, whistling some inane tune grinning all the while. Calling the lab, calling witnesses, dotting i's and crossing t's. At the end of the day his desk was neater than Danny had seen it in months.

By Tuesday afternoon he'd dragged out old unsolved files and was plowing through them, still whistling that inane tune. At lunch today, Danny could hold his curiosity no longer.

"What's up, boss? What's all this whistling about?"

"I'm a new man, Danny Boy. The world's a beautiful place."

"What's her name?"

Maxwell grinned. "Audrey. Audrey Williams."

"Where'd you meet her, this lady that's rocked your world?"

"Not yet. Not yet, Danny Boy."

"So? Give me the 4-1-1."

"You know the boy in that Dowling Street robbery? She's his mother."

Danny blinked a couple of times while he processed that information. He set his chicken leg down and cupped his hands around his mouth.

"Earth to Lieutenant. This is Earth, calling Lieutenant Maxwell. Come in, Lieutenant. Return to Earth immediately. That's an order."

"It's okay, Danny. I'm okay. In fact, I'm mighty fine."

Nothing he'd said had made a dent with the lieutenant. And now the woman was sitting here next to him. He'd been made an unwilling conspirator in her little scheme.

Audrey couldn't help but smile when she looked at the corsage, but she was put off by Danny's silent treatment.

"Doobie Brothers?" she asked, acknowledging his tapping and trying to break the ice.

He looked at her out of the side of his eye. "You a music buff?"

"Big time."

"Humph."

He switched beats and resumed his silence.

"So how long have you and Maxwell been partners?" she asked politely.

"Coupla years." Then silence, except for the tapping.

"La Bamba."

His finger stopped mid-beat, as he cut a glance at her.

"You like being partners with him?" she persisted.

"In this line of work, like ain't an issue. It's about respect." He took up the tapping again.

"So, you respect him?"

"Utmostly." His fingers didn't miss a beat. "Ain't a straighter cop on the force."

"How'd you come to be partners?"

Danny didn't try to hide his annoyance at her pestering him.

"Mighty Max was about to retire. I was up for promotion. Highest score on the exam. They sent me to him as his replacement. For him to 'train' me," he said, a wry twist on his lips. "Tame me, was really what they had in mind."

"Does a man who knows 'Sitting on the Dock of the Bay' really need taming?"

His finger stopped mid-tap. He glanced at her but wouldn't meet her curious expression.

"He has his methods. I have mine," he said, with an indifferent shrug.

"What does that mean?"

"He follows the party line. Goes by the book."

"And you?"

"I get the job done."

"So has he tamed you yet?"

"Nope. Doesn't matter. I'm stuck. His wife took down sick. Then she died. He hasn't said another word about retiring. I think he's using the job to fill the hole in his heart. He really loved that woman." Now maybe she'd shut up and leave him alone.

"Why did you tell me that?" Audrey said, looking at the corsage, then defensively back at Danny.

"He tries to hide it. But I can tell. He's real excited about you. As excited as he gets."

"And you resent that?"

As he stopped for the light, he turned his steel-gray eyes to her. "Listen lady. I know you're Malcolm Roberts's mama. Maxwell told me. If you're coming on to him just to get him to back off your son, I can tell you, your little ploy won't work." The light turned green, and he turned his attention back to the road.

"I really don't think that's any of your business."

"It's my case, too."

"Then you ought to spend your time finding out who really killed that man, instead of framing my son. My son is not a killer. A good cop would want to see the real killer brought to justice. Or is justice beside the point to a cop who needs taming?" She folded her arms across her chest, being careful not to smush the corsage.

*   *   *

Danny stopped the car in front of a bungalow on the Galveston side of Hobby Airport. "Listen, lady, I just don't want to see Mighty Max hurt. He doesn't have much experience with women."

"And I guess you do?" she asked, sarcastically.

"They come. They go . . . when they get what they want. The trick is to get what you want first." He nodded at her, then got out of the car.

By the time he got around to her side of the car, she had already opened the door. They walked to the door in silence. He rang the bell.

When Maxwell opened the door, he suppressed a grin. He looked from one to the other.

"Come on in. Thanks, Danny. I owe you one."

Danny stepped in right behind Audrey.

"Sure smells good," he said, with a grin. "What are we having?"

"We?" Maxwell asked, with a chuckle. "We are having seafood. You're having your favorite."

"My favorite?"

Maxwell held the door open. "Don't you remember? You were telling me how you were looking forward to having Popeye's tonight."

"Popeye's?" Danny looked puzzled, then the light came on. "Oh. Yeah. Okay. What time do you want me to come back for her?"

"You don't have to come back. You've done enough. You go enjoy your chicken." Maxwell shut the door behind him, and turned to Audrey.

"Welcome. I mean, come on in."

"I'm already in," Audrey smiled at his clumsiness.

The smile he returned showed he was aware of it. "I'm . . . sort of rusty at this."

"That's okay. I guess I am too." She looked around the room. She figured his wife had chosen the French provincial furniture. The matching table in the dining room was set with what she'd have bet was their wedding china.

"Sure smells good. Is there something I can do to help?"

"No. It'll all be ready in a short-short. Just let me go turn the fire down and grab some peppers." He walked through the swinging door to the kitchen.

Audrey stood there a minute, feeling awkward, then walked to the fireplace. A stern-faced couple stared at her out of an ornate silver frame on the mantle. She knew it wasn't Maxwell and his wife, because the clothes they wore were of another era. A bustle? She didn't know black women wore bustles back then. In the pictures in her mind of those times, the black women wore gunnysacks. Maybe she had the periods mixed up.

Then she saw the pictures of Cedric, with his snaggle-tooth

grin. The one of a scared little boy standing erect as a soldier with his hand in the big man's reminded her of the day she'd gone to his school. From the imprints in the layer of dust on the mantle, she could tell that other pictures had been removed recently. She appreciated the thought, but he could no more deny that Shirley had been a part of his life than she could deny that Sam had been a part of hers. At their age, folk had histories that just couldn't be denied. History is what made her who she was now. She liked who she was now, and she thought she liked who he was now, too. She turned and walked into the kitchen.

Maxwell wasn't there. A head of lettuce and three tomatoes were draining on a paper towel on the tiled counter. Audrey walked to the stove and took the top off the smaller pot—rice, white and fluffy. The top on the big skillet was rising and falling gently. She took it off and breathed in a heavenly aroma. She couldn't resist taking the big spoon and stirring the tomato-based sauce bubbling with onions, celery, and some lumps she couldn't identify. She tapped the spoon on the edge of the skillet, laid it back in the spoon rest, and replaced the top. Then she checked the fire and turned it down to just barely on. She ran her finger across the spoon, then licked her finger. Um-m-m, good, she thought.

A gentle breeze blowing the curtain drew her attention to the patio door in the den. She walked to the opening. On the fringe of the floodlight's brightness, she could see him walking from the back of the yard.

"I'm almost ready. Hold this," he said, handing her the bowl of sweet peppers, chives, and herbs. As he turned to lock the door, she took the bowl to the sink and began washing his harvest. By the time he'd positioned the stick in the track of the door and walked in the kitchen, Audrey was chopping the chives.

"You wield a mean knife, lady," he said, with an appreciative smile. "Since you're just taking over my kitchen, would you like an apron? I'd hate to see you mess up that pretty pantsuit." He sat on the bar stool.

"Nah, that's alright. I only wear an apron when I'm doing some serious cooking."

"Would you like something to drink?" he asked.

"Sure," she tossed over her shoulder, as she cored the tomatoes and quartered them.

He got up and held the refrigerator door open. "I've got beer, wine, apple juice, orange juice, some new peach stuff that's pretty good."

"Whatever you're having is fine."

He took out two beers, wiped the tops with the dishcloth, popped the tops, and set one near her on the counter. When he saw that she'd finished with the veggies, he reached past her and took down a large bowl from the cabinet over her head. He stood so close behind her, he could smell her faint cologne. He was tempted to plant a kiss on her neck, but Audrey turned and took the bowl from him, so he eased back onto the stool and watched her. He noticed that she cleaned as she worked. He liked a clean woman.

"Thanks for the corsage. It's beautiful." She held it to her nose. "And smells good, too."

"You're welcome. The lady at the florist shop said these are usually for proms and celebrations."

"So? What's this good news you're celebrating?" she asked, turning back to the salad she was making.

"I was gonna save that for after dinner."

"Nah. You gotta tell me now. You've had me in suspense all day."

"Okay. Here it is. I'm going to retire. I've been thinking about it for a long time. Now I've decided."

"Lucky you. When?" she asked, as she got down plates from the cabinet and served them. She was so comfortable in his kitchen that she forgot about the perfectly set table in the dining room.

"As soon as I get my cases wrapped up. It's not official or any-thing. You're the first person I've told."

"I feel honored." Audrey set the plates on the counter, and sat on the other bar stool. She took a forkful.

"Um-m-mph. This is really good. What is it? Looks sort of like shrimp."

"Mud bugs," he said, with a twinkle in his eye.

"Mud bugs? What the hell is a mud bug?"

"I could tell you like seafood. Thought you'd like this."

"I do." She pushed around in the mixture on her plate, speared one and held it up. "It kinda looks like a bug. Tastes good, though," she said, popping it in her mouth. "Tastes kinda like shrimp. What is it? For real?"

"You never had crawfish?"

"I thought they were something only Cajuns eat," she said, shaking her head.

"Well, I guess I'm sort of a Cajun. A black Cajun," he said, chuckling. "Grew up in Louisiana. Ruston. But I've been here ever since I've been grown."

"You were a cane cutter?"

"Nah. The cane fields are farther south. A lot of my friends would go down there to work, but I never had to. My daddy was a preacher, when he wasn't working in the lumber mill. The fire-and-brimstone kind. He did pretty good on revivals and such. I went into the army as soon as I was old enough. Wasn't really old enough, but I was so big they believed I was," he chuckled. "My ol' man was so strict, the army was like being on vacation for me."

"And now you're a cop. I hear you're the straightest cop on the force."

"I try to be," he said, with a wink.

"So how'd you become a cop?"

"I'd been an MP in the army. I had the training. The size. Back then the department was only looking for muscle. 'Course, now you have to have some college to get in. I picked that up along the way. VA benefits, you know. But I've risen as far as I can go. No way they're gonna make this ol' country boy a deputy chief. And the politics is a bitch. I'm not sure I want the headache anyway. Actually, I knew that a couple of years ago. But then . . ." he trailed off.

"Then Shirley got sick."

He looked in her eyes, then nodded.

"She's a part of you. You don't have to try to hide that from me."

Audrey could hear the relief in his sigh, as he pushed his plate aside.

"I want you to see something."

When he came back in the room, Audrey had cleared the plates away, wiped and dried the counter. He laid the pile of papers down on the counter.

"We'd planned to travel." He unfolded a worn map of the United States. There were big, red ovals drawn on it.

"Every year, we'd intended to do one circle," he said, pointing. "We planned to do all of these. Just take our time and see whatever there is to be seen. She sent off and got all these brochures from the different states' tourism departments."

Audrey took the brochures and picked through them until she found the one from Utah. She unfolded it and spread it out on top of the map.

"Here," she said pointing. "Right here. That's where you need to go. Zion Canyon. It's one of the few canyons that you see from the bottom up. Most of them, you have to see from the rim, like the Grand Canyon. I'm going to see all of them, one of these days. But I'm going to end up there, in Zion. Look at these pictures. Isn't this beautiful?"

"I'll show you something beautiful." He took a *Motorhome* magazine from the bottom of the stack of brochures. It fell open to a page that had obviously been looked at a lot. "I'm getting one of these. I think, this one," he said, pointing. "Or maybe this one," he said flipping to another worn page. "I haven't decided."

Audrey studied the pictures and the specs, then smiled.

"Which one drives better for you?" she asked.

"I haven't driven one yet. You know, when Shirley . . . well, I put this off. But I've made up my mind. I'm going on my next day off. I'm not as concerned about the driving as much as I am the bed."

"Bed?"

"I've always had to get an extra long bed. I'm not sure either of these will be. 'Course, they're all wide enough, since it'll just be me. And Cedric, sometimes. I've written both companies to see if they can modify it. Haven't heard back."

"I have no doubt they can. This is America. They'll blow sugar up your butt if you got enough money."

He laughed heartily. She smiled mysteriously, as she stood up.

"I've really enjoyed tonight. Dinner was wonderful. But I'd like to go home now."

"Why so soon? It seems like you just got here."

"Come on, take me home," she said, walking to the living room where her purse was.

"I know another good club we could go to," he said, grabbing his keys off the table.

"I'd like that. But another time. Tonight I'm expecting company."

"Sondra?" he asked, tentatively.

"Nope."

Maxwell pulled on his sports coat, then glanced at his watch, wondering who would be calling on her this time of night. He knew he shouldn't be jealous, but his brow furrowed with an emotion that had no other name.

*   *   *

Maxwell parked in Sondra's circular drive, then opened Audrey's door, wondering what to say to conclude the evening. The smile on her face pissed him off. He had thought she was having a good time with him.

"This way," she said, motioning for him to follow her. "Got something to show you." She walked around the side of the house to the back.

"Well, I'll be damned" was all he could say, when he saw the RV from his magazine.

Audrey unlocked the door. "You're my company. Come on in."

Inside, Audrey went to the refrigerator and took out two Coronas. "Make yourself at home."

While she searched the drawers for the church key, Maxwell walked around, opening cabinets and closets. He pulled the couch out into a bed, then pushed it back upright. He pulled off his sports coat and laid it over the chair, then squeezed into the driver's seat and pushed it all the way back. He grabbed the steering wheel and moved it back and forth. He reached the lever under the seat, then turned the captain's chair around. "I like this. It feels good. Roomy."

"I don't like being cramped up either," she said, setting the beer in the console for him. Then she sat in the passenger seat and sipped from hers. "I've really enjoyed this thing. The gas mileage is shitty, but tell me what fun doesn't cost money. Besides, I like having my own bathroom with me. I know it's always clean. No cooties."

Maxwell laughed, and sipped his beer. "Does this have the 454 engine?"

"Honey, all I know about the engine is that it starts when I turn the key." She reached the manual from an overhead cabinet and handed it to him. "Here. Maybe this will tell you what you want to know about that. I've got a good mechanic. Every woman needs a good mechanic—and her own bank account. You can look at the engine tomorrow if you want."

A slight frown crossed his face, as he thought again about the account, in Shirley's name only, he'd found while gathering papers for the probate lawyer. The thought had haunted him for two years. He'd thought that their trust had been total and complete. It hadn't been a substantial sum, but enough. The sense of betrayal he'd felt was eased somewhat when he learned that he was the payable-on-death beneficiary, but not enough. He forced his mind back to Audrey.

"Where all have you been?" Maxwell asked, as he flipped through the book.

Audrey told him about her trips. The kids loved the beaches, and she loved the water, but she couldn't keep the grit out of the bed. Desert's too hot and dry. The forests were her favorite places. She'd been raised in one, so she felt at home there. The tall pines, the cool air of Colorado. And northern California. The sequoias were humbling. Trees so tall, she couldn't see the tops, and big enough around for a car to drive through. They made the pines back home look like saplings. The Grand Canyon gave her an appreciation for the awesome power of water. Flying over it in a helicopter had been a religious experience. She planned to go back during the lightning season in September. The only way to get to the canyon floor was by donkey. Not her kind of thing. But Zion was. She couldn't wait to go. While she talked, she eased a footstool under his feet and set a bowl of chips on the console, and one with the picante sauce her friend Carolyn had made.

Maxwell noticed the way her eyes lit up when she talked about traveling. He felt so comfortable with her. He set his empty bottle down and walked to the back of the motor home. "Keep going. I can hear you." He stood over the bed looking from one end to the other, mentally measuring. Then he sat on it and bounced slightly to test.

"Lie down in it, if you want," she called out to him.

"Would that be okay?"

"Sure. Go ahead."

He stretched out on his back and scooched around until he was comfortable.

"The space is long enough, but I'd need a longer mattress. My feet hang off this one."

Audrey walked to the back and stood over the bed. "I see what you mean. But that shouldn't be a problem. I told you, they'll blow sugar up your butt." They both laughed. "Here, let me take your shoes off."

After she did, Maxwell scooted over toward the wall, turned on his side, leaning up on his elbow. "Sit down. Tell me where else you're going."

Audrey sat on the edge of the bed and began talking about her plans to see New England in the fall, the Amish country in Pennsylvania, and to drive the Natchez Trace from one end to the other. She had her own ovals drawn on a map in her head. Somewhere in northern Mississippi, she propped a pillow up against the back wall and sat up, resting her bare feet on the bed. When she got to the Blue Ridge Parkway, she heard a soft snore. She turned and looked at him. In his sleep he had a smile on his face, so she wasn't offended. It wasn't like Sam's disinterest. More like Maxwell felt comfortable enough with her to let go. She gently pulled his elbow, dislodging his fist from under his chin. Maxwell settled on the pillow. Audrey saw that his shirt was pulled tautly against his neck, so she undid the buttons down to the top of his pants. Maxwell didn't even stir. He looked so peaceful that she didn't want to wake him, so she leaned back against the pillow and closed her eyes, thinking of going to the Cherokee Nation, maybe this summer.

*   *   *

The insistent knock on the door awakened Maxwell. He was disoriented at first, but feeling her soft body next to him, made him remember. She slept on her stomach, her arms encircling the pillow. He put his arm around her waist, pulled her against him and snuggled against her warm body. But the knocking continued.

He eased over her and off the bed. He glanced at his watch: 1:45 A.M. As he passed the mirror on the closet door, and saw how disheveled he looked, he smoothed his hair and slipped his feet into his shoes. He peeked through the blinds and saw Sondra standing outside the door. Bright lights around the backyard illuminated the scowl on her face. He pushed the door open and was surprised to see Danny standing behind her.

"Morning," Maxwell said, a little embarrassed.

"What are you doing here?" Sondra asked, her hands on her hips.

"What do you mean by that?"

"You're putting it to her son. Now I guess you're fucking her, too." Her neck was working in righteous indignation.

Maxwell's face registered shock, then anger, as he self-consciously tucked his shirt in and began buttoning it.

"Listen, Sondra. This isn't what you think. But even if it was, we're both grown. Who are you to judge us? You quit that job. Remember?"

"Job or no, I'm not blind. I can see what you're doing. You and I both know—"

"You don't know jack, Sondra. You're always—"

"Lieutenant Maxwell!" Danny shouted above their argument.

"We gotta go! There's been a shooting. Another Vietnamese merchant. That Phim, Pham, whatever. The one you did the close patrol for. We gotta go!"

As Maxwell stepped down from the RV, Sondra grudgingly stepped back to let him pass.

Danny called over his shoulder, "I'm sorry I woke you up, Judge Ellis—I mean Ms. Evans."

ten

*M*axwell pulled his sports coat on as Danny followed him down the driveway. He couldn't help but cast an angry glance back at Sondra. She had crossed the line, calling him out that way and in front of Danny. It was one thing to have a professional disagreement. It was quite another for her to get in his personal business. Even as close as they'd been, he'd kept his misgivings to himself about her sudden decision to quit her bench and rush into marriage with a stranger. So what gave her the right to say such an ugly thing to him? She was supposed to be his friend. And Audrey's.

"Don't even ask," Maxwell ordered, when he got in the car and saw Danny's inquisitive look. "What've we got?" he asked, as Danny backed the car out of the driveway.

"All I know is, another Vietnamese merchant shot. Phim. Pham. Whatever. Still alive, last time I checked, but just barely. In a coma."

Even at two in the morning, the freeway was filled with the ever present Houston traffic. Danny flipped the switches that turned on the overhead lights and siren. He smoothly maneuvered the big cruiser around the cars as they moved out of his way.

★   ★   ★

Audrey awakened to the sound of their voices. By the time she got to the door she could see Maxwell over Sondra's shoulder, storming down the driveway.

"What's going on?" Audrey asked, then covered her wide yawn with her hand.

"I was just going to ask you the same thing."

"What do you mean? Come on in. Want some coffee?" She turned and moved to the kitchen area and began setting up the coffeepot.

Sondra walked up the steps and flopped in the chair.

"Audrey, do you have any idea what you're doing?"

"I sure do. I'm enjoying life for the first time in a long time." She pressed the button on the built-in tape deck, then snapped her fingers in time with her favorite Aretha. "I really like him, Sondra."

"You can't like him."

"Why?"

Sondra rolled her eyes at Audrey as she accepted the cup of coffee. "Don't you realize that he's trying to put Malcolm in prison?"

Audrey sat in the chair across from her. "Yeah, well, that's just his job. Malcolm is innocent. He didn't kill that man. The truth will come out."

"You are so naive. You don't understand. With them it's all about winning and losing. He's about to retire. He is not about to go out on a losing case. So when he wins, and Malcolm is on his way to the joint, are you going to celebrate with him?"

"The truth will come out," Audrey repeated. "That's your job."

Sondra gave her an exasperated look. "What if this comes to light? It could affect his job. Have you thought about the position you're putting him in?"

"I've thought about the position I want to put him in," Audrey returned with a sly smile.

Sondra drew her chin in and her eyes widened in surprise.

"This divorce has really thrown you for a loop, Audrey. You need to be more careful about your behavior until things have settled down. You have to be more reserved. Don't just jump at the first man who gives you a smile and a come-on. And the first thing you need to do is stop seeing Maxwell. Have you thought that he may just be lonesome? That he's using you?"

"I've been lonesome, too. Maybe I'm using him. Had you thought about that?"

"This is no good," Sondra said, shaking her head.

"You know Sondra, you've always been good at telling other folk what they oughtta do. Even when you don't have a clue what they're going through." Audrey took a sip of her coffee, a determined look on her face.

"I'm not going to quit seeing him, Sondra. If that's a problem for you, maybe I should move the RV. There's a place over by the Astrodome that I can rent by the month. I don't want to cause you any problems."

*   *   *

When Danny and Maxwell arrived, the street had been cordoned off and a crowd had gathered just outside the yellow tape marking the perimeter. The uniform moved the barricade to let the cruiser pass. Danny parked next to the Crime Scene Team van. When they got out, Danny stopped to talk to the techs who were in a huddle beside the van while Maxwell went inside.

Surveying the scene, Maxwell noticed that not much was disturbed, only one rack overturned. The officer who took the call broke from his conversation with the photographer and reported to Maxwell. Beginning with the time of the call, Maxwell took notes in the little notebook he pulled from his breast pocket. He made the entry explaining that the paramedics had knocked over the rack to get to the victim. By the time he finished getting the preliminary information, Danny had ambled in with the technicians. Maxwell cleared them to begin. The ID tech opened his briefcase and began intently dusting the counter and cash register. Another waited for the photographer to finish so he could gather blood samples.

Satisfied that the professionals had set about their work, Maxwell walked outside to look for witnesses. Just as he expected, no one in the crowd that had gathered was willing to claim any knowledge. Distrust of the police ran rampant in this part of town. He saw Stan, the ballistics man, talking to a tall man and started walking toward them. Then he saw that the tall one was Yudov.

"Stan. Yudov." Maxwell nodded his greeting to each of them. "Long way from your beat, isn't it, Yudov? You just passing through the neighborhood?" Maxwell eyed Yudov coldly. He still hadn't forgiven the lawsuit Yudov had filed to block his promotion. All that anti–affirmative action rhetoric. He knew it for exactly what it was. Even though the suit had been thrown out and he got the promotion, it still galled him. And what made it worse in Maxwell's book was that when they entered the academy together, Yudov hadn't been in the country five years. Hadn't taken him long to learn good old American prejudice.

"Heard it on the scanner. Just thought I'd come by and see if you needed any help. I was surprised to beat you here," Yudov said with a deprecating smile.

"I'm sure your lieutenant would appreciate you showing as much diligence in his sector as you have in mine," Maxwell said sarcastically. "Why don't you go study for the sergeant's exam—or go write some speeding tickets." Maxwell turned his back to Yudov. "What've we got, Stan?"

"Got the gun. Saturday Night Special," he said, holding up the weapon encased in a plastic bag. "You'll get the report in a few days. Just another ghetto robbery."

Watching Yudov walking away, Maxwell had come to the same

conclusion. The sooner he cleared the case the better, he thought. There would always be another one waiting.

"Tomorrow," Maxwell said with a firm smile that held no hesitancy to ask for favors. "Think you can handle that?"

"Anything for you, Lieutenant. Afternoon, though. You know we had that double homicide today over on the north side."

"Right after noon would be fine." Over Stan's shoulder he saw Danny walk through the doorway, then stop.

Danny turned around and looked at the plate-glass window covered with posters announcing events or urging a particular product. The hand-lettered sign next to the door drew his eye: DOOR LOCKED AT 10 P.M. USE WALK-UP WINDOW. He backed up and examined the doorjamb, then summoned the photographer and pointed to where he wanted pictures taken. He stepped outside the doorway to give the photographer room to work, then stopped and looked around with his "antennas up" look. Maxwell knew that look. When Danny walked to the edge of the tape, pulled it up and walked past it, Maxwell started after him. He was within earshot just as Danny approached the three young toughs in baggy shorts standing in the alleyway.

"Say, young brothas. What happened here?" Danny asked, showing his badge.

"Aw shi-it. I knew you laws was gonna come over here fucking with us. We ain't done nothing," one said.

"Yeah, but maybe you seen sump'um," Danny said, moving his head and arms just like he'd seen on a rap video.

"Aw, this mu-fucka thank he tuff," the second one said to the group. Then he turned to Danny. "We ain't seent nothing. Thought we wuz blind 'til we seent you," he said, laughing. He held up his hand toward the first one, who slapped it and joined in his laughter.

Danny gave them a look of feigned hurt, then turned to the third.

"Nemo. When'd you get back? Thought I just put you away a couple of months ago."

At the sound of his name, Nemo stiffened, and a look of apprehension crossed his face.

"How'd you like West Texas, Nemo? Your parole officer know you hanging out with these losers?"

"Who you calling a loser, mu-fucker?" the first challenged.

Danny turned to him with an eerie smile. "You. Why?"

"I don't have to take this shit off you."

"Yes, you do. 'Cause you ain't up to shit."

"Aw, fuck off. Punk-ass mother fucker. Bitch."

Danny rushed into him, spun him around, twisted his arm up, and pushed him against the wall. "You da bitch." He ran his hand in the man's pocket. "You da bitch with rocks in her pocket."

Across the alley, Maxwell moved closer and leaned against the building. Danny was always getting himself into situations. But to his credit, he usually got himself out of them. Still, Maxwell eased his hand inside his sports coat and fingered the revolver, just in case. No matter how it went down, he wasn't about to waste a bunch of energy wrestling with these young dudes.

"Listen up, dog," Danny said, still in his MTV mode. "I saw you fellas hanging around here the other night, too. This your turf, or what? I think you saw something tonight. I think you want to tell me about it. I think you'd rather do that than take a little trip down for possession."

"Fuck you!" the man muttered with his mouth pressed against the cold brick wall.

"And Nemo, you know you can't stand that," Danny growled. "So what's it gonna be, Nemo? Do I take him down, or what? Do I catch myself some small-time drug dealer wannabes or a killer?"

Nemo eyed Danny, then his compadre, then Maxwell. His stint

at the private prison in West Texas had taught him to keep his eye on the whole picture.

"Okay. Okay. I seen this dude run out of the store, got in a car, and drove off. That's all I seen."

"Shut up, Nemo! Don't tell this mu-fucker nothing," the tough called out.

Danny shoved his face harder into the wall.

"More, Nemo," Danny demanded. "That ain't enough. Come on wid it. What kind of car?"

Nemo hesitated, calculating whether to obey his partner or save his own ass, then said "Brown."

"Big? Little? What kind of car?"

"Regular car. Just a brown car. A Chevy maybe."

"A little more, Nemo, and I can let your boy here go."

"I saw a WH on the license plate. That's all. No, wait . . . Triff. Triff was on the back windshield."

"What'd the dude look like? Somebody you know?"

"Naw, naw, naw. Tall. Black all over. It happened so fast."

"Where exactly was the car, Nemo?"

"I don't know. Right over there where that van is, I think."

"Did the tall black man drive the car?"

"Naw. He got in the other side."

"You made the right choice, Nemo," Danny said, easing his hold and stepping back. With a wide arc of his arm, he threw the rocks far into the alley. "We appreciate the cooperation of citizens such as yourself."

As Danny walked past Maxwell, the tough called out, "I got yo badge number, mu-fucker."

Danny stopped and turned to him with that same eerie smile. "No, you don't. It's 4928. Better write that down now, before you forget it." Under his breath, he added "Small-brained motherfucker."

At the curb by the van, Danny stooped down and examined the spots on the concrete. He couldn't be sure if it was blood. He whistled to get the uniform's attention.

"Get the photo man and the blood girl over here," he said, pointing to the spot, as he rushed to the cruiser with Maxwell following.

★   ★   ★

In the car, Maxwell said, "That was a dumb thing you did. How many times do I have to tell you, you don't walk into—"

"I knew you had my back," Danny said, tapping out a beat on the steering wheel.

"Yeah, but I'm not always going to be here. You know, I'm going to retire soon."

"Sure, boss. Whatever you say."

"Cut the kidding, Danny. You've got to be more serious. When I retire, you'll be responsible for the younger officers. A role model. You can't go around jacking people up. And—"

"Citation."

"What?"

"S'cuse me, cap'n. While you're lecturing me on how to be a good cop, could you put in Citation. Chevy, brown, license with 'WH' in it. Bet you a dozen donuts you'll get one registered to Thrifty Car Rental. Now, what were you saying?"

Maxwell turned the screen toward him and typed in the information.

"I was saying that we're the keepers of the law. If we go around acting lawless, the criminals have nothing to aspire to. No reason to respect the law. When you—"

"What'd you get, boss?" Danny asked impatiently, leaning over, trying to see the display. "Bingo. You owe me some donuts." He flipped on the overheads and sped toward Intercontinental Airport. He knew those were the only rental car places open at this hour.

Maxwell saw the impatient look on Danny's face, but with his decision to retire it was more imperative than ever that he impart a tone to leave Danny with. So he continued.

"You didn't even ID him. Proper procedure calls for you to identify all witnesses—"

"I know who he is."

". . . and take an official statement. You could have at least taken him in for a statement."

"Don't have time. He'll be there tomorrow night. And the next. And the next. I can take his statement any time."

"And worst of all, you let the other one get away with a felony. There were uniforms there who could have taken him in. What is the man to think?"

"Think? He ain't thinking, Max. If he was thinking, he wouldn't be standing around on a street corner, trying to break into the big time by selling dime rocks. He's just riding the merry-go-round. Sell a few rocks, get busted, all the money he made goes to lawyers and probation. Sell a few rocks, get busted, money to the lawyers, he goes to the joint. Back again, sell a few rocks, get busted, and round and round she goes, and where she stops we all know. It's a chump game. I can bust him any night of the week. If it'll make you happy and get you off my case I'll do it tomorrow night. Promise."

Maxwell shook his head in exasperation.

Danny cast him a sidelong glance. "You know the Roberts boy got out on bond."

"I know," Maxwell said in a tired voice.

"Double the donuts says he rented that car."

Maxwell didn't say anything. He'd had the same thought.

"When we get his address from the rental company, we can radio to have a unit pick him up," Danny said, with an inquiring look on his face.

That would be an easy out, Maxwell thought. He could explain that to Audrey. Just standard department procedure. Then he thought of Audrey's eyes, of a mother's tears.

Danny saw the troubled look on Maxwell's face. He softened his voice.

"Maybe it would be better if we handled it. The two of us. You with me on that? Or should I go by myself? I'd do that for you, cap'n."

"Naw. I'm with you. It's my job."

★   ★   ★

Danny stopped the car in a "No Parking" zone and hopped out before Maxwell could tell him not to. By the time Maxwell had moved the car and entered the airport, Danny was already leaning over the counter under the Thrifty Car Rental banner and turning on the charm for the young woman in the green-and-white uniform. Maxwell sat down to wait, listening to the garbled announcements reverberating through the airport. He could gauge how close Danny was to scoring by the width of her smile. She was already past the "quality service" smile. By the time Danny signaled him, walking away, she was nearly to "Mama's really gonna like him."

"You told her you were going to call her, didn't you?"

"Of course," Danny answered not breaking his stride.

"But you're not gonna call her, are you?" Disapproval hung heavy in Maxwell's question.

"Of course not," Danny answered, undaunted.

"Danny—"

"I got what I needed."

"Danny—"

"She knows I'm not gonna call."

"Danny—"

"What? What!" Danny stopped in his tracks and gave Maxwell

an impatient glare. "You want me to go back and tell her I'm not gonna call?"

Maxwell shook his head and started toward the door again. "One of these days . . . one of these days, you're gonna get yours."

"I got mine already," he said, walking through the automatic door. "Name and driver's license number of the man who rented a brown Citation from Thrifty Car Rental this morning. Now all I have to figure out is how the Roberts boy got Vladimir Segeyev to rent a car for him. Maybe he hijacked Segeyev for the car."

When they reached the curb, Danny's smug smile turned to puzzled annoyance.

"Where the hell did you put the car, Max?"

$\mathcal{M}$id-afternoon, Danny pulled the cruiser to the curb in front of a rundown, two-story house not too far from downtown. He could see it had been a grand house in its day, but now showed years of neglect. A hand-painted sign in the front yard read ROOMS TO LET. An old man tended a scraggly flower bed. He stopped, leaned on the hoe, and watched them approach.

"Good morning. I'm Lieutenant Kirk Maxwell, HPD." Maxwell handed him his card.

"Afternoon. It's afternoon." His rheumy blue eyes didn't waver as he pushed strands of long white hair out of his face.

"You're correct," Maxwell said congenially. "Good afternoon."

"State your business," the man demanded impatiently.

"I'm looking for a man named Vladimir Segeyev. I understand that he lives here. Are you Mr. Segeyev?"

Maxwell saw a flash of fear in the man's eyes.

"I'm Benny Wilkov. Not that it's any of your business." He turned back to his flower bed. "Down the hall. Second door on the left. I don't know nothing about it."

"About what?" Maxwell asked.

When it was plain the man would say no more, Maxwell and

Danny headed for the steps. They crossed the wide porch, stepping carefully around loose boards. The ancient, rusty screen door weakly slapped closed behind them.

Inside, the grand old house had been cut up into apartments. The narrow hallway was musty, and dust covered what once had been beautiful hardwood floors. When Maxwell knocked at the second door, he heard movement in the room, but there was no answer. He knocked again, harder.

"Houston Police. We'd like to talk to Mister Segeyev."

After a minute or so, the door creaked open a crack, the length of the chain. Maxwell got a good look at the man's face.

"What do you want?" The voice was thick with a Russian accent.

"Are you Vladimir Segeyev?"

"No. Not here."

"When do you expect him back?" Maxwell asked in a pleasant voice.

"No telling," the man answered.

"Open the door," Danny demanded.

Maxwell gave him a hard look and shook his head. He tried to pass his card through the door.

"Have him give me a call, will ya?"

The man closed the door in his face. Maxwell stood there a minute staring at the door.

"You want me to do it my way?" Danny asked.

"No. I want you to pay attention. See that?" Maxwell said under his breath, pointing to a splotch on the wall near the door.

"Looks like—"

"Now you're paying attention. Got your pocket knife?" Maxwell asked, handing Danny his handkerchief.

When they were back in the yard, Maxwell stopped near Wilkov.

"Too bad about Mr. Segeyev's accident. When did it happen?"

The old man didn't even look up from his hoeing. "I told you I don't know nothing."

"Thanks anyway, Mister Wilkov." Maxwell turned to join Danny on the sidewalk.

"Rubleman's the one with the bandage." The old man said it so softly, Maxwell was certain he was afraid of being overheard.

In the car, Maxwell searched through the stolen car database and the hot list, but he didn't find the brown Citation.

"If the boy did hijack Segeyev for the car, wonder why he didn't report it?"

"Who knows? Maybe he has a little immigration problem."

"Maybe that's how Rubleman's arm got hurt. Wonder if he went to a hospital. I'll check that tomorrow. You get that handkerchief to the lab."

★   ★   ★

Audrey had already unhooked the electricity and tidied up inside the RV. Nothing was on the counters that could fall off. She sat on the couch, watching out the window and waiting. They'd agreed to leave work a little early so he could drive the RV before the evening traffic. She'd persuaded him that it would make more sense to test drive her RV rather than a new one. He could get a truer feel with the vehicle full of all the normal things. Audrey knew in her heart it was an excuse. She liked being with him. She liked the things he said to her, even if it was just a come-on. It made her feel good, and she needed that.

Audrey smiled when the Lincoln turned the corner, right on time. She waited in the doorway while he parked, then stepped down to the driveway and met him halfway.

"I hope Sondra won't mind me parking in her driveway." Maxwell's eyes were shining as he walked up the driveway, a gym bag slung over his shoulder.

"Y'all ought to quit. You and Sondra have been friends too long. You're both acting rather childish. She isn't here anyway. What's the bag for? This isn't for overnight. Shouldn't take but an hour or so."

"Just some stuff. Come on, let's get this show on the road."

Maxwell was surprised when she walked to the driver's door, but he shrugged and walked to the passenger side.

"I thought this was my test drive?" Maxwell asked.

"Yeah, I know, but it's better if I back it out and work down that narrow street. You can take the wheel on a straightaway."

"You scared I'm going to tear up your RV?" he asked with an amused smile.

"Not really. But why take a chance? A vehicle this size takes a little getting used to." She backed down the driveway and took them to the interstate. When she reached a straight part of I-10, she pulled over to the shoulder.

"Okay, you ready?" she asked, getting out of the seat and taking care not to bump her head on the overhead bed.

Ready? He'd been ready since last night when they'd made the plan. He was excited about being with her again. He could have driven a hundred RVs by now, but he'd been scheming up on an invitation. It had taken nearly a week of phone conversations to convince her that it was her idea. He moved to the driver's seat.

"Just pretend it's your Lincoln," she said, fastening her seat belt. "It's just a little wider, and about ten feet longer. Keep it at about sixty-five—you can't stop this thing on a dime, you know. When you've had enough, I'll take the wheel. Are the mirrors okay?"

He'd already checked them and the brake pedal. He put on the signal and pulled the rig back onto Interstate 10. She was right. It was like driving his Lincoln. He set the cruise control to sixty-five and relaxed into the seat. Then he told her how he'd driven big trucks for the army before he became an MP.

Audrey was impressed at the expert way he commanded the big

vehicle. She wondered why he hadn't mentioned that before. What else didn't she know about him? Everything she'd learned so far made her like him more.

With a broad smile on his face, Maxwell headed south on I-45, according to his plan.

"You like it?" she asked, as they passed the Hobby Airport exit.

"Love it. There's plenty of room, even for me. And the armrest is just the right height. I love these captain's chairs," he said, leaning his head back against the headrest.

"I had them put in special," she said.

Audrey grew a little concerned when they reached the city limits, even more when they passed the NASA exit.

"Haven't you had enough? We're almost to Galveston."

He shook his head, a mysterious smile on his face.

"I can't imagine you being so excited about a test drive," she said.

"I'm not. If I'm excited about anything, it's about being with you."

Audrey pressed her lips together, fighting a smile. She sneaked a glance at him. He was looking directly at her.

"You better keep your eyes on the road," was all she could think of to say, as she looked away shyly. She felt light as a feather inside. If a man had ever said something like that to her before, she couldn't remember it.

In Galveston, the road ended at Seawall Boulevard. Maxwell turned left and drove out of town. After the big rig rumbled across the bridge over an inlet, the road narrowed to two lanes. They passed scattered houses with hurricane shutters, occasionally a fenced pasture with a few cattle grazing on the thin coastal grass. After several more miles, Maxwell turned onto a beach access road. A few cars were parked along the beach, and he drove slowly past them, close to the water where the sand was firm. When he found a desolate stretch, he stopped and killed the motor.

"Come on, let's take a walk," he said, reaching for the gym bag.

When Audrey saw him take his shoes and socks off, then roll his pants legs up around his muscular calves, she took her sandals off too and tossed them inside the passenger door. He held his hand out to her and they walked down the beach, ankle-deep in the surf. For a while, neither of them said anything. The wind off the Gulf blew Audrey's denim dress around her knees. Occasionally, she reached down, picked up a shell and put it in her pocket. After a while, he led her out of the surf, across the dry sand to the top of a dune. He spread a blanket from his gym bag, sat on it and beckoned her to join him. The tumbling whitecaps of the Gulf were in front of them. Behind them, the sun sat low in the sky, in a fiery display of orange, pinks, and blues. When she was settled, he pulled a small cooler out of the bag.

"I brought some of that peach stuff I was telling you about. Thought you'd like it." He handed her a cold bottle. "Try it." She took a sip, while he watched anxiously.

"This is delicious."

"I'm glad you like it. I even brought dinner. Well, more like a snack." He set a package of saltine crackers on the blanket, then pulled a foil package from the cooler. Inside, there were slices of salami and squares of cheese. He stacked slices of each on a cracker and handed it to her, then made one for himself.

"This is nice," she said.

He nodded.

"Peaceful," she added.

"That's what I feel when I'm with you. Peaceful. I need that. I spend my days in a war zone. In some ways, it's worse than 'Nam. There was a time I felt I was doing some good. Now it's just counting casualties. They're getting younger and younger. I'm getting older and older. I'm glad I'm retiring. I'll be glad to be out of it."

"You know you're going to miss it."

He shook his head as he stretched out on the blanket. He leaned up on his elbow, his hand under his jaw.

"How can you not miss something you've spent your life doing?" Even as she said it, Audrey thought of the day she'd turned over the key to her house to the nice couple, the relief she'd felt in closing that chapter of her life, and her anticipation of the Canyonlands trip she'd planned.

"I'm ready for the next phase," he said. "I've been ready. I just need someone to share it with. What are you doing for the next, say . . . ten or twenty years?" His steady gaze said he really expected an answer.

Looking into his black eyes, Audrey could imagine her next phase. She could even imagine sharing it with him. But that was just a dream. She looked out across the water and sighed. "I had planned to travel."

"I'm up for that," he said with a little smile.

"That was my plan. But now, my life is turned upside down. There's so much weighing on me. I never imagined it would turn out like this. I don't know how this divorce is going to turn out."

"What do you mean? I thought you said you were divorced."

Audrey remembered the lie she'd told him the night they met. It wasn't a peace-breaking lie, so she decided she didn't have to be ashamed about it.

"Well, I'm not," she said, matter-of-factly. "I just said that because it was too much to explain right then. Sam filed three weeks ago. I told him I wanted everything, else I'd out him."

"Oh, a little extortion?"

"It's not extortion. It's a fair exchange. He was mad as a hornet, but he seemed to agree then. But as time goes on, he may change his mind. Or he may doubt I'll actually do it. I may end up penniless—"

"You won't be penniless."

A stern look came to her face. "I've watched it happen to some of my friends. Why couldn't it happen to me? And my son . . . I just don't know. I'm scared for him."

Maxwell knew they had agreed not to talk about him, but she'd brought it up, and the cop in him came out before he could stop it. He needed to know.

"Where is he?"

"Why do you want to know?" she asked. But her eyes said she knew the answer.

Maxwell would rather have taken a whipping than use her to find Malcolm. But he had to. He swallowed hard. "I need to talk to him."

"About the other shooting, right?"

He nodded.

Audrey tightened her lips. "I still don't believe . . . I tried so hard . . ." Tears welled up in her eyes.

"Come here." Maxwell pulled her to him and cradled her in the crook of his arm. "I know. I know," he said soothingly. He didn't want to tell her. Didn't want her to know his failure.

"You can't know," she said. "You don't even have a child. You can't know how it feels to have your hopes and dreams—"

"I have a child, Audrey. A son."

"I don't mean like Cedric. I mean a real child."

"I mean a real child. A junior, even."

"But I thought you said—"

"When I was in high school," he began slowly, "I got a girl pregnant. That's hard for me to say. For a long time after I found out, I said she 'got pregnant' like I had nothing to do with it. I didn't know about it until he was fourteen. The girl's family moved away in her senior year, somewhere up north. I was a couple of years behind her and I wasn't in love with her or anything, so I didn't think any more about it. I didn't go back to Ruston much after I went in the army. I don't even know how she found me. One day, she just called out of the clear blue. Told me she was having problems with him. I was skeptical at first. I knew it was possible. But fourteen years? The next day, she put him on a bus to Houston. The minute I laid eyes on him, I knew he was mine."

"How did Shirley take that?"

"Well, of course, she wasn't happy about it, but she accepted it. She was that kind of woman. Besides, we'd always wanted a child. It was a little awkward at first, but she and I both thought I could make up for lost time."

Maxwell thought again about Shirley's bank account. It had been opened around that time, and small deposits had been made regularly until the year she got sick. Maybe he'd assumed too much. He hadn't really given her a choice about the boy. But then, he hadn't had one either. He'd assumed other things too.

"I thought that one day he would follow in my footsteps. Even had visions of pinning a badge on him."

Audrey felt him shaking his head.

"It wasn't long before the streets claimed him. Nothing I did, nothing I said, mattered. Kirk was so angry. He felt I had abandoned him. That I'd left him to wallow in poverty while I had a nice house, a nice life. He never accepted the fact that I didn't know. I couldn't be his friend. And I didn't know how to be his father. Maybe if I'd known sooner . . ."

"Where is he now?"

"Prison. Down around Beaumont. He's in and out. Drugs. I got him out of juvenile a couple of times. Out of jail a couple of times, but after a while it didn't make any sense. No sooner than I'd get him out, he'd go right back. It was like he was on a crash course to destruction—trying to punish me—and there was nothing I could do to stop him. It wasn't anybody's fault. We just got dealt some shitty cards, me and him. Sometimes, I still wish . . ."

Audrey held him, as he held her. She understood that he knew about hopes and dreams. She understood about him and Cedric.

When they walked back to the RV, his arm around her shoulder, hers around his waist, the beach was dark, except for a million twinkling stars.

★　　　★　　　★

Audrey didn't like the looks of the neighborhood. She wasn't afraid, just wary. Along the streets, young men lounged idly against buildings and lampposts. Young girls pushed strollers on the broken sidewalk. Old women sat on porches of shotgun houses across the street, watching her with hardened faces. Not a sprig of grass in sight, just hard-packed dirt. She hadn't imagined Malcolm living in a place like this. Before she got out of the car, she turned her diamond around to the inside of her hand. The smell of burning grease wafted through the courtyard of the apartment complex. She climbed the stairs, being careful not to lean her weight on the rickety, metal banister.

She just had to be sure, had to look in his eyes. From Maxwell's question yesterday, she knew it wouldn't be long before they found him. She wanted to find him first. She was certain he would have an explanation for where he was when the second shooting happened. That poor man, she thought, still in a coma. She knocked at 207, and waited.

The door could use a coat of paint, or at the least a good scrubbing. There were three different kinds of deadbolts on the door. How could Malcolm live in a place like this? She knocked again, then looked at her watch. He must be at work. That was the only reason he was allowed to be away from the monitor. She wondered what kind of job he'd found.

Even though she'd already given it to him, she wrote her cell phone number on her new business card and stuck it in his door. She hadn't talked to him since his release, and she was a little hurt by that. A little "thanks for all your help" would have been nice. He never was there when she called him. She'd expected he would call her, that he would come over, that she would fix him his favorite dinner. Then she remembered he was grown. He probably had a girl that did that sort of thing for him. She wondered what she looked like. What kind of woman she was. As she descended the concrete stairs, she decided to grab a bite before her meeting. The board wanted to hear her preliminary plans.

★   ★   ★

Audrey felt stuffed. The T-bones Maxwell had grilled on his patio were delicious. She'd baked the potatoes and filled them with butter, sour cream, and chives. They sat on the floor watching the videotapes of the national parks he'd checked out from the library. He set their empty plates on the coffee table he'd pushed to the side so they'd have a better view of the TV screen.

"I saved your favorite for last," he said, putting in the one on the Canyonlands. He sat next to her on the floor and draped his arm on the couch behind her.

As the narrator's deep voice explained how the Canyonlands had been formed breathtaking aerial views of the orange formations of Bryce Canyon appeared on the screen. Audrey could see people walking among the tall, delicate-looking spires, and made a note to do that, too. Then the camera moved on to Zion Canyon. The rock formations were spectacular. At the end the camera zoomed down in to the canyon, traveled along the river at the foot of the tall, red walls. Audrey saw three white ducks skitter off into the water and swim away. Then the film credits began to roll.

Audrey leaned her head back against the couch, resting it on Maxwell's arm, and closed her eyes. She exhaled a contented sigh and a smile came to her lips. Maxwell couldn't help himself. He bent down and touched his lips to hers. That was all he'd intended to do, but he felt her lips pucker, so he went further, invading her mouth and tasting its sweet warmth. He cupped her chin in his hand and held her face to his, fingering the line of her jawbone. He massaged her throat, then her collarbone, his pinkie finger dipping into the cleavage of her breasts.

Whatever doubts Audrey'd had about him melted away in his kiss. She was not a tool to assuage his loneliness, as Sondra had suggested. A man this tender would not use her to get to her son. Nothing that felt this good could be wrong. The passion he was building in her was being met with his own. She'd never felt that before. Never been made this wet before.

Maxwell felt her hand on his forearm, not pulling it away, but fingering the hard muscle. Now she returned his kiss, and he felt her arm slip around his back, low near his waist. Her fingers tickled up and down the hollow of his back, raising sweet, fiery sensations in his groin. Maxwell opened his eyes, and pulled his lips from her. When he looked into her beautiful amber eyes, he saw a hunger that matched his own. He kissed her again and felt her drawing him down on the floor on top of her. She was a perfect fit, just as he'd imagined. Her arms wrapped around him, and her fingers raked down the back of his neck. The fire consumed him, driving him deeper into their passionate embrace, driving his thrusts against her. He knew he should slow down, slow the pace, but her hands under his shirt pulled him into her, and the flames licked at him. His hand slid under her dress, massaging her tender thigh, his fingers digging into her flesh. All of the times he'd thought of their first time together, he had imagined it slow and sweet. Hours of passionate kisses and caresses, exploring each other's bodies, culminating in simultaneous orgasm. Now he didn't have hours. An urgency he couldn't control propelled him forward. He rolled to the side and undid the button and zipper on his trousers, then pushed her dress up. The fire burned white hot. He lay on top of her, nuzzling her neck, then giving her a deep kiss. His fingers dug into her bottom, anticipating the moment he would dip into her feminine waters and find sizzling relief. Suddenly he felt her stiffen and push against him, but he was too far gone to turn around. Later he would give her long, slow pleasuring, any way she wanted it. He would satisfy her completely, over and over, until she would feel like her bones had turned to jelly.

Right now, though, the urgency was overtaking him. But she was struggling, pushing hard against him. With a mighty thrust, she pushed him off of her and scrambled to her feet. Maxwell lay on the floor, his breath coming in short bursts. He heard the bathroom door slam.

*   *   *

Audrey made it to the bathroom just as blood ran down her leg. She sat on the toilet listening to it drip. What could she do to make it stop? Nothing. She had no pads, no tampons, no cotton. Her purse was in the other room. But there was nothing in her purse that would handle this. She waited and waited, and still it dripped. She began to worry. It had never been like this before. She heard him call her name outside the door.

"I'll be out in a minute," she answered, as calmly as she could manage.

She could hear him saying he was sorry, that he shouldn't have tried to rush her, but all she could think about was towels. She heard him walk away. Only five steps to the cabinet, but she felt light-headed and leaned against it for support. Her dress was ruined. She struggled out of it, got a towel and put it between her legs. How could she face him like this? She heard him back at the door.

"Audrey, please come out. Let's talk about it."

"Bring me a pair of your pants," she said, between raspy breaths.

"My pants?"

"Pants," she said weakly. "A pair of pants. And a shirt."

She heard the tentative knock on the door, but she was too weak to reach the doorknob. The last thing she remembered was him calling her name.

TWELVE

*M*axwell sat in the chair, his elbows on his knees, hands tented against his mouth. A deep frown furrowed his forehead. The room looked just like the one Shirley had spent her last days in. He remembered sitting like this before, in a chair just like this one. He'd felt powerless then, and he felt the same way now. Everything about the hospital brought bad memories to him, memories of helplessly watching Shirley's transformation from a robust woman full of laughter to a gaunt skeleton. In the end, he'd lost her. The thought of losing Audrey too terrified him.

Audrey lay in the bed, within arm's reach. He had pulled the call button cord over to where he could reach it in a second. He watched her chest rise and fall under the sheet. Its crisp whiteness was a stark contrast to the blood-stained bedspread he'd brought her to the hospital in, after he'd found her on the bathroom floor.

He thought of the wild ride to the hospital, his dangerously weaving in and out of the traffic leaning on his horn, Audrey fading in and out of consciousness. He remembered shouting his desperate demand that the dispatcher find Sondra, and the calm in Sondra's voice when they finally patched her through.

She'd had her doctor meet them at the hospital. Dr. Johnson

asked Maxwell so many questions that he had no answers for. Maxwell signed so many forms without even reading them. When Sondra arrived, she somehow got the name of Audrey's doctor in Dallas out of her. Sondra had held his hand during the doctor's hurried phone call to Dallas, and sat with him as Dr. Johnson tried to explain to Maxwell about the surgery. Big words, strange words. All Maxwell told him was, "Don't let her die."

Maxwell wondered where Sondra was now. Audrey's eyes opened. When she saw him, a weak smile came to her lips. Then her lids fluttered closed.

He sat in the chair through the night while Audrey slept. He held her hand, careful not to disturb the IV needle taped to the back of it. The nurse who came in looked at him strangely. He recognized her too from the many nights he was here with Shirley, but he didn't bother to explain. Audrey finally came out of the anesthesia around three in the morning.

"They operated on me, didn't they?"

When he nodded, she turned her face away. Audrey felt groggy, but she wasn't in pain. The pain medication must be in the IV, she thought. Now her life would never be the same. She'd have to take the pills. She was embarrassed for him to be here, and at the same time, she was glad. But why would he want her now? Now that she was less than a woman. She wondered what the scar would look like. Two babies, and her stomach had been as unblemished as the day she was born. Now she was marred. She reached under the sheet and felt for it. She didn't feel anything. Must be the medication.

A little after seven the nurse came in and checked her vitals, making notes on her chart. Half an hour later, an orderly brought a full breakfast.

"Here, you eat this," she said, offering the tray to Maxwell. "There must be a mistake. I'm not supposed to eat anything this soon after the surgery."

"They must know what they're doing, Audrey."

Around eight, the doctor came in.

"Good morning. I'm Dr. Johnson. You look a lot better than when we first met."

"Did you talk to my doctor?" Audrey asked, not returning his smile.

"Yes. Dr. Salazar okay'd the procedure."

"Didn't he tell you I did not want a hysterectomy?"

"Yes, he did. He said you didn't want any more children either. That's why I suggested the endometrial ablation."

"Ablation? What's that?"

"It's a kind of laser surgery. A fairly new procedure, but I've done lots of them. We go in through the vaginal opening and burn out the lining of the uterus. That should stop the bleeding. We can do this as day surgery, but under these circumstances, I'd like to keep you under observation for another day. You'll probably go home tomorrow. I'll check on you in the morning."

"You mean you didn't operate?"

"I didn't cut you, if that's what you mean."

"So I don't have a scar?"

Dr. Johnson shook his head.

"And I don't have to take those pills?"

He shook his head again.

"And I'm still a woman?"

"You'll always be a woman, Ms. Williams. No matter what."

This time Audrey returned his smile.

*   *   *

Maxwell had raised the bed for Audrey and she rested comfortably as he read the newspaper to her. They both looked up when the door opened. Sondra walked in and gave her a peck on the cheek.

"Isn't Dr. Johnson a sweetie? He called me this morning. Said everything went fine. You gave us quite a scare last night. How do you feel?"

"I feel fine. He said I could go home tomorrow."

"You're coming to my house, of course."

Maxwell answered for her. "She's coming to mine."

Both women turned and looked at him. Sondra knew there was no point in arguing with him when he had that look on his face. She shrugged and turned back to Audrey.

"I brought someone to see you," Sondra said, walking to the door. She beckoned Maxwell to follow her.

When Audrey saw Malcolm, she felt like a ton of bricks had been lifted from her.

"Where have you been, boy? I've been so worried about you. I've been calling you and coming by your apartment."

He gave her a hug. "Don't worry about me, Mama. I've been around. Looking for a job. Laying low. I spent a couple of days with RL. Are you okay?"

"I'm fine, now, but I'm worried about you. How can you live in that awful place? And what were you doing in Dallas? You know you're supposed to—"

"What's that dude doing here?"

"Do you mean Maxwell?"

"That big cop dude. Is he bothering you, Mama? That lawyer lady can make him stop bothering you. It's me he's after."

"He's not bothering me, Malcolm. He's Sondra's friend. They've been friends a long time. And he's . . . been . . . a friend to me, too. In fact, he brought me to the hospital."

"Where were you? And what were you doing with him? Did he hurt you, Mama?"

"Of course not. I told you he's my friend."

"Your friend? How can he be your friend, when he's trying to put me away? I know you aren't falling for that. You can't trust these laws, Mama—even if they be black. And what about Daddy? Why isn't he here? I can understand him not coming to see about me, but you're his wife."

"Sit down, Malcolm. There's something you need to know. I didn't want to tell you like this, but there's no way around it. You may as well know now. Your father and I are getting a divorce."

"A divorce?" His disbelieving look turned to suspicion. "Did he leave you because of me?"

Audrey raised one eyebrow in surprise. "No. This doesn't have anything to do with you. And he didn't leave me." Her pride made her throw that in.

"Does RL know about this?"

She nodded. Malcolm was quiet for a minute, staring at a space near her feet.

"How can you do that to us?"

"It's not about you. Everything ain't about you, Malcolm. I gave you and RosaLee the best years of my life. You both are grown now. You have your own lives. Can't I have some life of my own?"

"Wait a minute, wait a minute." He looked up at her. "It's about this guy. That's it, isn't it?"

Audrey's surprise turned up a notch. Could Malcolm really think she was the kind of woman who would leave her husband for another man.

"You just kick Daddy to the curb, forget about your children."

She was speechless as her surprise headed toward anger. But she saw the frightened little boy behind the facade of sympathy for Sam.

"I can't believe you're gonna let this dude break you and Daddy up—and put me in prison."

"You're not going to prison, Malcolm. All you have to do is go to court and—"

"And you can get your precious house back. That's all that matters to you."

Audrey had had enough. She swung her feet over the edge of the bed and sat up facing Malcolm.

"Listen, little boy. I've had as much of you as I can stand today. I cannot believe I raised such an ungrateful, selfish child. Don't you know I can get my house back now. All I have to do is turn you over to that bondsman."

"Mama—"

"I want you to get out of my face now before I do something to you. Boy, I brought you in this world—"

"Mama—"

"Get out, Malcolm!"

★   ★   ★

Bright and early the next morning, Audrey put on the clothes Maxwell had brought and spread the covers on the bed. Then she sat on the edge of the bed, ready to leave. The night before she'd insisted that he go home and get some sleep. She needed some time alone to think things through. He left but was only gone a couple of hours, and had her tapestry bag with him when he came back.

Even though she felt a little weak, Audrey thought she could manage by herself in the motor home. She had some new books to read, and enough food to make a few simple meals. Maxwell wouldn't hear of it, though. They had argued about it all morning until she had shooed him out, insisting that he go get himself some breakfast.

Although she enjoyed his company and his fussing over her, she wasn't comfortable with the thought of staying in his house, and especially after what Malcolm had said to her yesterday. It was so unfair for Malcolm to blame her for the breakup. She couldn't really tell what RosaLee thought. In fact, when she'd called to tell her about the move to Houston, RosaLee's reaction had been so strangely unquestioning that Audrey wondered if she knew. But she couldn't tell either of them the truth. She owed that to her children. Telling them was Sam's responsibility.

Sam hadn't crossed her mind in a week. Between her new job and her time with Maxwell, she hadn't even thought of Sam or his little secret. The whole thing was unfair to Maxwell, too. He had been so kind to her, and she had nearly exposed him to a deadly disease. If she was really falling in love with him, as she thought, the best thing for her to do would be to leave him alone. Just go away from him and let him find a woman who didn't have so many problems. She was still turning it all over in her mind when the door opened and Dr. Johnson came in.

"Well, I see you're all ready to go home. Everything on your chart looks fine, so I'm discharging you. Just take it easy for a few days. If you have any problems, call me right away. I gave Mr. Maxwell my card. Wait a couple of weeks before you have relations. Do you have any questions?"

Audrey's face heated with embarrassment, but she had to know.

"Did you do an AIDS test?"

"Of course. We always test for HIV in any kind of surgery. Mr. Maxwell signed the consent form."

"And you did the surgery anyway?"

"We had no choice. Of course, we took precautions. I'm sure it'll be negative. You have none of the risk factors. But I'll see that you get the test results so that you won't be worried."

*   *   *

In the face of her reluctance, Maxwell insisted that she stay at his house "for just a couple of days." On the way from the hospital, Maxwell drove her to her RV. He wouldn't let her get out of the car, even though she insisted that she had no pain. She told him the things she wanted and where they were. It took him three trips to get everything, including Polly.

For a week, Maxwell was in heaven. He enjoyed taking care of her, fixing her meals, running her bath, reading to her from her romance novels or the newspaper. He enjoyed the comfort of having her near, of hearing her laugh at his jokes. He even got used to the bird and her incessant "Audee! Polly wanna seed!" The house was alive again, and little by little, it began to sparkle.

On the third day, she began resisting his pampering at every turn, but his will was stronger. On the fourth day, she'd insisted he go back to work. He may as well not have, since he checked by so often. The next day he caught her using the vacuum, and had a fit about it.

"Polly made such a mess. I was just getting up the seeds she threw out of her cage," she explained sheepishly.

"I guess she threw seeds way up here in the living room," he said, taking the vacuum cleaner from her. "Hell of a bird, that Polly. Threw those seeds up here on the mantle, too." He picked up the dust cloth she'd left on it.

Each night they separated—she to the flowery guest bedroom, he to the bedroom he'd shared with Shirley. Every night, when her light went out, Maxwell waited until the quiet told him she'd gone to sleep. Then he drifted into a contented sleep of his own, just knowing that she was in the bedroom down the hall.

Tonight contentment eluded him. The only illumination in the dark house was the night light he'd put in the hallway, in case she needed to use the bathroom in the middle of the night. He lay in the bed listening to the sound of the creaking mattress from the other room. He wanted to go in that room and make love to her until the sun came up. But he'd already done enough damage. How could he ever make it up to her, his loss of control? He sensed her presence, and when he looked up she was standing in his doorway. She looked like an angel in a white, lacey gown.

"Audrey, what are you doing up? Do you need something?"

"I need you."

The words flowed over him like cooling waters. He was tempted to throw back the sheet and invite her to join him, to hold her in his arms all night. But he knew he wouldn't stop there. There was only one way for him to be strong, to maintain his control.

"I think it's best that you go back to bed, Audrey."

"Kirk—"

"Go on, now. Go to bed."

Under the flowery bedspread, Audrey tossed and turned until nearly dawn. She was so ashamed that she had offered herself to him like some hussy. She could see her mother's lips curled around the words "wanton woman." But that was how she had acted. And for him to have sent her back to her bed like a child made her cringe. She thought about gathering her things and sneaking out of his house, but she did have some pride left.

*   *   *

The next evening when Maxwell got home, he found her tapestry bags and Polly's cage by the front door. He was confused. He couldn't get her to talk to him, and when she did respond, she wouldn't look at him. He saw the sadness around her eyes. All she would say is, "It's time for me to go."

As they shared the meal she'd cooked for them, Maxwell carried on a one-sided conversation, desperately trying to reclaim control of the situation and the warmth they'd shared. Even his compliments on her corned beef and cabbage didn't bring more than a nod from her. After dinner, she washed the dishes. Normally, it was a chore they shared. Now, to stall for time, he let her do it alone. When she finished, she dried her hands on the towel and hung it on the hook.

"I'm ready to go now," she announced, averting her eyes from his.

"I want you to stay here. Haven't I made you comfortable? What else can I do?"

"I need my own space."

Maxwell was so relieved. That's all it was. He was crowding her too much, not giving her enough breathing room. He had an easy solution.

"Well, why didn't you just say so, Ms. I've Got A Secret? I'll bring your RV over here. We can put it right there in the driveway. There will still be room for my Lincoln."

She shook her head, walked to the living room, and picked up her bags.

"You can't go," he said from the doorway. "I won't take you. So you may as well come sit down and let's talk about how we can work this out."

"I'll call a cab."

*   *   *

When they got to Sondra's driveway, Maxwell wouldn't get out of the car. While she made three trips to the RV with her things, he sat in the Lincoln with a hard look on his face. He couldn't stop her from taking the joy from his life, but he sure as hell wasn't going to help her.

THIRTEEN

*F*rom the top floor of the office building, Audrey had a great view of the city. She sipped lemon-laced water, her eyes alternately scanning the door to the restaurant and the embossed leather folder that held a menu with no prices. She was glad Mary-Beth was here in Houston, even if it was only for two weeks, and even though MaryBeth was here for her job. Audrey looked forward to spending some face time with her friend. She couldn't wait to tell her about Maxwell. Maybe MaryBeth could make it make sense to her.

For three days after she moved back to the RV, she hadn't heard from him. They had been three miserable days. She'd had more than one crying fit. His rejection of her hurt so bad. She tried hard not to think of how she had shamelessly offered herself to him. But she was still a woman. And she didn't have AIDS. Dr. Johnson had called and told her that. What was it about her that he didn't desire her sexually? He seemed to like her. Maybe he just liked her as a companion. Maybe he had been grossed out by all the blood. But that hadn't been her fault. And it was fixed now. In one crazy moment it even crossed her mind that he might be like Sam. She remembered that Sam had courted her persistently at Bishop. She wondered what it was about her that had attracted a man like that. Why couldn't she attract a man like the ones in her romance books? That was silly. She knew the answer. They don't exist. Then, just before she got really crazy with it, Maxwell had shown up— acting just like a hero from one of her books.

That night, he quietly knocked on the door, but she wouldn't answer. Never again would he or any man get the chance to reject her. And she refused to be just his companion. If he didn't want all of her, she thought as she flopped on the couch and picked up her book, he could just go to hell.

But he wouldn't. His patient knocking continued. When it was quiet, she couldn't concentrate on the book, for listening for the sound of his motor starting. She went to the potty. She sat back down to read. She got up and poured herself a glass of lemonade. She sat down to read. Finally, she got up and peeked through the blinds. He had taken two folding chairs off the back of the RV and was sitting in one, waiting. She had to give it to him. He was patient. Finally, she poured him a shot of bourbon and took her glass of lemonade outside. She handed him the glass and sat down.

"I'm not going to let you go, Audrey," he said, in a quiet, deep voice.

"So, you're going to stalk me now?"

"If I have to."

And he did. For three weeks. Every day, he was there, soon after she got in from work. If he didn't bring dinner, she whipped something up. They fell right back into the routine they'd enjoyed before. Except instead of separate rooms, they went to separate houses. Even the laughter came back. More than once, she'd caught him staring at her, a look in his dark eyes she couldn't quite fathom. Once he'd put his arm around her, but she withdrew. She found herself willing to be just his companion. Maybe that was just her role in life. She wondered what MaryBeth would think of it all.

There was no doubt in her mind what MaryBeth would think of how she was handling the divorce.

The thick package of papers had come last week. She'd tried to read them—the decree, the deeds, "deeds to secure assumption," stock transfer documents, affidavits. It was too much, the words too strange. She couldn't tell if there was a trick in them. She put them all back in the package, added a cryptic note—"Does this say I get everything?"—and mailed the package to Sondra in Pine Branch.

When MaryBeth appeared in the doorway, Audrey glanced at her watch again. Just like her. Late, as usual, but not too. Audrey really had hoped she'd be on time this once, so she would have time to fill her in.

MaryBeth was dressed to the nines. But then, she'd always been a dresser. In fact, Audrey had her to thank for turning her on to the full-figure designers. Now MaryBeth probably got a good discount in the store. Still, Audrey thought the skirt was a little short for a woman her age. MaryBeth breezed over to the table and tossed her designer purse in the other chair as she sat down.

"Why me, Lord?" MaryBeth exhaled breathlessly, rolling her eyes heavenward. "I don't know why they went to the expense of sending me here to train this girl. Little Miss Sunshine. She's cute as a button. Dumb as a brick. I figure she's either sleeping with the boss, or she's his daughter. How else could she get this plum position at her age? Of course, at first, before I met her, I thought two weeks was too long. Now I figure a year would be about right." MaryBeth flicked her bangs off to the side and looked around. "What do you think of this place? The VP at the store recommended it."

"There're no prices on the menu. And the maitre d' has a really stiff upper lip, but—"

"Don't worry about it. I've got an expense account."

"No, it'll be my treat. I invited someone else." Audrey's lips were pursed, but she couldn't hide the smile around her eyes.

"Someone else?" MaryBeth disguised her disappointment at not having Audrey to herself. Who else could she tell about her disastrous trip to Tahoe? How Mr. Seemed-So-Perfect had turned out to be an uptight tightwad who seemed to think she should be a virgin—at nearly fifty. "Like who?" MaryBeth asked, turning from her disappointment and noticing the look on Audrey's face.

Audrey took a sip of water. "I wanted to tell you last night when you called, but you wouldn't let me get a word in edgewise. Anyway, I'm . . . sort of seeing somebody. I want you to meet him."

"You're what? Seeing somebody? You mean like, *seeing* somebody?"

"So?" Audrey asked defensively. "What's wrong with me seeing somebody?"

"Not a thing. It just seems so soon. I mean, you and Sam . . . it's been so long . . . I mean, I never thought of you that way." MaryBeth smacked her forehead with her palm. "Jeez, that sounded stupid. I'm happy for you. Tell me about him. How'd you meet him? You just got here. Is he someone you work with? You just got the job, Audrey. You ought to be careful—"

MaryBeth stopped her headlong rush, turned, and looked behind her to see what brought such a big smile to Audrey's face. "OhmyGod, Audrey, is that him? He's gorgeous."

Audrey's smile broadened as Maxwell approached their table.

"Sorry I'm late," he said, returning her smile. He leaned over and pecked Audrey on the cheek. "We got a call. In fact, we won't be able to stay. I just came by to let you know."

"We?" Audrey asked, blushing at his show of affection.

"Danny's waiting in the car," he said, turning his smile to the other side of the table. "You must be MaryBeth. I'm Kirk Maxwell. It's a pleasure to meet a friend of Audrey's."

"MaryBeth Solomon. Pleasure to meet you, too," she answered, looking up at him and offering her hand.

"Can't you just stay for a salad or an appetizer?" Audrey asked.

Maxwell chuckled as he sat. "You know me better than that. I'll catch a burger later. Audrey tells me y'all have been friends forever," he said, turning to MaryBeth. "I'm so sorry I can't stay. How long will you be here?"

"A couple of weeks."

"If you don't have plans for tonight, can I take y'all to Roxy's? Scott Gertner is performing. He does a sort of Luther Vandross set. Do you like that kind of music?"

"I'm not familiar with the name, but that sounds good. I like Vandross. Audrey gave me his new CD for my birthday. Is that okay with you?" When she looked to Audrey for confirmation, she saw the frown that creased her forehead. She glanced over her shoulder to determine the object of Audrey's disapproval.

The man in the corduroy blazer looked out of place in the elegant ambience of the restaurant, and the maitre d' would have had to be a lot taller to look any farther down his nose at him. The classism irked her. Put that good-looking man in blue pinstripes and the maitre d' would be falling all over himself trying to find him the best table. Midnight blue, she thought, would be the perfect compliment to his shock of black hair. She wondered if he cut it close on the sides to hide the gray. Suddenly the man pointed and started walking in their direction. MaryBeth sat up a little straighter, in case he noticed her. But with each long stride, he got younger and younger. Disappointed, she turned back to Audrey.

"Did you say that was okay?"

"Ms. Williams. Good afternoon," Danny said, acknowledging Audrey in a curt voice. "Lieutenant, we really have to go. The dispatcher called again. I left the car in a 'no parking' zone." He glanced at MaryBeth, then did a double take. "Don't I know you from somewhere?"

MaryBeth turned an appraising eye to him and what must have been the oldest pickup line in history, then cut her eyes to Audrey in a question.

"This is Danny. Kirk's partner," Audrey explained, crimping her mouth.

Taking her cue from Audrey, MaryBeth turned back to Danny. "I doubt it, but nice to meet you," she said, dismissing him and turning to Maxwell. "What time should we be ready?"

"I'll pick you up for the ten o'clock show," Maxwell said, pushing his seat back and standing. "Come on, Danny. Let's go."

Danny's eyes were glued on MaryBeth.

"It's a shame I have to leave so soon. But if you'll give me your phone number, I'll call you later."

"For what?" MaryBeth asked, with a wide-eyed, skeptical look.

Danny shrugged and turned on his disarming smile. "You never can tell."

MaryBeth was not disarmed. In fact, she was offended at his obvious and clumsy pass.

"Sweetheart, I've already raised my children. And you're a little big for a grandbaby." Rolling her eyes, she turned back to Maxwell. "We'll be ready. I'm looking forward to it."

"You'll have to excuse my partner, MaryBeth. He's a little rough around the edges. I'm working on him. Duty calls," he said, bumping Danny with his elbow.

★   ★   ★

"I think that was the first time I've ever seen you at a loss for words with a woman," Maxwell teased, as they rode the glass-front elevator down to the bottom floor atrium of the office building.

"Aw, I was just bullshitting," Danny said, still smarting from the rebuff. "Some women don't know how to take a compliment."

Maxwell chuckled. "Some women just don't go for bullshit. Weak bullshit, at that."

"So, who is she?" Danny asked when they were in the car.

"Friend of Audrey's."

Danny tightened his lips in annoyance. "Well, I could see that. What's her name?"

"Why?" Maxwell's brows raised as he glanced sideways at Danny.

"Just wondered, that's all." Danny shrugged his shoulders.

Maxwell's crooked smile showed. "She really put you in your place. *Grandbaby*. I love it," Maxwell chuckled, then became serious. "What've we got?"

"Gas station. Perp shows a gun. A big gun, according to the female attendant. Third day on the job. She gives him the money. Medium height, medium everything. Doesn't know if he's white, black, or Martian. Big gun is all she remembers. I guess they're all big when you're looking down the barrel. Dispatcher says she's so shook up, couldn't identify her own mother. Perp got maybe fifty dollars. I don't even know why they called us on this one."

"It's a robbery. We're Robbery. We take them all, not just the glamorous ones."

"I know, I know. Taxpaying citizens."

"There you go."

At the scene, Maxwell spoke with the white-haired Ms. McGuffin. Danny was right, perp could have been a Martian. He calmed her down as best he could and stayed with her until her son came to pick her up. Not much to investigate.

Back at the station, Maxwell filed his report. He wondered if poor Ms. McGuffin would show up for work tomorrow. He straightened up everything on his desk, then gathered his things to call it a day.

"Say boss, what you got up tonight?" Danny asked, nonchalantly.

"Just taking Audrey and her friend out for a nice evening on the town."

"I don't really have any plans for tonight."

"Well, it's Monday. Not the hottest night of the week. Maybe this would be a good time for you to call that girl from the airport."

"Nah, I told you about that. Wanna grab a quick brew?"

"Not this evening. I'm gonna catch a couple of winks before my date. Thanks anyway," Maxwell said, pulling on his sports coat and heading for the hallway.

Danny hurriedly pushed his CDs into his backpack and fell into step with him.

"Two women too much for you, old man?"

Maxwell chuckled. "Gotta pace myself. You'll learn that when you get a little older."

Crossing the parking lot, Danny tried again, "So, where're you taking them, The Ambiance? Cody's? I hear they have a good show there."

"Roxy's."

Danny stopped at his BMW motorcycle, pulled the cover off, rolled it up and put it in the saddle. "Heard they have a good show there, too," he said, as he mounted the motorcycle, and eased it back off the kickstand. Maxwell didn't see the triumphant smile on Danny's face as he roared out of the parking lot.

★   ★   ★

The cop working overtime as security guard recognized Maxwell standing at the back of the line under the neon-lit marquee. He walked up to him and with a wink said, "We've been waiting on you, sir. You all come with me please."

Inside the plush club he introduced Maxwell to the owner. They were shown to one of the best tables in the house. They had a great view of the stage. Audrey thought it was unfair to those who'd bought their tickets presale, but MaryBeth didn't have a problem with it.

"Relax, Audrey. Sometimes you get a blessing when you don't deserve one. Sometimes you get screwed when you don't deserve it. It all comes out in the wash," she said, as she snapped her fingers to the beat. The band set a smooth groove for the intro. Goertner came on and played the audience like a pro, then took an intermission. A dj began spinning records, and Maxwell took Audrey on the dance floor to show off their swing-out number.

Alone at the table, MaryBeth scanned the room. The crowd was predominately female. Lots of young ones, she noticed. Her eyes roamed the bar, where the single men would be. Nothing interesting. She turned back to her glass of burgundy, just as the tempo changed to a slow song. She saw Maxwell pull Audrey to him, and imagined how good it would feel to have a man put his arms around her that way, to look at her that way.

"What's a beautiful lady like you doing sitting here all by herself?"

MaryBeth turned to face him. "Where do you get all these old, tired lines? The Classic Movie Channel?"

"Mind if I join you?" he asked, even as he sat. "Good show, huh?"

MaryBeth didn't respond. Audrey had filled her in about Danny and what he'd said to her. She didn't feel a need to even be polite to a man who would accuse her friend.

"Wanna dance?" he asked.

"With whom?"

"Aw, come on. You don't want to go home and have to say you gave up a chance to dance with the best-looking fella in the place?" He turned on his best lady-killer smile. When he saw her annoyed expression, just before she turned her head away, he changed his tack.

"Do me a favor, then. Don't make me have to go back to the station and tell the guys that the most beautiful woman in the house wouldn't even give me a little dance."

She turned back to him, and saw the hangdog look on his face. He saw the uncertainty creep into hers.

"Just one? Please?"

The music changed to an upbeat number.

"Just one?" she asked, skeptically. "Then you'll go away? Promise?"

He grinned and took her hand. He winked at Maxwell's surprised look when the couples passed each other.

MaryBeth fell into the groove of the crowd on the dance floor, doing the step Audrey had taught her. Over the thumping bass line, Patti was screaming "When You Talk About Love," and the backup singers were crooning "Love, love, love." Under hooded lids, she glanced around to make sure she was on the beat. The brother next to them was jerking his shoulders up and down in double time. His partner was doing a slow hully-gully in time with the beat. Mary-Beth added that move to Audrey's dance. Satisfied, she turned to Danny.

She was horrified to see him skipping around, wiggling his body, flailing his arms about, not even near a beat. His eyes were closed, so he couldn't see the other dancers moving back grudgingly to give him room—or to keep from being injured. MaryBeth knew from the heat she felt that her cheeks were bright red. Not only were they the only white couple on the dance floor, but the age difference was too obvious to miss. She hoped it was a short song. Mercifully, it was.

MaryBeth started off the dance floor as the music segued into another LaBelle song. Danny pulled her back into his arms to the strum of a sweet guitar and Patti's voice effortlessly trilling up and down the scale into "I Like the Way It Feels." MaryBeth felt his hard grip around her waist as he started off in what she guessed would be a round dance at the rodeo. After being dragged only a few steps, she planted her feet. Other dancers pouring on the dance floor trapped her, preventing her escape. If she was going to have to do this, then it would have to be her way.

"Wait. Stop," she demanded. "Just feel the music." She began to lead him, swaying at first. When she felt he was with her, she pressed her hand against his, and her thigh against his, to show him the way. After a couple of missteps, he easily followed her urging. MaryBeth liked leading him. She liked being in control.

The guitar strummed and Patti sang. By the time she got to the chorus, his tight grip had loosened into a soft embrace and Mary-Beth relaxed into it. She liked the way his body felt, pressed against hers. Where her hand rested on his back, the long muscle stretched taut and strong under her fingertips. Just the right feel to erase the memory of the soft, sponginess of Mr. Seemed-So-Perfect. So what if he was just a baby only a few years older than her son? It was just a dance. Just a fantasy. She didn't notice when he pulled her other hand around his waist and put his arm around her shoulder. I like the way it feels, feels, feels. He resisted her forward movement just enough for her to feel the strength in his chest, the hardness of his thighs. She could only imagine the rest as he pressed her body against his. She didn't even realize when he took control. She only heard, I like the way it feels, feels, feels . . .

*   *   *

Danny only heard the strumming of the guitar—and the beating of his own heart.

Fourteen

*M*aryBeth kicked the door shut behind her, pulled off the high heels, and collapsed on the bed. It had been a long day, after a long night. There had been a time when she could have partied all night, then met the day with a smile. She hadn't met this day that way, or Little Miss Sunshine. That poor girl was never going to "get it." And the day had ended with the vp hinting that MaryBeth's next promotion depended on Little Miss Sunshine "getting it."

Lying on her back, she unbuttoned the suit jacket, then her blouse. She lay there a while, pondering whether to pamper herself with a hot bubble bath or take a trip to the exercise room. The thought that it had been three days since she'd had a workout forced its way into her mind, so she dragged herself up. It was an everyday fight—for the rest of her life, apparently.

She hung the suit up, then wiggled into the spandex bra and shorts. Pulling on the nylon pants, she saw the red message light on the telephone. Audrey could wait until after her workout. If she didn't go to the exercise room now, she would put it off again. She pressed the button anyway.

"MaryBeth? Give me a call. 555-3780."

She recognized his voice and frowned at the phone. Call him? "You can't be serious," she said, as she pulled on the matching nylon jacket. At the elevator, she was still fuming. She couldn't believe he'd expected her to leave the club with him last night. She could hear her daddy's grizzled voice: "MaryBeth, you always leave with the one who brung you—unlessen he does something unmanly. Then you stay put, and call me." She smiled to herself at the thought of Danny doing something unmanly to her. It wasn't the first time she'd had the thought.

*   *   *

The department was empty this time of morning. MaryBeth hung the robe back on the rack and tried once again to explain to Little Miss Sunshine why that particular line didn't fit with the sophisticated look the corporate office was striving for.

"Miss? Could you help me?"

MaryBeth turned around at the sound of his voice. Her emotions pulled her in different directions. Anger that he would show up at her job. A keen appreciation for how good he looked. "We're busy. We'll find a clerk to assist you," she said, in a no-nonsense tone.

Little Miss Sunshine patted MaryBeth's hand as she would her doddering grandma's. "I'll help him," then nearly tripped over her high heels getting to Danny.

"What can I help you with?" she asked, flashing half her dentist's Mercedes worth of perfectly capped teeth, batting her eyelashes as she scanned his finger for a wedding ring.

"I'm looking for something special, for a special lady."

"Oh," she said, disappointment barely hidden in her voice. "What kind of special lady? Mother? Sister?"

"Neither."

"I see." She covered the disappointment with a total quality smile. "Did you have something in particular in mind?"

"Something like this," he said, lifting a red lace teddy from the rack and holding it up.

"Well, like, what size does she wear?"

Danny looked uncertain. "I don't know . . ." He looked up and down her lithe body, then past her. "Her," he said, pointing to MaryBeth. "About her size. What size would you say she wears?"

"I dunno. Maybe—"

"I'm sure about it. This lady is that exact size. Would you mind asking her what size she wears?"

He watched as the young woman spoke to MaryBeth, saw MaryBeth's mouth drop open, then crimp in annoyance at the girl's question.

Danny strode over to them, wearing his quirky grin. "Ma'am, I know this is a lot to ask, but would you mind trying on one of these for me?"

"I most certainly would!"

"But it's for my special lady. She's your exact size. I want to see how it will look on, before I buy it. I noticed your sign said 'no returns on lingerie.' I'd consider it a special favor," he said, holding the teddy up against her.

She stepped back, pushing the flimsy garment away from her. "I don't do favors for perverts."

As he watched her storm off, he turned his quirky grin to Little Miss Sunshine and handed her the teddy and his credit card. "I need one a size smaller. Wrap it up real pretty."

★   ★   ★

Danny whistled as he thumbed through the files on his desk. It was time to file away all the little scraps of paper cluttering his desk. It had gotten to the point he couldn't find anything. He realized he was whistling the same inane tune Maxwell had. He didn't even know the name of it. But he wasn't in love. He'd never be all moon-eyed over a woman like Maxwell had become lately. Still, he kept whistling the tune. He looked at one phone message, but there was no name and he didn't recognize the number. He dialed it. It was the blood bank, reminding him it was time to donate. He snapped his finger. Stacye, down in Blood, should have called him back by now. It had been nearly a month. He picked the phone up again.

"Stacye, Danny. Remember me?" "Yeah, the guy who promised to call. I'm calling now." "I know it's been a month. That's why I thought you might have something for me on the Pham shooting. You did get the spot on the sidewalk, didn't you?" "I figured it was blood. Do we know whose? Not Roberts, huh? Damn. Okay, what about the stuff I brought you in the handkerchief?" "What the hell do you mean, you lost it?" "I know it was wrapped up in a hand-kerchief. What the fuck difference does that make?" "What?" "Dinner?" "Tonight?" "I'd love to have dinner with you, but right now I'm so worried about my case, I just don't have an appetite." "Come help you look for it? Tell you what, you find my sample and a match, and you can pick any restaurant in town."

Danny fumed after he hung up the phone. He didn't have time to be bothered with Stacye tonight and especially since she didn't have what he wanted. He had another plan for tonight. He picked the phone up again.

*   *   *

No sooner than MaryBeth sat on the bed and pulled her shoes off her aching feet, there was a knock at the door. When she looked through the peephole, she recognized the bell captain, so she opened the door.

"Package for you, Ms. Solomon," he said, handing the box to her.

"Just a minute. Let me get my purse."

"Aw, that's all right, Ms. Solomon. The gentleman already tipped me. You have a good evening, now." He bowed curtly, then started toward the elevator.

As she closed the door, MaryBeth noticed her store's emblem on the box. She immediately thought of the vp. He'd said a couple of suggestive things, but she had managed to deflect them without insulting him. She had two cardinal rules. Never date a married man, and never, never, never date the boss. He was both. She tossed the box on the coffee table, found the classical music station on the radio, then walked to the bathroom to the strains of Debussy's *Clair de lune*.

Tonight was her maintenance night, her weekly ritual. She undressed, put on her silk, shortie pj's, then started into her routine. Wash and condition the hair, pluck the eyebrows, depilatory for the upper lip, mudpack for the face. It seemed that each year added to the number of potions required just to stay even. With a towel wrapped around her head, she took the nail polish and remover to the couch. Her eyes kept roaming to the box on the table. Judging from the size of it, she guessed a scarf. She wondered what kind of taste he had. She fanned her hands around until the polish dried. How on earth was she going to finesse this, she wondered. To give it back to him might be insulting. To accept it would unbalance the relationship. To give him something back of equal value would give him the wrong idea. Finally she opened the box. The card read "For a special lady." When she pulled back the tissue, she saw the red lace teddy.

*   *   *

"Say, boss. You know, something's been bothering me about that shooting."

"Which shooting?" Maxwell asked, without looking up from the file on his desk.

"Phim. Pham. Whatever. Don't you think it's peculiar that the robber left money? Over a hundred dollars in bills. Usually they take all of the bills."

"Maybe he got spooked. Thought he'd been seen. Had to leave quickly."

"Maybe so," Danny said unconvinced. "Let me see the file on that other ch . . .Vietnamese shooting."

Maxwell gave him a sidelong warning glance, flipped through the files in his drawer, and tossed it onto Danny's desk.

Danny opened it and turned to the inventory. "See. Says right here, $379 in bills, $7.49 in coins. And no prints on the cash register. You reckon he got spooked twice?"

"No telling. He's an amateur."

"So you think it's the Roberts boy, too, huh?"

"He's the only suspect we have."

"What I'd like to know is, how did he get inside the stores. Both of them locked the doors at ten. Why would the clerks let him in?"

"Who knows? When a gun is sticking in your face, you might do anything."

"Not that Phim. You heard him. He has a gun himself." Danny closed the file and reared back, deep in thought.

"Say boss, maybe it's not a robber. Maybe just a killer."

"A serial killer, huh? I guess that's possible, but that would rule out our suspect."

"Why?"

"Black folk don't get down like that. We'll kill you over something insignificant like a quarter, or stepping on our toes, but not over nothing. Plus, he's too young. If it's a serial killer, we need to be looking for some middle-aged white man, maybe a Vietnam vet."

"Roberts said it was a white man. Mama got you going for his story now?"

"You were the one who brought up a serial killer," Maxwell said, giving Danny a hard look. "Don't bring Audrey into this."

Danny knew he was treading on thin ice, but he couldn't help himself.

"Max, I don't know exactly how to say this . . . I mean, it seems to me that maybe you should reconsider what you're doing with this woman. Even if her motives are pure, there are just too many opportunities for conflicts of interest."

"What do you mean, 'even if her motives are pure'? What motives?"

Danny tightened his lips. "Had it occurred to you that she might be using you to save her son?"

"We have an agreement not to discuss that. She has never brought it up. And she would never ask me to do anything unprofessional. Even if she did, do you think I'd actually consider it?" Maxwell glared at him.

"I'm just saying that there are too many ways this thing could backfire. I'll bet his lawyer is going to make hay out of it. She didn't seem to like you very much."

"We had a little spat, but it's all over now. Sondra wouldn't do anything to hurt my career. And neither would Audrey."

"Tell that to the review board when we lose the Nguyen case. You could get busted. No telling about those pricks. They might even try to mess with your retirement."

Just then, the door opened. Ockletree hobbled in on one crutch, holding a sack from an upscale department store. "What am I? A fellow takes a bullet in the leg for his department and gets promoted to delivery boy," he said, dropping the sack on Danny's desk.

"Your mother left this at the front desk for you," he said, flopping in the chair. "She's a real looker. Ol' Barnes was trying to get her phone number. Let's see what's in the bag."

"She's not my mother," Danny said, with a crooked smile, as he reached in the sack and pulled the box out. When he opened it, they all saw it. Danny's face turned as red as the teddy that he hurriedly stuffed back in the box.

Ockletree let out a low whistle. "Looks like our boy has hit a home run," he said, winking at Maxwell as he pulled himself back up on the crutch. "I've heard of guys robbing the cradle, but I don't know what you call this. I can't wait to tell the guys on the desk."

Maxwell fought a grin, waiting until Ockletree was out of hearing range. "That's the perfect shade of red for you."

"Can it, Max," Danny said angrily.

"It looks a little small for you, though," Maxwell chuckled.

"I mean it, Maxwell. It's not funny."

"Aw, grandbaby—"

"Shut the fuck up!"

"Or what . . . grandbaby?"

Maxwell unbristled when he realized that that was the first time in their nearly two years together that Danny had spoken to him in that tone.

"She did this to embarrass me," Danny said, his lips drawn tight.

"No more than you embarrassed her. You embarrassed me. At the restaurant, at the club. You come on like gangbusters. Acting like a man out for a quick lay. Did you really think she would leave the club with you? That was insulting, Danny."

"I didn't mean to insult her. She just seemed like an interesting person."

A skeptical look crossed Maxwell's face. "You sure it's not just that you can't stand being turned down?"

Danny's mouth drew tight again. "I'm not used to that."

"Then you oughta stay in your league. A woman her age has heard a lot of lines. Met a lot of jerks, I imagine. And here you come acting just like one. If you're only trying to get her in the sack, looks like you've blown that," he said, thumbing toward the bag Danny had set on the floor behind his desk.

"Okay, I admit it. I wouldn't fight her off me," Danny said sheepishly. "But it's not just that."

"I guess I don't have to point out the obvious. You weren't even born when she went to the prom. And you're trying to tell me about conflicts. What could you possibly have in common?"

"I don't know. But it'll be interesting trying to find out."

"Well, if you're serious about it, let's go to Tino's," Maxwell said, grabbing his jacket. "Chile relleno is the special today. I'll give you a lesson in subtlety—grandbaby."

*　　　*　　　*

No exercise room tonight, MaryBeth thought, as she flipped on the radio. As the soft strains of a soothing violin concerto played, she pulled the caftan over her head, letting it fall over her body. She smoothed her hands over her breasts, down her waist, and over her hips. Her body felt tight through the thin fabric. She could skip a day, she thought with a nod.

This evening, she wasn't so much tired as bored. It hadn't even been a week, and she was too fed up with living in the hotel. She was tired of eating salad with no dressing from the deli next door to the hotel. Going without meat was the penance she paid for the fact that she wasn't keeping up her exercise regimen. The suite was elegant, but too impersonal. None of the touches that said some-body lives here. She was beginning to really dislike it. What was there to do? Watch TV? Not hardly. It was only two weeks out of her life, she reminded herself.

She rummaged in her suitcase until she found the Beverly Jenk-ins book Audrey had given her. Looking at the cover she thought, if all the buffalo soldiers looked like this one, surely they'd have won the war—whatever it was. History wasn't her strong suit, but Audrey had said this was a history lesson she'd enjoy learning. She took the book to the little terrace outside the living room, sat in one chair, and propped her feet up in the other. As she became en-grossed in the story, the lights of Houston began to glitter below for as far as she could see.

The buffalo soldier was about to show the beautiful and prim schoolmarm some decidedly unmilitary moves, when MaryBeth heard a knock on the door. She folded the corner of the page so she wouldn't lose her place and reluctantly placed the book on the table. The man she saw through the peephole was taller than the bell captain she knew. His back was turned.

"Room service."

"I didn't order room service," she called out through the door.

"This is room 1916," the man insisted.

Disregarding the warnings in the plastic holder on the door, she opened it. "I didn't—"

Danny turned around to face her.

"What the hell are you doing here?" she demanded, with her hands on her hips.

"I came to apologize." No quirky grin, not even a smile.

MaryBeth fixed him with a stony stare.

"I'm told I've been acting like a jerk."

"And you've quit? What's with this 'room service' bit?"

"Would you have opened the door if you had known it was me?" he asked, cocking his head slightly.

"No."

"See? I was right. Can I come in if I promise not to act like a jerk?"

"Your promises aren't worth diddly. You promised you'd go away after one dance," she answered, not moving.

Danny raised his eyebrows and tightened his lips in an apology. "I said I'm sorry. I admitted I acted like a jerk. What else can I do? Can't we just pretend the past two days never happened?"

"Honey, I'm way past the pretending age."

"Well then, how 'bout we just start over. Hello. I'm Daniel O'Connor," he said, extending his hand.

MaryBeth looked down at his hand, but made no move to take it. She leaned her head to the side to look for his other hand.

"Oh, these are for you," he said, thrusting a slim-necked vase wrapped in green florist's paper toward her.

She reluctantly accepted the vase, peeled back the paper, and saw two white roses in full bloom and one pink bud.

"One for each day that we've known each other," he said. "My clumsy attempt at being deep and meaningful." When she still didn't move, he added, "Guess I need a little more practice, huh?"

MaryBeth slowly stepped back from the door. Danny walked in and sat on the couch where she'd pointed. She set the vase on the coffee table.

"Nice suite," he said, looking around.

She nodded, sitting in the chair opposite him.

"What do you want, Daniel?" she asked in her forthright manner.

"I'm not sure." Danny shifted on the couch, crossing one leg over the other, resting his shin on his knee. "I guess I just wanted you to see a different side of me."

The man she saw now bore little resemblance to the cocky, self-absorbed man she'd met before.

There was a knock at the door. MaryBeth frowned as she started up from the chair.

"I'll get it," Danny said, already starting for the door.

As she settled back in the chair, MaryBeth noticed the confident way that he walked, the swagger that said "I'm in charge here." Danny opened the door wide and stood back.

A tuxedoed waiter pushed a cart into the room and stopped it at the place where Danny pointed. Covered dishes, crystal glasses, and a silver candelabra sat on a gleaming white tablecloth that reached the floor. With quiet and practiced precision, the waiter set about his work. He positioned two chairs from the desk on either side of the cart. He reached underneath the tablecloth, pulled out a bottle of wine and set it on the table. He lit the candles, uncorked the bottle, then stood back, still as a statue. As if on cue, Danny walked over to MaryBeth and offered his hand.

"I figured this is the only way I'd get you to accept a dinner invitation." The quirky grin was back.

When she sat, he pushed the chair under her, then took the other chair. The waiter came to life, uncovering the dishes, and stashing the covers under the tablecloth. He filled each glass halfway with burgundy liquid before resuming his still-life pose.

MaryBeth surveyed the asparagus, steamed new potatoes, and the rare prime rib that she had denied herself for years—even after she could afford it.

"I hope this is okay," he said. "I didn't know what you like, so I got what I like."

"This is fine."

The waiter acknowledged Danny's one-finger signal of dismissal with a quick nod, then took his leave.

"So tell me about yourself," he said, cutting into the thick slab of meat on his plate.

"How far back should I go? To when you were born, Daniel?"

"How about to when you were born."

"Okay, I was born and raised in Oklahoma. My mom was a housewife. My dad worked himself up from the service department to manager of a car dealership. So, we weren't rich, weren't poor. I got a scholarship to a small and prestigious liberal arts college in Georgetown, Texas. Dad wanted me to have a good education, just not too far from home. I had been thinking about Wellesley, but Texas was as far as he would allow. I majored in fine arts, married a lawyer, had three kids. When they got up some size, I went to work for the department store. That's about it. My whole life in one paragraph."

Danny frowned as he chewed a bite of meat. It hadn't occurred to him that she might be married. He'd checked for a ring that day in the restaurant. A couple of married women had come on to him, but he wouldn't give them the time of day, not even a promise to call. He liked to keep his life free of complications like husbands. He couldn't blame her, though. She'd spurned all his advances. Maybe that's what she had been trying to tell him. Still, she hadn't thrown him out tonight. Maybe she was game. Maybe he could play, but he wanted all the cards on the table. He picked up her hand and caressed it, looking into her eyes.

"Do you always leave your ring at home when you take a trip? Or do you have one of these open marriages?"

"Marriage?" MaryBeth frowned, then laughed. "Honey, I've been divorced longer than I was married."

"Well, you left out that little fact in your paragraph." Danny took a sip of wine to hide his relief. "So what do you do for the store?"

"I'm the head buyer in Dallas. Worked my way up from clerk. The store was bought out by a national chain a couple of years ago. I'm being considered for a position in the corporate office. In the meantime, they're sending me to their other southern stores to train their buyers. I hope the rest aren't as challenging as this one." She shook her head, just thinking about the silly girl. "Okay. Your turn. And try to keep it to a paragraph."

"I grew up in Chicago. My parents were as different as night and day. My mother was a cultured woman from a fairly wealthy family. Happened to fall in love with a 'dumb Irish cop.' That's how he always referred to himself, although he was very proud of his job. She must have really loved him, because she gave up a substantial inheritance for him. I never knew my grandparents."

"Probably just as well, if they could turn their backs on their own child."

"Maybe. Mother was satisfied, maybe resigned, to her life, but she wanted something different for me. I was an only child. I spent my childhood being pulled between them. He made sure I played every sport. She took me to art museums and the symphony. She'd have to sneak me off to piano lessons, because he would complain that she was making a sissy out of me. That was the only thing I ever remember them arguing about. I played football at Iowa State—definitely not pro material—finished with a degree in history. My senior year, they were in a car wreck. She died instantly. He hung on a few days. On his deathbed, he made me promise that I'd become a cop. So here I am."

MaryBeth saw the resigned look on his face before he covered it up.

"What would you have done otherwise?"

"Oh, I don't know. I enjoyed school. Probably would have stayed until I got a PhD, then taught. Maybe at some small and prestigious liberal arts college." He smiled at her.

"So, what's being a cop like?"

"Most of the time it's like a dog chasing his tail. Every now and then, you get to do some real good. That's when I think about my father. And why he stayed in it. Anyway, I've got too much invested in it now. Fifteen years. I can leave and draw a full retirement in five more. I can stand that."

"Then what?"

"Then, I'm going back to school and get a PhD. That'll make her happy."

"You've made your father happy. You're planning to make your mother happy. What makes Daniel happy?"

Danny looked uncertain, then recovered. "Would you like some dessert? There were several that sounded good, but I thought you should decide."

She shook her head. "I'll have to fast for three days just to get over dinner. It was perfect."

Danny nodded at her compliment. He pulled another bottle from under the tablecloth, set it and their glasses on the coffee table, then pushed the cart into the hall. When he came back he raised the wine bottle in a question. "Let's sit on your terrace."

Mellowed from the two and a half glasses she'd already had, MaryBeth rose from the chair.

On the terrace he filled the glasses and handed her one. When she sat, he did, too. He stretched his long legs and propped his feet on the railing.

"I've never seen Houston from this angle. The part I see is never pretty. What's this you're reading?" he asked, picking the book up.

"Just a history book Audrey gave me," she said, reaching for it.

He held it out of her reach and turned it over to the front cover. A bemused look came to his face. "History, huh?"

"The buffalo soldiers played a distinguished role in our history." She reached for the book again.

He flipped it open to the page she'd folded. "Hmmm, I see. Stroking . . . nibbling . . . sucking. I'll bet they did. Somehow I didn't take you for a romance reader."

"I'm reading it for the history, I told you. Not that there's anything wrong with reading romance novels," she added defensively.

"Women's stuff," he snorted.

"Oh, yeah?" she laughed. "What's guy stuff?"

"Newspapers. Magazines. Detective books. A guy wouldn't be caught dead reading a romance novel."

"That sounds like something your dad would have said. I was reading in the newspaper the other day that of all paperbacks, romance novels sells more than all other categories combined. It must be something in them that women like. Maybe if more men read them—sort of like a training manual—they'd be better lovers. Then maybe women would do less reading." A drowsy smirk crossed her lips as she took the last sip in her glass.

"But then, how would they learn history?" His smirk matched hers, then softened into a half smile. "I think we should go in."

MaryBeth looked up at him. She supposed he intended that little smile to be sexy. If so, it worked. She saw the suggestion in his eyes and on his lips, and was surprised to find herself considering it.

Danny took her hand and led her back into the living room. His hand was warm and strong. She liked the way it felt. It reminded her of how hard his body felt on the dance floor. Something stirred deep inside her, as she imagined those hands roaming over her body, imagined her breasts pressed against his firm chest, imagined his hard thighs against hers.

He turned and looked at her. "I've really enjoyed this evening." He pulled her close and planted a slow kiss on her cheek. MaryBeth swooned at his nearness, the heat from his body, the woodsy smell of his cologne. Maybe it was the buffalo soldier that got her in this mood. So what if he was a baby, she owed this to herself. Eyes closed, she raised her lips to meet his.

"I hope we can do it again, real soon," he whispered close to her lips.

Then he was putting on his jacket. Then leading her to the door. Then he was gone.

Eyes wide open now, MaryBeth expelled an exasperated sigh to the door that had closed in her face.

FIFTEEN

$f$riday evening, MaryBeth walked out of the store, grateful for the respite the weekend would bring. Her mouth turned down at the thought of standing up on the bus for thirty minutes. Too tired for that. She thought of flagging a taxi, but in this traffic a taxi wouldn't be able to go much faster than the bus—it would just cost more. So she trudged the two blocks to the bus stop, wondering what to do with herself for the weekend.

Originally she had planned to fly back to Dallas for the weekend. Now she didn't have the energy to face the packing, the crowd of tired businessmen and excited children at the airport, and the cab ride home. And to what? No husband, no children, not even a dog. On the other hand, the prospect of spending the weekend holed up in her hotel room wasn't enticing either. Maybe she'd go in the store on Saturday, just to see what kind of weekend crowd they had, but immediately rejected the thought. She'd had enough of the store—and that silly girl.

There was a crowd at the bus stop. She didn't like crowds, so she continued walking to the next stop. Maybe it wouldn't be so crowded. She remembered the message Audrey had left for her at the store. As soon as she got to her room, she'd call her. Maybe they could do a movie marathon tomorrow at the twelve-screen theater near the hotel. She was thinking of the latest movies she wanted to see when she heard his voice.

"Can I give you a lift?"

MaryBeth cut her eyes toward the street and saw Danny astride his motorcycle, walking it at her pace. She'd spent the whole night and most of the day trying not to think about him. Wondering what kind of game he was playing. Trying to get the feel of his soft lips on her cheek and the smell of his cologne out of her mind.

"How long have you been here?" she asked, still walking.

"About a block. So, how about it?"

"How about what?"

"Can I give you a ride?"

She stopped, looked from the motorcycle to her short skirt and sheer panty hose, then back to him.

"Thanks, but no thanks," she said, shaking her head.

"Have you ever ridden a bike before?"

"Not in this lifetime," she laughed.

"You'll like it. It's safe." He pushed the helmet into her hands. "Or would you rather spend your time standing up on a packed bus?"

MaryBeth thought about the prospect, as she looked at the helmet in her hand. She rolled her eyes back at him.

"You'll go slow? Promise?"

Danny nodded with a grin, then patted the seat behind him.

MaryBeth didn't even have to raise her skirt as she sat astride the seat. Looking over his shoulder, Danny took her hands and pulled them around his waist. He roared off, weaving between the cars sitting at a standstill in the Friday evening traffic. He ignored her protests about the speed.

At the stoplight, he asked over his shoulder, "How about dinner?"

She thought about the dinner in her room. No way she'd let him pull that little stunt again. No telling what might happen.

"Thanks anyway, but I'm just having salad tonight. Gotta make up for my recent excesses."

The light turned green and he roared off, again.

"This isn't the way to my hotel," she yelled in his ear, when he got on the freeway and headed away from town.

MaryBeth wasn't afraid, but she didn't like the feeling of his being in control of her. She wondered if this would be considered a kidnapping. But who would she tell—the police?

He just nodded. Smooth as silk, he weaved in and out of the traffic like it was an obstacle course, sometimes driving on the shoulder. He finally pulled off at the Clear Lake exit, then sped down a wide, winding road, whizzing past tall pines in the median. He stopped at the tall, wrought-iron gate of an upscale apartment complex, punched the buttons, and the gate slowly opened. When it was just the width of the cycle, he roared through it, then stopped next to one of the buildings.

Danny let her off, then leaned the bike on the kickstand. He stood closer to her than necessary, put his hands on the helmet, and lifted it off her head. Then he stood there, staring at her so long, she nervously fluffed her hair and inched back from him.

"What are we doing here?" she asked.

"Since I intruded on your home, I'm inviting you to mine. Sort of even the score." He put his hand on her waist and urged her in the direction of the stairwell.

*   *   *

Inside he tossed his keys on the coffee table and his jacket on the couch. He turned his back to her, pulled his shoulder holster off and put it on the mantle over the fireplace.

"Make yourself at home," he tossed over his shoulder. "I'm glad you could come."

"Ha! Like I had a choice."

Danny turned around to face her and fixed her with his steel gray eyes.

"You had a choice. You made a choice." A slight smile crossed his lips, challenging her to deny it.

MaryBeth turned away from him and cast an appraising eye around the room. It was nothing like the bachelor's pad she'd expected.

The evening sun streamed through partially opened mini blinds, at ceiling-to-floor windows on the front wall. The large room had a homey feel. A buckskin couch sat in front of the tall windows. The wall opposite it was covered with shelves built around a stereo system. The shelves held CDs, cassette tapes, and books. Facing the fireplace was a buckskin club chair, wide enough for two people, and a matching ottoman. A handmade quilt was folded over the back of the chair. She assumed the television was in his bedroom. Framed prints of modern art covered the walls.

MaryBeth walked to the window and looked out. Colorful sailboats dotted the lake.

"I can see why you'd live way out here. It's quiet, and you have a great view of the lake."

"The view is better from my sailboat. When the time is right, I'll take you out on it."

"What do you mean, like the weather?" she asked, turning back to him.

Danny wore that same little smile. Then he walked to the stereo and put in a CD.

MaryBeth was surprised that so much sound could come from such small speakers. Mozart's *Andante* flooded the room. Definitely not what she was expecting.

"This one's my favorite," she said, sitting on the ottoman. "I'm surprised you have it."

"I told you, my mom was into classical music."

"Are you saying I remind you of your mother?" This time the challenge was in her eyes.

"Oh, no. I don't know enough about you to compare you to her—yet." His steel gray eyes, focused on her, appeared soft as velvet.

What kind of game was he playing? Little boys shouldn't play with fire. Grown women shouldn't either, she thought. MaryBeth broke the contact between their eyes.

"I'll whip us up some dinner right quick," he said, and walked to the kitchen.

MaryBeth kicked out of her high heels, then stood and quickly freed her body of the hot pantyhose. She stuffed them in her purse, then scanned the shelves. Most of the books were history, a lot of them about Ireland. The music was divided by category and alphabetized. He not only had a good selection of classical music, but oldies, Chicago blues, and jazz. She found urban contemporary and all the latest rock groups, but none from what should have been his youth. And no country and western. She reached up to a high shelf among the oldies, pulled out a Buddy Holley CD, and read the cover.

When she looked up, he was leaning casually against the doorframe, holding two wine glasses, staring at her. The bemused look on his face somehow made her feel off balance.

"It's impolite to stare, Daniel."

"More impolite than returning a gift?"

MaryBeth turned back to the shelves and pretended to be interested in a particular CD. He'd done it again.

"Dinner will be here in a minute," he said.

"I thought you were cooking."

He laughed. "That's one thing that I have no interest or ability in."

MaryBeth needed to regain some sense of control. Boldly, she walked over to him and took one of the glasses from him.

"What *are* you interested in?"

"The same things you are. What are you interested in?"

MaryBeth turned her back to him and took a sip. "You have a great music collection," she said, holding the glass toward the stereo.

He ambled past her and changed CDs. "Check this out. Remember this one?"

Tommy James and the Shondells singing "Crystal Blue Persuasion." How could she forget? She wondered what they were doing now. She chuckled at the thought that they were probably grandfathers. Then he put on Gary Lewis and the Playboys' "This Diamond Ring." Before she knew it, she was sitting cross-legged on the floor. He played DJ from the ottoman, putting on songs that were popular when she was young. He even played Jan & Dean's "Dead Man's Curve" for her.

The doorbell rang on "Johnny Angel." He suggested that they move to the big antique dining table at the other end of the room, but she didn't want to move. Danny put the pizza box on the coffee table and went to the kitchen for the wine bottle. MaryBeth didn't even think about fat or calories, biting into the pepperoni pizza loaded with bell peppers, olives, and onions, as the Beatles sang "I Wanna Hold Your Hand." Then Leslie Gore, Petula Clark, and Otis Redding. Any name she called, he had it and played her favorite cuts. She snapped her fingers and shook her head to the beat, a smile on her face as she tripped down memory lane. When the pizza box was empty and the wine bottle nearly was, he slowed the tempo with the Righteous Brothers's "Unchained Melody" and pulled her up from the floor.

"Okay, show me how to do this again," he said, looking into her eyes, a hint of a sensual smile on his lips.

She walked into his beckoning arms. Only their hands touched, and he showed her he'd mastered the lesson. And more.

This time, he was leading her—and she let him. He released her hand and pulled her closer and closer, until her nipples pressed against his chest. She didn't push him away. What are you doing, MaryBeth? It's just a feel good. He leaned down and softly touched his lips to hers. She didn't push him away. Then he kissed her. And she let him, closing her eyes and enjoying it. What are you doing, MaryBeth? It's just a little kiss. His hands roamed down her back, coming to rest on her buttocks. His lips were nibbling on her throat and he was pressing her against his hard passion. What are you doing, MaryBeth? Treating myself.

Then he was sucking hard on her neck, then biting her. She winced and pushed his head away. His hands were under her skirt, squeezing her against his hardness, in quick jerky motions. He walked her backward, as his hands found their way under her blouse and he squeezed her breast. She flinched and grabbed his hand and pushed it away. In his urgency, he fumbled at the clasp on her bra, then jerked on it. This was not turning out to be the treat she'd anticipated.

MaryBeth shook her head and pressed her palms against his chest, forcing him back to arms' length. She saw the hungry look in his eyes and remembered being young, and impetuous, and in a hurry. But she was past that now.

"Not like this," she said, shaking her head. "Honey, I'm way too old to have bad sex. It's been real, but it's time for me to go. Why don't you just take me home." She turned to get her purse, but he held her arms.

"Why don't you teach me?"

"Teach you?" she asked, looking up into his eyes.

"Show me how to love you."

She searched his eyes. She saw surrender there. She realized that since the moment they met they had been fighting each other for control. Now he was laying it at her feet. She accepted his gift.

She took hold of his hands and pulled them to her sides, resting them on her hips. Slowly, she began moving her body sensually in time with the music.

"You did fine, setting the mood. Now this part should be slow and easy. Not this herky-jerky stuff. Nice and easy, see?" she said, guiding his hands down, then back up. When she let him do it, he got it right. She guided his thumbs to her nipples and showed him the motion. She held her hands away and let him do it. She raised her lips and kissed him slowly. Then she pulled back and looked at him.

"Rule Number 1. First and foremost, never jerk or tear a lady's clothes. That's just too primitive. You don't want her thinking about how much she spent on them." She pulled one of his hands behind her back to the clasp of her bra.

"Put your thumb here and press. If that doesn't work, then . . ." She pulled his other hand behind her. "Press in opposite directions. See how easy that was?" she said, as the clasp unfastened.

His hands slowly eased around until his thumbs were on her bare nipples, making just the right motion. She breathed deeply. She felt herself slipping, surrendering to the sweet desire that was coursing through her. Not yet, though. There was more he needed to learn.

MaryBeth reached down, placed her hand between his thighs and slowly moved it upward until she fingered his manhood through the fine gabardine fabric. She heard his short moan when her hand rubbed the most sensitive spot. Then she pinched it.

"Ouch!" He flinched back and stared at her in disbelief.

"Rule Number 2. It shouldn't hurt. Never. Pain isn't sexy. The correct amount of pressure is way this side of pain. Just imagine that every place you touch a woman is just as sensitive as this is," she said, as she touched him there again, gently this time.

He nodded that he understood, so she put her hands on his cheeks and guided his mouth to her breast. He pushed her sweater up and exposed her bare breasts. The wondrous things he did with his tongue, while his thumb rubbed her other nipple, made her massage the muscles around his waist. When his warm lips closed softly on her nipple, she arched her back and ran her fingers through his hair. His lips and thumb traded places, and he gave the same attention to her other breast. He pulled away slowly, his teeth barely grazing her nipple. He gazed into her eyes, as he led her to his bedroom.

He saw the dreamy expression on her face turn to a frown, as she surveyed the room.

"Looks like a locker room, doesn't it?" he said sheepishly, expressing her very thought.

MaryBeth leaned back against the dresser, arms folded, shrugging her agreement. It looked like Jason's room used to, after she stopped picking up behind him.

Like a whirlwind, he swept up the socks and pants off the floor, grabbed shirts off the chair and weight bench, and stuffed them all into a hamper in the closet. He made up the bed and smoothed the covers, then turned to her. "Better?"

She nodded.

"Now, what's Rule Number 3?" he asked, sitting on the bed. He held one hand out to her and began unbuttoning his shirt with the other.

"Hey, not so fast. Number 3—you must use protection."

Danny grinned, leaned over, pulled his wallet out of his back pocket, then he held up the proof for her to see. She wondered why he didn't keep them in the nightstand. Maybe he didn't entertain his women here. She walked over between his legs and took it from his hand. She leaned down and gave him a long, slow kiss, pulling his arms around her and resting them on her hips. He caressed up her back, pushing the sweater up and over her head. He pulled the lacy bra forward and down her arms.

With a little smile dancing around his lips, he relished the sight of her breasts for a long moment. When his tongue touched her nipple, MaryBeth's eyes fluttered closed. She nimbly undid the remaining buttons on his shirt and pushed it back over his shoulders. She nibbled on one shoulder, then his neck. He caressed her bottom, pulling her against him, rubbing her against him, letting her feel his power.

Danny's hand found its way under her skirt. His fingers worked inside her panties, pushing her hips back away from him. With his other hand, he eased the zipper down the back of her skirt. The skirt fell to the floor, revealing her lacy bikinis. She pulled his hand between her thighs. He turned it sideways, and she moved her leg to accommodate its width. She stiffened when she felt his finger snaking inside her, dipping into her honey. He eased it out and pushed his thumb into her, rubbing his wet finger back and up between her cheeks, into the opening that had never known an invasion other than her Ob-Gyn's. She nearly fainted and had to lock her knees to keep them from buckling. She threw her head back, surrendering to it, letting him pleasure her in a way she hadn't known was possible. When he withdrew his fingers, she gasped and looked down into his eyes.

"Did you like that?" His voice was husky. His eyes were serious.

"I'm supposed to be teaching you," she answered breathlessly.

"Well, teach me," he said, pulling her to him, lifting her astride his lap until her knees rested on the bed on either side of him. Holding on to her thighs, he arched his hips, rhythmically rubbing himself against her.

MaryBeth slipped her hand between them, released the button on his waistband and carefully slid the zipper down. Her fingers reached into his briefs and freed him. She kissed a trail down his torso as she removed his clothes. When she finished, he took off the only piece left of hers.

MaryBeth played with him, teased him, until their protection was fully in place. She laced her fingers through his and pushed him back on the bed. Inch by inch, she taught him the full meaning of slow and easy. On every downstroke, she teased his lips and nipples with her tongue. Each time he freed his hands, she captured them again, laced her fingers through his and held him down. When he tried to rush her, she stopped and held stock still. "Not yet." Then she took him to Slow and Easy—Second Semester.

MaryBeth saw the look of urgency building on his face, and felt it in the thrusts of his hips. She pressed the heels of her hands against his chest for leverage, raised herself and released him. Danny shuddered and blew out an exasperated sigh. Then another, then another.

"Rule No. 4. It's better together," she said, smiling down at him.

Danny's breaths still came in short puffs. His eyes narrowed and a determined look came to his face.

"Okay. All right. Give me a minute here." He pulled her down hard against his chest, caressing the length of her body, until his breathing slowed. When he regained his composure, he turned her on her back. He tickled her nipple with his tongue, then with his lips. And when he used his teeth, he could tell by the way she massaged his shoulders, he had passed Pressure 101. When he trailed kisses to her navel, he felt her fingers raking through his hair, so he continued. He pressed her knees apart and held them open while he teased her with his tongue and lips, lower and lower, slow and easy. When he reached the center of her desire, he felt trembling in her thighs, straining against his hold. He gauged her pleasure from his artful manipulation, by the strength of her fingers gripping his shirt, twisting and pulling the cotton fabric. So much for Rule No. 1, he thought.

He closed his lips on it and lovingly caressed it until every inch of her body trembled, telegraphing her need. Her fingernails dug into his back. She grabbed a hand full of his hair and twisted strands of it around her fingers, pulling so hard it hurt. And there goes Rule No. 2.

Her grip was so strong, he could feel the muscles tensing in her arms. Pulling, pulling him up. When he got to her breast, he covered it with his mouth, massaging it with his tongue, then sucking it until he drew soft moans from her. Her thighs rubbing and squeezing against his hips made him harder than he'd ever been. Could he hold himself? He had to.

Danny pulled her hands from his hair and pinned them against the bed above her head, as he rose and entered her—slow and easy. He knew how she liked it. He stroked her like she had stroked him—slow and easy. Long, slow, deep strokes until her fingers squeezed his so hard he couldn't tell pleasure from pain. Now she was the one trying to rush him, urging him with her hips. He freed his hands, pushed her knees toward her chest and held her still as he drove into her molten heat.

He felt himself climbing, pushing her ahead of him, as he stroked her, deeper and deeper, faster and faster. Her contracting around him drove him to greater heights, but he held on, pushing her higher and higher, until she cried out for him. At that moment, he surrendered to a shattering, growling release. He collapsed into her embrace.

Danny lay in her arms, breathing hard, licking the sweat off of his top lip. A feeling of contentment enveloped him as he realized he'd never worked so hard for it before—and he'd never enjoyed it so much.

"You should have told me you were a screamer, Professor Solomon."

sixteen

$\mathcal{M}$ aryBeth kept a proper distance from him as they walked through the lobby of her hotel. As soon as the elevator door closed, Danny was kissing her all over, his hands under her clothes.

"So, did I pass the course, professor?" he asked between kisses.

"You definitely passed," she giggled, pulling his hand from under her sweater when the elevator door opened.

"Did I get an A?" he asked as they walked down the hall.

"I'm not sure. You may have to retake the exam," she said, with a beguiled smile.

She unlocked the door as he pulled her into his arms, and they fell into her room, locked in a passionate embrace.

"Let's see if I can pass Aquatic Sports for extra credit." He grinned wickedly as he began undressing her. Just as he pulled her in the shower, MaryBeth heard a knock on the door.

"It must be the bell captain. I'll be right back."

She grabbed a robe and pulled it around her wet body. At the door, she peeped through the hole. Her eyes widened.

"Mother? It's Paula. Open up."

MaryBeth started, then slowly turned the knob.

"Surprised to see me?" Paula asked. She wore a big smile.

Speechless, MaryBeth nodded her head.

"Well, can I come in? I came all the way from Galveston to see you. This is the only day off I've had this semester. Don't I get a hug or something?"

"Of course, baby," MaryBeth said, putting her arms around her daughter. "I just wasn't expecting you, that's all. Come on in."

Paula looked around the spacious room and let out a low whistle.

"The store is really taking care of you these days." She tossed her crocheted knapsack on the table and flopped on the chair, swinging her legs over one arm, and hanging her head over the other arm. Her long hair brushed the floor. She pushed the clunky sandals off her feet and they dropped to the plush carpet without a sound.

"It's just for a couple of weeks." Mary Beth sat gingerly on the edge of the couch.

"What I wouldn't give to live like this for a couple of weeks. I'll bet you get room service and everything. You should see the dump I live in at med school."

"What brings you to Houston?" MaryBeth asked, with a weak smile.

"I drove my new roommate up here to visit her parents. I wanted you to meet Elizabeth. She's cool. I called the store and couldn't reach you. But you know how persistent I can be. They finally gave me the name of the hotel. I came by earlier thinking we could have dinner, but you weren't here. Anyway, I had dinner with Liz and her parents. Boy, I couldn't wait to get out of there. Talk about stiff. I'm glad I didn't have a mom like hers. Anyway, I'm supposed to pick her up at midnight and we're going on back. We both have a lab in the morning."

"Well, I'm always glad to see you." MaryBeth's lips were pursed in a tight smile, as she looked at the clock. Ten-thirty.

Paula raised her head and cocked an ear. "Sounds like the shower's running, Mom."

MaryBeth started, and her eyes darted toward the bedroom door. "Ah, yeah."

"I'll turn it off for you," she said, throwing her legs on to the floor. Paula started for the bedroom.

"No!" MaryBeth said, rising and trying to block her way. "Just let it run for a while. It takes a while for the hot water to get way up here."

Just as Paula reached for the doorknob, Danny opened the door. His eyes bucked when he saw Paula. Her eyes bucked and her mouth dropped open when she saw him, dripping wet and buck naked. They were all speechless.

"How did you ladies get in my room!" Danny demanded. "I'm calling the management about this!" He backed into the bedroom and closed the door.

Paula closed her mouth and looked at her mother. MaryBeth had that "deer in the headlights" look.

"Mother!"

"Paula—it's not what you think."

A sly grin crossed Paula's face. "Well, I sure hope it is. You go, girl."

MaryBeth blushed a deep rose.

"He's cute. And so young. I guess I'd better go," she said, putting her sandals on, and picking up the knapsack purse. "I've been ousted again. I got used to it with my roommate last year."

"You don't have to go," MaryBeth said, embarrassment still burning her cheeks. "Well, maybe under the circumstances . . ."

At the door, Paula said, "Next time, I'll call first. I just wasn't thinking . . . I mean I never would have thought . . . I just want to know one thing, Mother."

MaryBeth looked at her, eyebrows raised in a question.

A big grin came to Paula's face. "Is he always so quick on the uptake?"

"Paula!"

Paula slipped out the door and closed it behind her.

As soon as the door closed, Danny walked into the room, this time with a towel wrapped around him, tucked at his hips.

"Your daughter's beautiful. And so are you." He tried to put his arms around MaryBeth, but she pushed him away. She collapsed on the couch and put her face in her hands and rested her elbows on her knees. He sat next to her.

"Bad timing, huh?"

She took her hands down and gave him an annoyed look.

"I'd say that, Daniel."

"Why do you call me Daniel? Everybody calls me Danny."

"Danny sounds so young. Something you'd call a little boy. How old are you anyway?"

"Almost thirty-six. Why?"

"Well, that's a relief," she said, wryly.

"Why?"

"I thought you were twenty-something."

"So you're a real cradle-robber. Are you disappointed?" He wore his quirky grin.

"I'm not in the mood for jokes, Daniel." She stared soberly at the coffee table. Then, she turned to look at him.

"Don't you want to know how old I am?"

"Nope."

"Why?"

"I don't care," he shrugged.

"You don't care about my age, or you just don't care about anything?"

"This is a trick question, isn't it?"

MaryBeth stood and walked across the room. She stared out the patio door, mindless of the twinkling lights below that stretched out into the distance. For a few wonderful hours, she had soared to the heights. She had been free. Now she wrapped her arms around herself. Her body was still taut from their lovemaking. With Paula's surprise visit, reality had intruded hard, crashing her back to earth. She wasn't free. She never would be. She'd been robbed of her best years, being the responsible parent, struggling alone under a load made for two. She'd been the role model, teaching them responsibility and respectability. They'd absorbed the lessons. She'd been lucky. Now she'd been reduced to "Way to go, Mom," like it was a game or a joke.

"You'd better go, Daniel."

"Go? Why?" He frowned at her back.

"You got what you wanted. You got your lesson. You can just go now."

"So, I'm being dismissed? Like a schoolboy?" His frown deepened.

She threw her chin up. That was her answer.

Danny walked over, stood behind her, and put his hands on her shoulders.

"I thought we had something together. Something we could build on."

"There's nothing to build on. There're too many years between us. We both knew that in the beginning. It was just a nice way to pass the evening. Go home now, Daniel." She shrugged her shoulders from his hands. She wouldn't turn to face him because she didn't want him to see the tears in her eyes.

Danny smoldered with anger.

"I won't let you treat me like that. You can't just play with me, then send me home like I'm some kid. I'm a man, MaryBeth. If you're just into toy boys, I'm not the one."

MaryBeth whirled around to face him, her eyes blazing. Just before her palm landed against his cheek, he grabbed her wrist and held it. She struggled to wrest her hand away, but his grip was firm, his strength greater. Slowly he forced her hand down, turned it behind her back, and pressed her against him. He grabbed the back of her neck and crushed her lips against his. When she refused to respond, he thrust his tongue in her mouth, claiming her, forcing her to accept him. He held her tight until he absorbed all of her anger, all of her fear, all of her insecurity. He felt her surrender to his strength, spent from the release of emotion. Then he released her wrist, put his arm around her, and held her gently.

★　　　★　　　★

The shapely blonde waitress set their plates on the table. Maxwell wore a perplexed expression, as he watched Danny cut into his chicken-fried steak. Danny was going on and on about how unfair it was for them to have to work on Saturday.

"We've worked a bunch of Saturdays. We've always worked every other weekend, Danny."

"Yeah, well, you need to change that. You're the lieutenant. You ought not to have to work on the weekend. If you ever retire, that's the first thing I'm going to change."

"You never complained before. And you've never let a pretty girl like that one get away without getting her phone number and promising to call," Maxwell said, nodding to the pert, young woman in the starched pink uniform behind the counter.

Danny shrugged without looking in that direction.

"What's up, Danny? Some lady finally stole your heart?" Maxwell chuckled.

Danny gave him his quirky grin, as he chewed on a bite of steak.

"All right, come clean. I've got to hear this," Maxwell said.

"You don't want to know."

"O-o-oh yes I do," Maxwell said, setting his knife and fork down. He propped his elbows on the table, his hands under his chin, his eyebrows raised in an expectant look. "The conqueror gets conquered. Come on, out with it. Who is she?"

"Ms. Williams friend. MaryBeth."

Maxwell's mouth dropped open. Then he sat back against the high back of the booth and let out a laugh, shaking his head.

"What?" Danny asked with a frown on his face. "What?"

"You can't be serious," Maxwell chuckled. But when he saw the look on Danny's face, he knew he was.

"Well, I'll just be damned, grandbaby."

★   ★   ★

"Turn around. Yeah, that one looks good on you," MaryBeth said, pulling the elastic neckline of the peasant dress around Audrey's shoulders. "The color is right for you, too. You've just got to get it."

Audrey twirled around in front of the three-way mirror. The full skirt of the hot pink, gauzy dress settled around her knees. She agreed with MaryBeth. She did look good in it.

"But I can only afford two. And I need work clothes. Not something frivolous like this."

"Get them all, Audrey. When was the last time you treated yourself? You need to do that often. You owe it to yourself."

Audrey turned and looked at MaryBeth. "Oh no, not Ms. Penny-pincher herself? But I guess it's easy if you're spending someone else's money."

"You only live once, Audrey. And these are really a bargain. The prices are even better than at the store with my discount. I'm getting all these over here," she said, pointing to a pile of clothes. "Besides, you need to have something sexy to wear. A woman just feels good in sexy clothes. And it wouldn't hurt for you to wear something sexy for Maxwell. And you really need to do something about that gray. A woman has to keep herself up. A woman has to—"

"Okay, okay. Come on, let's get these, then go by the bookstore. I want to pick up a few books Sondra recommended."

"Sounds good to me. I'd like to get a few myself. I enjoyed the other book you loaned me. Say, how about we grab a bite at that new coffeeshop in the bookstore."

★   ★   ★

Audrey sipped from her cup of hazelnut coffee. MaryBeth was reading the back of Audrey's new book, munching on a salad, thinking about how to tell her.

"What would you say if I told you I was interested in a younger man?" MaryBeth blurted out.

"I'd say you've been drinking too much coffee and not eating enough meat. Are you?"

MaryBeth just smiled.

"I haven't seen you this calm in a long time. Maybe a younger man is what you need. You're just fair glowing. Tell me about him. How much younger?"

"Well, let's just say a lot. But Audrey, he makes me feel alive. Energized. I've done things with him I've never done before. I've ridden a motorcycle. I'm even going sailing. He's more of a man than all these old geezers I've been seeing put together." MaryBeth hesitated, then said, "His name is Daniel . . ." Holding her breath, she waited for Audrey's reaction.

Audrey frowned. "That jerk?"

"Oh Audrey, he's really not like that, once you get to know him."

Audrey sucked her teeth.

"It's important to me that you like him."

"It's not for me to like him. If you like him, I love him." Audrey sucked her teeth again, crimped her mouth, and looked off.

"Oh Audrey," MaryBeth sighed, her shoulders slumped. "This is going to be hard enough without you acting like that. I mean, I'm not stupid. I'm not thinking about forever after and all that."

"Yes, you are. You know you are."

"Okay, okay. I'll admit I've thought about it. But I know it can't be that way. I know it's just for now." MaryBeth sat up and threw her shoulders back. "But you know what, Audrey? I've figured out just for now is all you ever get. At my age, it would be stupid to miss out on now, worrying about later."

"Throwing caution to the wind, is that it?"

"Isn't that what you're doing?"

Audrey stared at her for a long time, trying to deny it to herself. She reared back in the chair and folded her arms across her breast. A hint of a resigned smile came to her lips.

"I guess if you like him, he must not be too much of a shithead. All I can say is, you've paid your dues. If he makes you happy, I'm happy for you."

*　　　*　　　*

No need to go to the exercise room today, not after the workout she'd had earlier this morning. MaryBeth felt downright decadent, lazing around in bed so late. The Sunday edition of the Houston *Chronicle* was spread all over the bed and the floor. The breakfast dishes were on the cart by the side of the bed. She could still smell his woodsy fragrance on the pillow.

Danny had gone home to change clothes and then go to work. They planned to go to the movies that evening. He wanted to take her to some artsy theater where a film that had won an honorable mention at the Cannes Film Festival was showing. She was up for that. When the phone rang, she just knew it was him and answered on the first ring. Jason's voice surprised her instead.

"Mom, what are you doing down there in Houston?"

"I've got this temporary assignment—"

"That's not what I mean."

"Oh? What did you mean, dear?"

"About this guy?"

MaryBeth pursed her lips. Her good mood was broken. She didn't know what to say. There was a long silence on the line.

"I talked to Paula," he said.

"Oh?"

"She thinks it's cute. She says he's cute. Cute, Mom. *Cute.*" The disparagement was clear in his voice. "How young is this guy anyway?"

MaryBeth took a couple of breaths before she responded.

"What? No, 'Is he nice to you, Mom?' No, 'Are you happy, Mom?' Huh, Jason?"

"Mom," he whined into two syllables. "You're embarrassing me."

"Embarrassing you? This doesn't have anything to do with you, Jason. What right do you have to criticize me? I'm the one who took care of you. I'm the one who changed your diapers. And now, I'm embarrassing you?"

"I just don't think it's right for you to be parading around here with a guy half your age."

"Who are you to say what's right for me, Jason?"

"Do I get to be the ring-bearer in the wedding? Huh, Mom?"

"Who said anything about getting married? And I don't remember you objecting to being a groomsman in your father's wedding when he married Jennifer. And in fact, I paid for your tux."

"That's different, Mom."

"How so, Jason?"

"He's a man."

"I see. So it's okay for a man to have someone half his age, but not okay for a woman?"

"You're a mom, Mom."

"I'm a woman, Jason. When you come to grips with that fact, you call me back. Good-bye, Jason."

MaryBeth slammed the phone down and fumed. How dare he talk to her like that! The little snot-nose. After all she'd done for him. All the sacrifices she'd made. Helping him buy his car. And the insurance. By God, she still carried him on her automobile policy. Then a bit of remorse crept in. She'd only spoken to him in that tone once before. But even then, it hadn't sounded so final. What if he never called her again?

At least Paula was on her side. Jeez! This wasn't about sides. And would she have a mouthful for Paula, spreading her business that way. She'd probably told Ryan, too. He'd probably call next, whining. She had a mind to call Paula and let her have it.

All she was doing was having a little fun, she fumed, as she paced back and forth in front of the dresser. You'd think after all she'd sacrificed for them, they would want her to have a little fun. Oh, but no. Fun isn't for moms. Fun is just for sons and daughters—and, apparently, dads. Financing fun is for moms. Why couldn't she have a little fun?

But she knew in her heart it was more than that. Danny was fun, but he was more than that. He had touched her in a way she hadn't thought possible. He made her feel young again, and alive and full of energy. She had caught herself thinking about forever. But deep inside, she knew forever wasn't something she should be thinking about with him. Just a day at a time. Just for now. But was just for now worth being estranged from her family?

seventeen

*M*axwell was unaccustomed to feeling this excited, but he liked it. He liked it a lot. He was sure he would enjoy the Essence Music Festival. He'd heard a lot about it. Ockletree had gone last year and had talked about it for weeks afterward. But his real excitement stemmed from the prospect of spending the weekend with Audrey.

"Put your bag on that bed in the back," Audrey said, as she checked the cabinets, making a list of things she was short on— eggs, grits, potatoes. "You can put those hang-up clothes in the closet on the left."

As he put his things away, Maxwell noticed her bag was on the overhead bed, next to Mighty Max. Well, that answers that question, he thought. He followed her outside, feeling useless, but watched intently as she unhooked. Back inside, she settled in the driver's seat. That answered his question about who was driving.

"The copilot's job is the shake down," Audrey said, as she started the motor.

"Shake down?"

"Yeah, clear the decks. You have to make sure there's nothing that can fall off. Nothing on the countertops. Check the table.

Check the bathroom, too. Make sure all the cabinet doors are closed."

When he'd done as instructed, Maxwell relaxed into the seat and put on his seat belt. As they weaved through the Houston traffic, he stole glances at her. Her arm was outstretched, her hand casually resting on the steering wheel. She was in charge. She had been in charge. He'd allowed her to be. He had been willing to give her all the time and space she needed. He could have forced her, but he didn't want it that way. He wanted her to come to him willingly. He'd done everything he knew how to make her feel willing. But now, enough time had passed, much more than the doctor had allotted. And it wasn't Shirley's bed. It was her space. And he had the whole weekend.

When they were ten miles past Beaumont, Audrey pulled off into a roadside park, then put the gearshift in park. She eased out of the seat and walked to the back. "Potty stop."

"In Vidor?" Maxwell asked with a smile and a frown. "You picked the infamous place where they don't let black folks live? You better make that a quick stop."

"You brought your gun, didn't you?" she returned with a wink.

When she came back, she stopped just behind the seats. "Okay. Your turn to drive."

"Who me?" Maxwell asked.

"I'm not doing all the work on this trip."

Maxwell moved over to the driver's seat and Audrey settled into the passenger seat.

Two hours later, when they got to Lake Charles, Audrey said, "All right, you can pull off there by the beach, I'll take the wheel."

"Just relax. I've got it. How about a soft drink?"

"Sure. Are you hungry? Wanna stop?"

"I'll bet you've got something back there I would like."

While she made sandwiches, she thought how different his request was from Sam's "Fix me something to eat" after miles of silence. She thought of all the differences between them. She enjoyed just being with Maxwell. She even enjoyed their lighthearted arguments.

When they got to New Orleans, Audrey got her campground book down from the cabinet.

"The closest ones to the Superdome are all on Chef Menteur highway, and that's still a good piece out. We'll have to take a cab. I should have towed the car." She gave him directions.

"Have you stayed at any of them before?" he asked.

She shook her head. "Never even stopped in New Orleans before. I like being in the country."

"Well, how about we drive by all three, you can smoke 'em over, then pick the one you want."

She picked the newest one. They went into the office together. Since he'd bought all the gas, she insisted on paying. When he pulled into the assigned spot, he got out with her.

"Let me. Tell me if I'm doing this right, now." He pulled the cord out and plugged into the electricity. Audrey understood he was learning, so she taught.

"We can hook up to the water, too. Get the hose out of that compartment." Then, she showed him the hookup for that.

"That's it. We're all set. Would you like to shower before the show?"

*　　　*　　　*

The cab left them in front of the Superdome. The traffic was bumper-to-bumper with cars bearing license plates from nearly every state. Excitement buzzed all around them. Along the sloping promenade up to the arena, the crowd was thick. Every age, from young to old. Young women in short skirts, young men sporting bald heads. Groups of sistahs her age, couples of every age, children Audrey thought were too young for this kind of affair. She and

Maxwell waded through the crowd and found their seats in the huge arena. They were good seats, but the view of the large screens was better than that of the stage.

Audrey had heard RosaLee talking about the young performer who was the opening act. He stomped back and forth from one end of the stage to the other, beckoning the crowd to join him in a syncopated "Oh yeah! Oh yeah!" She couldn't remember if she had ever thought a man that thin was attractive, and wondered why he took off his shirt. His gyrating around on the stage was comical to her, but the teenage girls sitting in front of them were really turned on. She looked at the program and saw that the Dells were in one of the superlounges. No contest.

She pulled Maxwell through the crowd. On the way they stopped at one of the concession stands. He got a hot sausage po' boy on French, dressed. Since she hadn't heard of it before, Audrey had to get the alligator sausage. She sampled his sandwich, but he turned down her offer of a bite of her sausage.

"Aw, come on. Try it. You'll like it. It tastes like chicken," she teased.

"Everything tastes like chicken," he chuckled. "I'd just as soon eat chicken."

There weren't nearly enough chairs in the superlounge for the number of people standing around conversating, but Maxwell spotted two together. This crowd was definitely older. All the young folks were in the main arena swooning over the young fellow with the gyrating pelvis and a chest that might develop one of these days.

Audrey and Maxwell were surrounded by a sea of standing bodies by the time the Dells took the stage dressed in matching black tuxedoes and red cummerbunds. They crooned the love songs that had thrilled several generations: "There Is," "Always Together," "Love Is So Simple," "Oh What a Night." That they'd been on stage together forty-five years was obvious. That gyrating boy could sure learn something about stage presence from them, Audrey thought. When they sang "Stay In My Corner" and the lead singer held the note for so long, the crowd went wild. The crowd tried to bring them back for an encore, but they obviously intended to conserve their energy for the second show.

When Audrey and Maxwell made it back to their seats in the main arena, stagehands were scampering around preparing the stage for Ms. Patti. Audrey made friends with the dignified lady sitting next to her. Willie had come by herself from Mobile. This was her fourth year straight. Audrey admired her spunk and felt encouraged about her own trip.

Diva Patti strode on the stage in her signature high heels. The girl tore it up. Just kicked out of her shoes and sang her ass off. Audrey was surprised that all of her backup singers were male. After three of Patti's hits, Audrey found herself on her feet, doing the bump with Willie on "Lady Marmalade." After several more, Patti went spiritual on them with "What a Friend We Have In Jesus." Willie shared a tissue from her little bag with Audrey. Then another on Patti's monologue about the love, and loss, of her sister that led into "Wind Beneath My Wings" and another on the closing: "Somewhere Over the Rainbow." Patti finished to a thunderous standing ovation.

Audrey scanned the program, took Maxwell's hand, and dragged him off to another superlounge to catch a little of the Emotions while the main stage was being set up for the last act.

"All this walking is tiring me out," Maxwell complained.

"I'm not missing a minute of this because you're hardheaded. I told you to wear your tennis."

"Now what would I look like wearing tennis, out here with all these dressed-to-kill brothers?"

"You'd look like a man whose feet didn't hurt," she answered with a smile.

This time they were in the sea of standing bodies. Audrey was surprised that these classy ladies were so much more "mature" than when she'd seen them that time in California. Then, she remembered how "immature" she'd looked twenty years ago. Their timing was perfect to catch "Don't Ask Your Neighbor."

They returned to their seats just as Luther danced on stage, singing "I Can Make It Better" with his backup singers. He wore a high-collared black suit; they wore lavender tuxedoes. Their syncopated three steps, pause, three steps, pause, was perfectly choreographed. Luther tried to make it appear that his wasn't. He seemed to be enjoying himself more than anyone in the room. When the number ended, the singers eased onto stools at the side of the stage, continuing their harmonious crooning. Luther walked to the front and sang his heart out: "A House Is Not a Home," "A Thousand Kisses," "Never Enough," "Power of Love," "Your Secret Love." It would have taken all night for him to sing all of his hits. An hour later he closed the show with "Love Won't Let Me Wait." He took a deep, royal bow and left everyone in the arena on their feet.

Bright lights flooded the huge arena. Audrey immediately picked up her purse. Maxwell took her hand and pulled her back into the seat.

"Just sit down. No point in us rushing out with this crowd. I'd act worst than one of these kids if somebody steps on my toe." He didn't turn her hand loose, and she didn't make him.

"I told you to wear your tennis."

"I would have, if you'd worn yours," he said, looking pointedly at her toes wriggling in high-heeled sandals.

"You wanna go to a club?" she asked. "Or to the French Quarter?"

"I've had enough of crowds for this night. Do you have something to drink in the RV?"

"Beer and maybe some bourbon. That's all."

"That's enough. And you've got good music. Let's just make our own club."

"I'll make some nachos, too."

★   ★   ★

Maxwell paid the cab driver and pressed the three-number combination to open the gate to the RV park. They walked to the RV, still arguing over whether Patti or Luther should have been the closing act.

The first thing Maxwell did when they got inside was take off his shoes, then his sports coat, then his shoulder holster. Although departmental policy required him to carry his weapon at all times, he knew he was out of his jurisdiction. It was just an ingrained habit after all these years. He pulled the folding door closed and changed into shorts and a T-shirt. Then he remembered the little box that Danny had given him yesterday with his quirky grin. "Just in case you get lucky, old man." Maxwell opened the box and put one of the packages in his pocket. Then he hung his clothes up, put his gun in the suitcase, and slipped his feet into a pair of thongs.

Audrey fished around in the back of the cabinet over the couch until she found the bourbon bottle, then poured him a glass. She poured herself a glass of lemonade.

"Let's sit outside," she said, as he folded the door back. "You look so comfortable. Here, take these out while I change."

Audrey was relieved to be free of the new bra she hadn't quite broken in yet. She slipped the hot pink gauzy dress on and, admiring herself in the mirror, pulled the elastic neck around her shoulders like MaryBeth had done. Then she dimmed the lights and went to join Maxwell at the table outside.

Maxwell leaned back on his elbows on the table, his long legs stretched out in front of him. Sipping his drink and staring up at the big moon, he thought how peaceful this was, even with the security lights and the sounds of the highway nearby. Yep, he was definitely going to buy the RV. He envisioned many nights like this. He was certain he didn't want to spend them alone, though.

When Audrey appeared in the doorway, silhouetted by the light inside, he could see her voluptuous form through the flowing dress. His vision of her walking to him and sitting astride his lap aroused him in a way that made him sit up straight. She started to the other side of the table.

"Here," he said patting the bench, "come sit next to me."

When she sat, he put his arm around her shoulder.

"So what's on tap for tomorrow?"

Audrey sipped her lemonade. "There will be a lot of vendors at the convention center. I'd like to go down there for a couple of hours. See what's for sale. Then, more good music tomorrow night at the dome. We ought to catch some of the acts in the jazz super-lounge this time."

"Don't even say superlounge to me."

"You better wear your tennis."

"I will, if you will," he said with a smile.

Maxwell looked up at the moon. He thought about the picture Audrey had shown him of Zion Canyon.

"I'll bet that big ol' moon is even prettier from the bottom of a canyon," he mused.

Audrey looked up. "I can only imagine," she said, with a dreamy smile.

When she looked back at him with that dreamy look on her face, he couldn't help himself. He leaned over and kissed her. Just a touching of lips at first. When she didn't shrink from him, he kissed her like he really wanted to. He put his arm around her and turned her toward him. Her full breasts pressed against his chest. To force himself not to touch them he picked up her hand and laced his fingers through hers. He had waited for this moment so long, he didn't want to ruin it by taking her too fast. When he drew his lips from hers, he heard her soft intake of breath, as though she was disappointed. He planted kisses on her face, then nibbled at her neck, breathing in her aroma.

All of her promises to never put herself in a position to be rejected, all of her acceptance of her role as his companion, just melted away in his kiss. Once she had wondered how she would react if he ever did approach her again, but that wasn't until after she'd mentioned that she was going to the festival.

She hadn't exactly invited him, and he hadn't exactly invited himself. One thing had led to another. They had just started talking about the logistics of it as though an invitation had been extended. She hadn't objected. She enjoyed his company, and he seemed to enjoy hers. She felt safe with him. He knew Sam's secret and it didn't seem to matter to him. It had never come up again since that first night, months ago. Maybe that's what being a real friend is about. Occasionally she found herself wondering if he had a woman. She didn't see how he could, because he spent so much time with her. But in all the quiet nights they'd spent together since that night at his house, he hadn't acted like he wanted her as a woman. So she'd set up the sleeping arrangements on the trip to make it plain that she didn't expect that from him. From the look of acquiescence on his face when he first stepped into the RV, she thought it was settled.

But now, her sweet dream, the one she'd had the night she met him and almost every night since, was intruding. And his lips on her neck were warm, and his fingers were entwining in hers, and his other hand was rubbing her back.

When Maxwell felt her fingers relax, his lips wandered down seeking the sweetness of the melon. They lingered on the swell of her breast just above the elastic neckline of her dress. He felt a jolt, then realized his pager was vibrating. Annoyed, he turned it off without even looking at the display. Whatever it was, he couldn't do jack about it from this distance. Danny would just have to handle it. Even Cedric would have to wait. Right now, this beautiful woman was in his arms, and his dream was coming true. He cupped her face in his hands and pulled her lips to his, massaging his thumbs down her neck.

"Nice night."

They both blinked at the bright beam from a flashlight trained on their faces. Instinctively, Maxwell's hand reached for his gun. He felt naked without it, but was on his feet in an instant to face down the intruder bare-handed. The thin-framed man in a security guard uniform took a step backward at Maxwell's quick movement and the size of the man. He put his hand up in apology, taking another backward step.

"Didn't mean to disturb you folks," he said, a hint of nervousness in his voice. "Just making my rounds. Y'all just, uh, have a good night. If you need anything, just holler. I'll be around."

Under Maxwell's stern glare, he hurriedly slinked away.

Maxwell muttered under his breath, "Barney Fife, motherfucker. Bet' not come back around here."

Audrey could see the adrenaline on Maxwell's face. She giggled. "So how does a cop feel when he's busted?"

His frown melted into a chuckle.

"You wanna go in?" she asked. "I'll fix us some nachos."

He reached for her hand, led her to the door and held it open for her.

Inside, Audrey reached inside the refrigerator for the block of cheese. Maxwell walked up behind her and placed a gentle kiss on her neck. Then he turned her to face him trailing kisses to her lips. He traced their contour with the tip of his tongue, then probed the depth of her mouth. He withdrew his tongue, inviting her to reciprocate. And she did.

Audrey felt herself surrendering to his tenderness. His big hands were massaging her back. After all her promises and vows, she wasn't sure she was ready for this, but she sure liked the way it felt. Sweet, mellow feelings were inundating her. Without releasing her lips, he took the cheese from her hand, dropped it on the counter, and wrapped his strong arm at the small of her back. Audrey put her arms around his neck, inviting him to kiss her more deeply. And he did. She felt his hands massaging down her back to her buttocks, pressing her against him. She felt a sweet pulling in her pelvis. He raised the back of her dress, gathering the fabric in one hand and rubbing the other along the back of her thigh. His finger easing inside the leg of her panty brought the fear forward. She tried to pull away from him, but he wouldn't let her go.

"What?" he whispered. "What is it?"

Audrey drew back, but couldn't meet his eyes. "I haven't . . . It's been a long time since . . . I don't know that I want you to see my body."

He cupped her chin and raised it to force her to look at him. "Why?"

Audrey blushed. "It's not exactly my cheerleader body, anymore," she said, looking away from him.

"I've already seen your body—twice. I want to see it again. This time, I want you to be conscious."

Audrey looked up into his black eyes and saw the depth of his sincerity in them, and in his smile.

Maxwell released her chin, stepped back from her, reached up and turned the bright light on. Then he pulled off his shirt and stood vulnerable before her.

"This one hasn't been on a football field in a long time either. Are you gonna run, screaming from the RV? Or will you stay—and let me give you the pleasure that you deserve?"

Audrey felt all of her defenses crumbling. She reached out and touched her fingertips to his chest. Her hand looked small against its broad expanse. She fingered the keloid scar that ran diagonally down his rib cage. Then she looked up into his eyes.

"Only if you turn this spotlight off."

He reached up and turned the light off, then eased the elastic neckline down over her arms, baring her breasts in the soft glow of the dim light. "You couldn't have looked this good when you were a cheerleader."

Audrey blushed again under his appreciative gaze. He touched his lips to hers, then covered them with a passionate kiss. He leaned back and looked in her eyes. Then he cupped her breast in his hand and lowered his lips to it. Waves of passion coursed through her, as his tongue made circles around her areola and curled around the tip of her nipple. He slowly sucked it into his mouth. Then he lavished the same loving on her other breast, while his hands sensuously caressed her body, rolling the dress down over her hips. It fell in a soft puddle on the floor. His lips found hers again and she put her arms around his neck, surrendering to his kiss. He scooped her off her feet, and carried her the few feet to the bed. Audrey felt light as a feather as he gently lowered her on it and eased himself on the bed beside her. He pleasured her breasts for a while, then dribbled kisses down her stomach. When he touched his tongue to her navel, Audrey sucked in at the feelings that were unfamiliar to her. Then she relaxed and enjoyed a freedom that she hadn't known with any other man.

The night he'd lost control, Maxwell had promised her a long, slow pleasuring, and now was the time. He untied the ribbons on both sides of her hips that held her panties on. He pushed aside the scant, silky fabric, and sought her bud. Like a loving gardener, he encouraged and coaxed it to flower. As it bloomed, petal by petal, he tasted the sweetness of each one, until he brought her to the brink of ecstasy. Then he nudged her over the edge.

As she lay quivering and spent, Maxwell kissed his way back to her breasts. When he reached for the button on his shorts, Audrey pulled his hands away.

She felt like a wanton woman, as she released the button on his waistband and slowly unzipped his pants. But she didn't care, she wanted to give him as much pleasure as he'd given her. She slipped her hands around his hips and pushed his shorts down, freeing him. She took his maleness in her hands and caressed it, up and down, until he moaned. She gently rubbed her thumb across the broad tip, drawing a throaty groan from him.

Maxwell locked his lips to hers in a greedy kiss, and reached under her so that he could touch the firm, smooth skin of her buttocks. He pulled her to him and rubbed his silken shaft against her soft wetness. He felt himself being drawn up in a vortex of swirling passion, but caught himself in time to protect them.

As they laid on the bed, Audrey guided him to the place that only he could satisfy. The moment he entered her, she felt whole for the first time. He entered her gently, and slowly filled her to her core. He held still for a moment, then eased out to the tip and filled her again. The age-old rhythm of lovers became their dance. Their coupling rose to a fevered pitch, seeking and searching. They were mindless to the RV swaying from the motion of their lovemaking.

Audrey put her arms around his neck and held on for the wild ride. She reached a height that she always sought, had always known was there, but had never reached. She felt herself spinning, spinning in the whirlwind. With his last powerful thrust, they spun out of control, holding on to each other for all that they needed.

Audrey had always known something was missing. Now that she knew what it was, she felt complete. Maxwell knew he wanted her forever. Lying exhausted in each other's arms, they drifted into a sated sleep.

*   *   *

The next morning, Audrey awoke cradled in Maxwell's arms. A big smile came to her face. She hadn't had such a restful sleep in months. Maybe years. When she stirred, he kissed her good morning. She started up from the bed to get the coffee going, but he held her back and gave her something else she'd never had—early morning love.

When he got up to use the restroom, she started the coffee and breakfast. When he came out, he kissed her and fondled her until she almost let the toast burn. They sat at the little table and ate a hearty breakfast of grits, eggs, and sausage, watching some of the other RVers packing up and pulling out. Then they showered and dressed. Audrey insisted that Maxwell wear his tennis.

★   ★   ★

The taxi let them out in front of the convention center. They milled around the rest of the morning and most of the afternoon looking at the wares that vendors from all over the country had to offer. Audrey found she had to be careful about what she admired, because he bought everything she said she liked. Famished and loaded down with packages, they took a cab back to the RV park.

After they'd eaten the sandwiches she piled high with thinly sliced smoked turkey, Maxwell looked at his watch.

"It's three o'clock. We ought to have just enough time to take a quick nap before the show tonight," he said as he closed the blinds.

But nap wasn't what was on his mind. Or hers either. They slowly undressed each other and ravished each other's bodies.

★   ★   ★

When the phone rang, Audrey pulled away from Maxwell.

"Don't answer it," he said, pulling her back into his arms and nuzzling against her neck dreamily. "It's either the wrong number or somebody trying to sell you something."

"Only a few people have this number; I have to be sure. If it's a salesman, I'll tell him I already have everything I need." Audrey kissed him gently and rose from the bed. She pulled a towel around her as she walked to the living area and answered the phone.

"Hello." "Sondra?" "Talk louder, I can hardly hear you. I'm in New Orleans. You ought to come next year. You won't believe the music." "No, I'm not by myself. Why?" "Malcolm? No, I don't know where he is. Why?" "Don't give me that bullshit. What's going on?"

Audrey slumped against the counter. Maxwell slipped on his shorts and walked to her side. His dark eyes said he already knew.

"I'm on my way. I'll call you as soon as I get back. Five or six hours."

She punched in a number.

"RosaLee? This is Mama. Is Malcolm there with you?" "This is serious, girl. They've issued a warrant for him. The bondsman has a bounty hunter looking for him. Do you know where he is?" "When was the last time you talked to him?" "He what?! What girl? What's her name?" "Jesus! Do you know how to get in touch with her?" "Call his friends. We've got to find him before the bounty hunter does, RosaLee. Call me the minute you find out anything." She pressed the off button and threw the phone on the couch.

"I've got to go—"

"What can you do?" Maxwell asked.

"I don't know. I've just got to go."

"And miss the show tonight? We already have tickets."

The look on Audrey's face gave him the answer. He walked outside and began unhooking. By the time he came back inside, Audrey had cleaned up and put everything away. When she started for the driver's seat, Maxwell held her back.

"I'll drive. You have too much on your mind."

Maxwell settled in the driver's seat and pulled out of the RV park.

The drive to Houston seemed interminable. Audrey thought about her house and all she had put into it. She could hear Sam's voice— "What if he runs?" Then she thought of her child being hunted down by white men with guns and bloodhounds.

Maxwell picked up the phone and dialed Danny's number. When he got no answer, he dialed Danny's pager and put in Audrey's cell phone number. He wondered how he was going to explain this to the captain. Danny had been right. The situation was fraught with opportunities for conflict, although he never anticipated something like this. Just the week before, he'd been surprised to find himself thinking how easy it would be to forget a little detail, just enough to provide reasonable doubt. The captain would be mad as hell that they lost the case, but he wouldn't be able to take away his retirement. Even if the captain had his suspicions, the only way he could take his retirement would be to fire him. And Maxwell was sure he could do it in such a way that that wouldn't happen. Even so, it could mean he'd leave the department with a cloud on his otherwise spotless record. Audrey would be happy that the boy was free, and he would be happy that this thing was no longer between them. He'd reasoned that, if the boy was really bad, he'd do something else, and it would be another officer's case. In the end, he knew he couldn't do it. He could live with a cloud on his record; he just couldn't live with the knowledge that he'd compromised his ethics.

Maxwell was irritated that Danny hadn't returned his page. Danny was on call for the weekend, so he should have had the damn pager on. And departmental policy required that every page be returned promptly. So why the hell didn't Danny call back? He punched the number in again.

EIGHTEEN

*D*anny held the motorcycle while MaryBeth climbed off. She pulled the helmet off and shook her hair out. She stretched her arms, then bent over to stretch the muscles in her back. He put the kickstand down and leaned the bike to a secure footing. It was quiet on the cul-de-sac.

"This is a nice place," Danny said, looking around. The fat moon illuminated the condos nestled among the pine trees.

"Yeah. Audrey and I have had some good times here. It's so peaceful."

She remembered the hard times after the divorce, when she'd been really crazy. Audrey had brought her here. Audrey always seemed to know when she was just about to go over the edge. "Just a little getaway for the kids," she'd said. In their excitement, the kids had believed that. MaryBeth knew better. After the kids were settled in for the night, she and Audrey would sit on the deck. Audrey's pitcher of lemonade sat next to her bottle of wine on the table between them. She would rant and rave until the bottle was empty and Audrey had to help her to bed. They'd weathered her storm together. The last few times, it had just been the two of them, the pitcher and the bottle. Peaceful.

Danny unhooked the strap that held their bags to the back of the bike. He slung his nylon duffel bag over his shoulder and hefted her leather one in his hand.

"What did Audrey say about us coming up here?"

"Well, I didn't exactly ask her," MaryBeth said, with a sheepish look in her face. "She was so excited about going to New Orleans, I couldn't get a word in edgewise."

"That's hard to believe," Danny said with a crooked grin. "So how'd you get the key?"

"Oh, that's easy. The key is always here," she said, running her fingers on top of the doorframe. She opened the door and turned back to him with a smile.

Danny dropped their bags in the middle of the living room and grabbed her in a bear hug.

"Wait! Let me show you around first." She showed him the kitchen, the deck, and the two bedrooms on that level. "Now for the best part." She took his hand and led him downstairs.

The spacious bedroom was dark. Heavy curtains covered the glass wall. When MaryBeth started to open them, Danny pulled her back into his arms and kissed her deeply. She melted in his embrace. He lifted her onto the dresser and stood between her legs, planting kisses on her face and neck.

"Quit it, quit," she said, pulling away and pushing against his chest. "Let's shower first. I'm all sweaty and covered with road dust. Go get our suitcases. I'll start the shower. After that . . ."

Danny's eyes lit up at her provocative promise. Then he bounded up the stairs two at a time.

MaryBeth walked into the bathroom and pushed the shower curtain back. A gasp escaped her lips and she stumbled backward at the sight of a young woman cowering in a corner of the tub. The girl's eyes were wide with fright.

"What are you doing here?" MaryBeth put her hand over her heart to still its pounding.

The girl cringed further against the wall and covered her mouth with her hands. She hunched her shoulders and lowered her head, as though she could draw herself into a ball. Her blunt-cut coal black hair fell across her face like a mask.

MaryBeth held both her hands up. "It's okay. It's okay. I'm not going to hurt you. How'd you get in here?"

The girl didn't say anything.

"Did you hear me?" she demanded.

The girl was mute.

"Do you speak English?"

The girl nodded her head.

"Who are you?"

The girl lowered her hands from her mouth. "I'm Mimi."

*   *   *

Sometimes you catch a break, Danny thought as he crossed the living room. Before he could ask Maxwell last week to trade his on-call duty, he had to hear all about Maxwell's upcoming trip to New Orleans. He owed Ockletree big time for trading with him. The store had extended MaryBeth's time by several weeks, but this was the last one. He didn't know what would happen when she moved back to Dallas, but he wasn't going to think about that this weekend. Instead, his mind roved pleasantly from one event to another that he hoped to experience with her. He was definitely going to ask her to go with him to the jazz festival in northern California. He wondered if she was game for that long a trip on the bike.

He started to the bike to get the cooler with bottle of the champagne. He saw the figure of a man bending over it, his hand on the keys in the ignition.

"Nice bike, huh?" Danny called out from the doorway as he eased his hand toward his waistband.

The man was startled and took off running across the cul-de-sac. Danny gave chase, hopping over the low hedges just as the man turned the corner of the next house. Danny didn't break his stride turning the corner and starting down the steep hill, slipping on the way down, nearly losing his balance. At the foot where the slope was more gentle, he stopped and peered into the darkness, breathing hard, adrenaline making the blood pound in his temples. He could see the reflections on the lake and dark outlines of trees, but the man was nowhere. Damn! he thought. Jerk! Danny walked across the backyard and started up the hill between the houses.

When he rounded the corner a fist met him squarely in the jaw. Despite the pain, he got a grip on the man's shirt as he went down, pulling the man with him. They struggled, trading blows and grunts. As they fought their way onto the patio, both of them took brushes against the hard concrete. In the thrashing of bodies, a trash can was kicked over, its contents spilling as it rolled down the hill toward the lake. Danny felt the man's hand on his waist, and they struggled over the gun. He managed to get a knee between them and pushed the man off of him. When he looked up the man was standing over him with the gun trained on him.

"Don't move, motherfucker." Breathing hard, the man backed up to the patio door and made three hard raps. "All right, on your knees. That's it. Now, crawl over here." When the door slid open, the man backed through it. "Come on, motherfucker, keep crawling. Don't make me shoot yo' ass."

"Malcolm!" Both women screamed his name.

Malcolm turned and looked at them, "Aunt Bet?" He frowned in confusion. "What are you doing here?"

In that moment of distraction, Danny leaped for him. Malcolm kicked him in the chest and wrested his foot away, backing further in the room.

"Come on, motherfucker. Sit in that chair."

"Put the gun down, Malcolm! He's my friend!" She started toward him.

"Your friend?" His confusion deepened. He shouted, "Stay there, Aunt Bet!"

"He won't hurt you, Malcolm. Put the gun down."

"He already hurt me," he said, rubbing the abraded skin on his arm. "Mimi! Go upstairs. Look in the kitchen. Bring me some tape, some rope, anything."

"What are you going to do, Malcolm?" MaryBeth asked.

"I'm going to tie him up. I ain't gonna shoot him unless he makes me. I'm not going back, Aunt Bet. I ain't gonna be locked up. I didn't kill nobody. Me and Mimi are gonna take that bike and head for New York."

MaryBeth saw the desperation on his face.

"That's ridiculous, Malcolm. This girl says she's pregnant. She can't travel on that bike."

"It's all we got. Her car broke down about a mile down the road. I couldn't fix it. We got to get outta here."

"If you do this, your mother's gonna lose her house."

"We can't go back. Mimi's family will disown her. They hate black people. They hate me. And they don't even know me. Something to do with a stupid ol' war before she was even born. Some black soldier got her aunt pregnant. It's stupid. I haven't done nothing to them. I love her."

"And what about your mother's house?"

"My father can figure something out. He's a smart lawyer," he said, his lips curled in disdain.

"Danny will help you, won't you Danny? We can take you back. We can say you were with us, can't we, Danny?"

"Make him put the gun down, MaryBeth. Then we'll talk." Danny's eyes were fixed on Malcolm, looking for an opening.

"I've known this child all his life, Danny. He's not a killer. Can't you see he's just young and scared. He's not dangerous."

"He has a gun pointed at my head."

"Will you help us, Miss?"

MaryBeth turned to Mimi, standing in the doorway. Her frightened look made her appear small and childlike. Too young to be carrying a child of her own.

"I know you."

At the sound of his voice, MaryBeth turned back to Danny.

"You're the girl whose ol' man got popped in that Dowling street robbery," he said.

"He didn't kill my father."

"Shut up, Mimi," Malcolm warned.

"He didn't kill my father. They did."

"Shut up, girl! He's a cop! He's one of the cops who questioned me."

"They, who?" Danny pressed.

"The men who come to take our money. The Russian men."

"So it was a robbery."

"Not a robbery. If we don't pay them a share, they break things in the store. They threaten to hurt the women. They do this to all of our stores. The nail shops. They come every Saturday night, when the stores close."

"You know them, don't you Mimi?" Danny pressed. "The one with the scar. Segeyev. He's one of them, isn't he?"

She nodded slowly. "They warned us what would happen. My father called the men of the association together. He wanted to fight back. Some wanted to join him, but there is so much fear. My father, my uncle, and my cousin. They refused to pay."

"So they killed your father."

Mimi started to cry. "And then my uncle. I talked him into going to the police. But he said the police wouldn't help. That they were in on it."

"So you were just going to let your boyfriend fry for this?"

"We didn't know what to do. You see what they did to my uncle. We are going to go away. To someplace they can't find us. To someplace we don't have to sneak around to be together. We have been sneaking around, hiding from my family for almost a year. With the baby coming, we couldn't hide much longer. That night my father was killed, we were going to tell them. Malcolm was coming to the store and we were going to tell them."

Danny's mind started clicking. Malcolm's story was beginning to make sense. His prints all over the gun, but none on the trigger. The bullets with other fingerprints on them. The car rented to the Russian. The tall white man. He turned to Malcolm with a look of disgust.

"So this is your plan? To run away?" Danny threw up his hands and rolled his eyes. "You think you can outrun a computer? It's scary to think somebody dumb as you can be a father. And the one person who believed in you, you're just gonna run away and let her lose her home? You ought to be ashamed. You need to grow up. Why didn't you tell us? Or your lawyer, at least?"

"I told the truth. I told everybody who would listen. Nobody believed me. Not that lawyer lady. Not even my own mama. I didn't know about the shake-down operation until I got out of jail. When they shot her uncle two weeks later was when she told me about it. Y'all thought I did it. Y'all were looking for me. They were looking for me. If the cops found me, I'd end up in prison for life. If them dudes found me, I'd be dead. I wasn't going out like that."

"I've got to go," Danny said, standing.

"Sit down!" Malcolm brought the gun to full attention

Ignoring Malcom, Danny walked to the dresser, raked his fingers through his hair, and straightened his clothes. He walked back to MaryBeth and planted a kiss on her cheek.

"MaryBeth, you stay here with them. Don't let him leave. I'll come back for all of you." Then he turned to Malcolm.

Malcolm backed up a step, his eyes wary, still firmly holding the gun. Danny rolled his eyes, then held out his hand.

"If there's any hope of you getting out of this, I'm gonna need that gun."

NINETEEN

The sun was coming up when Danny hit the Houston city limits. He drove straight to the rundown house on the seedy side of downtown. He eased up to the side of the house, every muscle in his body tense. When he peeked in the bedroom window, the place looked deserted. The closet door stood open, revealing only a few hangers. The bed was stripped. Vodka bottles and trash were strewn about on the floor.

"They moved."

Danny jerked around, his hand on his weapon. He saw Mr. Wilkov leaning on a hoe.

"Good riddance, I say. Nothing but trouble." He shook his head. "This used to be such a nice neighborhood. Now, nothing but riffraff. Those two were the worst. Drinking and rowdy. No class. Dreck. Making noise all times of the night. Disturbing the whole house. My other tenants were threatening to move."

"Where did they go?"

"Who knows? Who cares?"

"When?"

"Couple of days ago."

"Could I look in the room?"

"I don't care. Clean it up while you're in there, if you want. I'm an old man. I'm tired. Too tired to—"

Danny was already on the porch.

In the room he found envelopes from the INS addressed to Segeyev. He opened a drawer and found bullets. He was looking around the room for something to pick them up with when he heard Maxwell's voice in his head.

"Do it right. Impatience loses cases. When in doubt, get a warrant."

He had consent from the landlord. That should be enough. But what if it wasn't? Danny looked at his watch. No judge would be in this early. By the time he got to the station and typed up an affidavit for a search warrant, maybe one of them would have meandered in. He closed the drawer.

On his way out, Danny called out to Wilkov.

"Don't go in that room. Don't touch a thing. That's an official police order. I'll be back."

Danny roared off on his bike.

"Order, smorder," the old man muttered under his breath, as he turned back to his scraggly flower bed.

*   *   *

Danny's fingers flew over the keyboard, typing the affidavit. Intermittently, he dialed Maxwell's pager, then the judge's office. Maxwell hadn't called him back—even though he'd added their code red at the end of his number. The judge's receptionist was clearly getting irked by his calls. As the pages came off the printer, he opened his drawer for a stapler. There was his own pager where he'd left it before his trip. Maybe that's why Max hadn't returned his pages. Maybe he'd taken his pager off for his trip, too. He dialed Maxwell's home phone and left a message.

Danny toyed with the idea of getting approval for his plan. Since he couldn't reach Lieutenant Maxwell, Captain Holt was next up the chain of command. But what if Captain Holt wouldn't authorize it? This was Saturday. If it wasn't tonight, he'd have to wait another week. And another man could lose his life in that time. Danny would not have that on his conscience, no matter what the captain said. Surely he could convince him. But what if he couldn't? He placed the two calls again.

★   ★   ★

Danny stood at the captain's door, still toying with the idea of just going ahead with his plan. Better to have to say "I'm sorry" than being denied permission and then punished for insubordination. He rapped on the door.

"Come in," the captain growled.

Danny pushed the door open, nodded to Captain Holt, and stood in front of his desk.

"O'Connor. What do you want?" An impatient look settled on the captain's face before his eyes went back to the papers on his desk.

"I need authorization for a stakeout."

The captain looked up at him, and pushed his eyeglasses on top of his balding head.

"Chain of command is through your lieutenant. Where's Maxwell anyway?"

"He's off today."

"Yeah, well, so am I, but I'm here. Ask him Monday."

"It can't wait 'til Monday, captain."

"Well, call him at home. I need to talk to him anyway. I'm taking both of you off the Roberts case. Giving it to another team."

"Why?" Danny's eyes jerked open in surprise.

"I've been hearing rumors. Rumors I don't like. If they're true, I'm gonna have his ass. And yours too, O'Connor. I want you both in here, first thing Monday morning."

"I'll tell the lieutenant you want to see him."

"Both of you, O'Connor. In my office. First thing."

Danny backed out the door in a hurry. The captain hadn't exactly said no. He knew then what he was going to do. Fuck procedure.

*   *   *

Danny stood in front of his dresser, his own angry face staring back at him from the mirror as he loaded the bullets in his gun. He knew what Maxwell would say. "Go through proper channels. Follow procedure." But he'd tried that and it hadn't worked. He didn't need some prick sitting behind a desk playing politics all day, telling him how to do his job out on the streets. Guys like him and Maxwell were risking their lives everyday out there where the rubber meets the road. And it really burned him that the judge turned down his search warrant. While that pompous fat ass was pondering the niceties of probable cause from the safety of his desk, a man could lose his life. He put the last bullet in the clip. He already had loaded his .357 with Black Talon bullets. He fastened the thick vest around himself and pulled the loose black shirt down to cover it. Then he strapped on the belt with the extra ammo. He pulled his pant leg up and fastened on the ankle holster, then slid the smaller gun into it. The extra weight felt good when he shook his leg to straighten his pants. Since he expected two, he grabbed an extra set of handcuffs. What else? Pepper spray and, finally, the shoulder holster. Now he was ready.

As the wind blew through his hair and the roar of the motor droned in his ear, there was a determined look on his face. Maxwell would caution him against going into this situation alone. But he worked best alone. Maxwell would advise him to get a team. There was no one else he wanted on his team, except Maxwell. No one else he trusted with his back. Maxwell would advise him to devise a plan, to construct scenarios, to prepare contingencies. "Plan your work, then work your plan." Sometimes, you just have to play the cards as they're dealt. That was Danny's plan.

*　　　*　　　*

Maxwell parked the RV a block over. He didn't like the idea of leaving Audrey alone in this neighborhood, and especially at this time of night. But if his hunch was right, time was of the essence. Audrey looked worried, as she had since Sondra's call, but she didn't appear fearful. He didn't plan to be gone long. He checked the door to be sure it was locked, then walked down the alley.

*　　　*　　　*

The streetlight at the end of the block provided the only illumination. Audrey sat in the darkened motor home watching Maxwell walk away and praying that nothing happened to him. She hadn't thought about the danger of his job before. Just when she had found real happiness, she had to worry about losing him. What had she done to deserve this roller-coaster life—up one day, cast to the depths of despair the next. Why did it seem that just when everything was going to work out for her, it all went to shit? She'd always tried to live right, to treat other people right. She'd even given Sam the building. Maybe it was the happiness that had come to her life that made her relent. Maybe she was just being a fool. But the divorce was final now, and she was glad she'd given him the building. It seemed fair to her, and her conscience was clear. When MaryBeth called with the news about Malcolm, she had been ecstatic. Then Maxwell told her what he was going to do.

Now she sat in the dark RV, alone, wringing her hands and watching the street.

*　　　*　　　*

When Maxwell got to the end of the alley, he stopped and looked up and down the street. Not much to see. Not a soul in sight, except a man sitting in a car. Maxwell crossed the street and sauntered past the store to the end of the block with his hands shoved deep in his pockets. He saw all he needed to see. Through the car window, open to the hot and muggy night, he got a good look at the man's profile.

Halfway back down the block, Maxwell crossed the narrow street, walked straight to the car, and punched the man in the mouth through the open window. He felt bones yielding under the force of his fist. He jerked the door open, dragged the man to the ground, and cuffed his unbandaged hands to the car door. He left him face-down on the pavement. Then he took the keys out of the ignition and put them in his pocket.

*　　*　　*

Danny hated stakeouts. All the waiting nearly killed him. Usually he had someone to talk to to pass the time. The little man's jacket was way too small, but he was glad to have it. It was cold as shit in the refrigerated room behind the coolers, but it provided the best view of the entire store. He couldn't just walk around the store pretending to be a customer. They wouldn't make their move with a customer present. Plus, it would be a dead giveaway, since the front door was locked at 10 P.M. and customers had to use the walk-up window. He hoped Phong would remember the signal. Shivering, he looked at his watch—12:10. The other shootings had been around midnight. He hoped like hell he had picked the right store. The girl had said this cousin was the one who'd refused to pay the protection money. If they didn't come, he would never tell Maxwell that he'd sat in this damned cooler two hours for nothing.

Danny tensed when he heard the can drop on the floor. The signal. Then he heard the lock being turned. Two men came in, both wearing long black trench coats. The second one locked the door behind him. Phong was on cue, moving behind the counter, just as Danny had instructed. Danny recognized the scar-faced Segeyev from his mug shot but couldn't see the other one's face.

"What you want?" Phong asked.

Right by the plan, Danny thought.

"You know what we want, you little gook. Five hundred dollars. And make it quick."

He'd heard enough to testify. Danny eased to the door of the cooler.

"I not give you my money. I work hard for this money."

Oh shit! Phong was off the script. He'd told him to give up the money. That way, nobody would get hurt.

"Say Frank, this little gook says he ain't gonna pay. Should I shoot him now? Or give him another chance?" Segeyev's gun was pointed at Phong's head.

Danny knew time had run out. He had to act now. He jumped into the aisle, both hands on his gun.

"Drop the gun! Police!"

Both of them turned to him and Danny recognized the tall, pale white man. Danny's eyes met Yudov's just as the ball of fire hit him.

Danny lay sprawled on his back, writhing from the pain that roared through his chest. He knew if he could feel pain, he was alive. That was a good sign. The shadow of a man standing over him with a gun was not. He couldn't force his eyes to focus, but Danny knew who the man was. He felt real terror for the first time in his life.

"You can't get away, Yudov," Danny said, every word a stabbing pain in his chest. "Cut your losses now. Aggravated assault," he coughed. "Say he did it." Danny rolled his eyes toward Segeyev.

"My cousin? Why would I turn on my dear cousin from the old country like that? We've got a good thing going here. Gook money's financing our organization. You know, O'Connor, you could have made something of yourself. If you had gone with me way back when, you could have been accepted by the real police.

The ones who count. Certain people high up in the department would have noticed you. Smart guy like you could have gone places. You could have even gotten invited to the compound in Idaho. But you took up with the wetbacks first. Then the niggers. What did it get you? Look at you now."

Danny could see his gun on the floor behind Yudov, but there was no hope of him reaching it, even in a "Lord have mercy" play.

"I got backup." Danny could hear the desperation in his own voice.

"Yeah, I can see," Yudov said with a sneer. "Where's your big, black Sambo when you need him, O'Connor?"

"He's coming."

"Late. Always late. That's the way they are. You can't count on 'em, O'Connor. Too bad for you."

Then the door exploded and glass showered into the room.

*   *   *

"You 'bout a lucky fool," Maxwell said, looking down at Danny on the hospital bed. "If you hadn't had on that vest, you'd be a goner. Whatever gave you the notion to take them on by yourself? Procedure calls for you to—"

"I knew you had my back." Danny gave his quirky grin, then winced from the pain in his chest.

"You knew no such of a thing. If MaryBeth hadn't called Audrey, you'd be a dead duck now, instead of laying up here with a couple of cracked ribs."

"Did I hear Ockletree say you killed Yudov?"

"Naw. Bastard ain't worth killing. Got him in the arm. He'll live—at least until he gets to Huntsville. I 'magine the brothas down there will give him a nice warm welcome. Him and his cousins, too."

Danny looked pleased, then he frowned.

"Guess that means desk duty for you for a while, huh?"

"Probably. Regulations say anytime there's an officer shooting, that officer will be—"

"They oughta give you a medal."

"Doesn't matter. I'm going to retire as soon as I'm cleared."

"Sure, boss. Whatever you say." Danny crimped his mouth, then closed his eyes, exhausted. His breathing was quick and shallow.

Maxwell just smiled. Whether Danny believed him or not, he knew what he was going to do. The first thing would be filling out the retirement papers he had picked up at Personnel last week. Then he would use his time on the desk to close out his cases. Then, he was going shopping for an RV.

"You know, I had figured out it wasn't the Roberts boy," Danny said, with his eyes still closed.

"Yeah, right, Danny."

"I did. It was that clean trigger. There should have been prints on it."

"Sure Danny. Whatever you say."

"No kidding. And the blood didn't match his."

"Okay, Danny."

"That little punk couldn't kill anybody, anyway. Got a pretty good right hook, though. Ms. Williams was right all along. Tell her that for me, will ya'?"

"Shut up, Danny. You're supposed to be resting now. You can tell her yourself later. She'll be up here after a while."

Danny opened his eyes. "Say, Max. I need you to do me a favor."

"Anything Danny Boy. You name it."

"They say I won't be outta here for a couple of days. I need you to drive to Shreveport and pick up my woman for me."

"Your woman?" Maxwell asked, with raised eyebrows in amusement.

"MaryBeth. I left her there with the Roberts boy."

Maxwell gave him a rueful look. "Sorry, Danny. Can't do that."

"Why not? I promised her I'd come back."

"She's not the kind of woman you can tell what to do. She rented a car and is on her way here now. I keep telling you, you're outta your league, grandbaby."

Once the sun had passed the west rim of the canyon over-head, the temperature began to drop. Even in late August, it wouldn't be long before jackets would be required. Audrey's eyes were glued to the window and the panoramic view of Zion Canyon below them. The road zigzagged back and forth, descending into the canyon.

"It's even more beautiful than the pictures," she exclaimed. "Cedric, can you see?"

"There's a river down there," he said, with his forehead pressed against the window over the couch.

"That's how canyons are made, Cedric. Running water. Running for a thousand years."

"Are we going down there?"

"We sure are. All the way to the bottom. We can even put our feet in that river."

On the last pass before they reached the floor of the canyon, Audrey peered hard out the window.

"Looks like some black folk over there," she said.

"Are you sure?" Maxwell asked. "Way out here? I doubt it."

"I'm pretty sure. I don't believe I've seen any of us since we left

New Mexico. I hope we park near them. I wonder where they're from?"

"What about those people from Los Angeles we met at the Grand Canyon?" Cedric broke in.

"You're right, Cedric." Audrey turned to Maxwell and corrected herself. "Arizona."

Maxwell pulled in front of the park headquarters and shut the motor off.

"Come on, Cedric." As he climbed down from the driver's seat, he gave Audrey a sly grin. "If there are any black folk here, I'll bet they'll put us right next to them."

"Quit being so paranoid. This is a government park."

*   *   *

"Daddy, you said the other little boy was coming today," the boy whined, tugging at his father's sleeve.

"They'll be here today," the father said, looking up from the book he was reading. "Why don't you go play with your sisters until they get here."

"I'm tired of playing with them. They're girls. And they're just babies. They're taking their naps, anyway."

"Well, maybe you'd like to take a nap, too."

"I'm a big boy, Daddy. I don't take naps anymore."

"Then go see if the ladies need some help. You know they're fixing a big dinner."

"Say, Corey," Ike called out from his seat at the picnic table. "Why don't you come over here and give me a hand?"

"What you need, Mr. Ike?" Corey asked, intrigued by the array of fishing tackle on the table.

"This morning I was down by the river, and I saw this great, big fish. Thought I'd catch him for the big dinner. Except I can't decide which one of these things he'd like."

Corey climbed up on the table and looked over the offerings.

"This one," he said, pointing to the silver, metal teardrop with blue feathers. "This one'll get him."

"You reckon?"

"Sure. This is the prettiest one." Corey grabbed the lure. "Ouch!" He stuck his thumb in his mouth. "There's a hook in those feathers!"

"Sure there is. What? You thought that big fish was just gonna grab onto those feathers with his lips and hold on tight while we reeled him in?" Ike chuckled. "Nobody ever taught you to fish?"

Corey shook his head, still holding his thumb in his mouth.

"Come on. I'll teach you. In fact, we'll have a contest. You get that lure—and watch out for the hook. I'll use this red one here. I'll bring the rods, you bring the tackle box."

*   *   *

When Maxwell and Cedric came back to the RV, they were both grinning like the cat who ate the canary. Maxwell pulled the rig into their assigned spot and killed the motor.

"The men will do the hooking up. Right, Cedric? Why don't you put on something pretty, Audrey. Then we'll take you for a walk. We've got a surprise for you. Right, Cedric?" Maxwell said, nudging Cedric with his elbow.

"A surprise?" Audrey asked. "And I've got to change clothes? What's wrong with the clothes I have on?"

"What about that dress Max got you in Santa Fe?" Cedric asked, barely suppressing an excited grin.

"The leather dress?"

"Yeah, the Indian princess dress. The one with all those beads on it. It looks real pretty on you, Ms. Williams."

Audrey didn't trust the angelic look on the little imp's face.

"We can pretend we rode our ponies from Mesa Verde and found this canyon," he said with the same impish smile. "And I could put on my headdress with the feathers."

Audrey knew it was just a ruse to wear the headdress Maxwell had bought him. He'd been dying to take it out of the long, flat box. Maxwell insisted he save the elaborate, feathered headdress until he got home, but had let him have the tom-tom drum and the flute. Cedric had beat that tom-tom drum for fifty miles before she'd taken it from him and read him stories about the Hopi and Anasazi from the books they'd bought at Mesa Verde National Park. She looked from Cedric to Maxwell. He wore an expectant look.

"Okay, okay," she conceded. "But you have to wear yours, too."

He nodded, then he and Cedric went outside to hook up.

★　　　★　　　★

Their space was next to the RV where she thought she'd seen the black people, but no one was in sight now. The leather dress felt soft as butter against her skin, and the beaded fringe tickled her knees. She even put on the matching moccasins. Audrey pushed the door to the RV open and stood taking in the grandeur of Zion Canyon. It was everything she had imagined—and more. The majestic red walls rose on both sides of them. She could see the river from the doorway.

Wearing the three-feather headband and a silly smile on his face, Maxwell reached out for her hand to help her step down.

"You look beautiful in that dress. I don't know about an Indian princess, but you're my princess." He pulled her close and looked down into her eyes. "Are you happy, now that you're here?"

"Couldn't be happier," Audrey said, glowing. She raised on her toes to kiss his cheek.

"So, can I take off this feather thing now?"

She smiled and shook her head. "You wouldn't want to disappoint Cedric."

He crooked his arm and she laced hers through it.

"Come on, Cedric. We're going for our walk now," Maxwell called out.

Cedric appeared in the doorway. When he stepped down, the bright colored headdress almost reached the ground. The tom-tom drum was strapped over his shoulder, and the wooden flute was tucked in his pocket.

"I'll lead the way," he said, and began beating a steady, slow beat on the drum.

"You're going to disturb the other campers with that drum," Audrey said. "If you just have to make some noise, play your flute."

Cedric looked at Maxwell for approval to change their plan, then stuck the drumstick in his pocket. He took the flute out and began to blow on it, emitting shrill, screeching sounds.

"Jesus, he's gonna run all the ducks off with that thing," Audrey said, under her breath to Maxwell.

As they passed the RV in the neighboring campsite, Audrey commented that the license plate was from Texas. When they got to the next one and it had a Texas license too, she said, "There goes the neighborhood."

When they passed it, a group of people yelled, "Surprise!"

Audrey's eyes bulged and her mouth dropped open. Sondra stood with her arm around her Ike's waist. Audrey recognized him from the picture Sondra had shown her of their wedding. Two of the prettiest little girls. A tall man she didn't know, and a boy about Cedric's size.

Before Audrey could say a word, the door to the RV opened and a woman stepped out. She and Audrey stared at each other a long time. The woman wore a hesitant smile. Audrey pressed her lips together as hard as she could, but no power of earth could have kept the tears of joy from her eyes. She and Vivian hugged each other for so long, Sondra tried to break them up. But her effort only turned into a group hug. Marc had his camera ready and snapped a picture.

Maxwell introduced himself and Cedric, shaking the men's

hands. Since it appeared the women would be occupied for a while, the men sat down to get acquainted. Ike passed a cup and a bottle of brandy to Maxwell. The two pretty little girls crawled up in Marc's lap. Corey took Cedric behind the RV to show him the fish he'd caught and was keeping in a bucket. Maxwell took the fancy headdress from Cedric before he and Corey ran down to the river to chase the ducks. The women finally broke from their embrace and giggled their way into the motor home to catch up. After a while they came out, bringing the utensils, dishes, and a tablecloth.

In the quiet of the canyon, their attention was drawn to a distant rumble that grew into a roar. They watched a motorcycle zigzagging down into the canyon. Then it pulled into their campsite and stopped. Both riders wore black leather pants and matching fringed jackets. The driver put the kickstand down and pulled off his helmet.

"Well, I'll be damned," Maxwell said. "What the hell are you doing here? I thought you were going to California."

"We are, but we didn't want to miss the party," Danny said with a grin. "We've been following you all day, old man. You're really getting rusty."

"We didn't miss the shindig, did we?" MaryBeth asked as she pulled off her helmet and shook her hair out.

"You're just in time," Audrey said, hugging her. She held Mary-Beth at arm's length. "You could have told me about this, you know."

"I would have, Audrey, I swear," she said, very seriously. "But a gun-toting cop threatened to shoot me if I told."

"Liar. I love you anyway. Come on, meet my friends. You can help us with dinner."

The day took on a festive air, as a kente tablecloth was spread over the picnic table. Pretty soon food was piled high from end to end. There were briskets Marc had brought from Noel's Catering, a big platter of steaming corn on the cob slathered in butter, and a huge pot of beans that Ike had cooked all day on a tripod over the campfire. Sondra and Vivian had made mashed potatoes, cole slaw, and several breads and desserts.

When all was ready, Marc asked everyone to join hands around the table and give sentence prayers. He led with: "Lord, I thank You for the blessings You have bestowed on me through my family—my wife, Vivian, my son, Corey, and my two beautiful daughters, Passion and Joy."

Vivian was next. "Thank You, Lord, for answering my prayers and reuniting me with my friend." Passion, with her grown self, said hers—then another one for baby Joy, "since she can't talk good like me yet." Cedric was thankful for his fancy headdress and for Maxwell being his "almost daddy." Corey gave thanks for catching the fish and promised to release it from the bucket back into the river tomorrow, since it wasn't quite big enough for everybody to eat. Ike, Sondra, Danny, and MaryBeth followed, in that order. Maxwell and Audrey were last.

"Lord, you know I ain't much of a praying man," he began. "But I do want to thank You for sending me an angel to bring joy back into my life. And for Cedric, and for watching over him. Heal his mama, Lord. And touch that judge's heart. And Kirk Jr.'s heart too, while You at it. I thank You for giving me my good health and clothing me in my right mind. And then, for letting me live to see Your wondrous works on this trip. Then, Lord, I want to ask You to look after Danny Boy. He's really gonna need You, now that I've re-tired. And—"

Maxwell felt the sharp poke in his side from Audrey's elbow, and realized he'd gotten carried away, all the way back to his daddy's church in Ruston, Louisiana.

". . . and for these new friends. Amen."

Then it was Audrey's turn. She tried to think of a one-sentence prayer, but she had so much to be thankful for it couldn't all fit into one sentence. Her job, Malcolm's freedom, her expected grand-baby, her reunion with Vivian—and this sweet, thoughtful man who had brought it about. Tears welled up in her eyes and she fought them so hard, she couldn't speak. There was a long silence. Maxwell put his arm around her shoulder to encourage her. Finally, he spoke.

"I'll speak for her. Lord, You know what's on her heart, so she don't have to say it. Amen."

They all echoed Amen, and sat down to a noisy and jubilant feast.

*   *   *

After dinner, after the sun set, a cool wind blew through the canyon. The children were put to bed. Vivian insisted that Cedric stay with them in their motor home so that "Maxwell and Audrey could have a little privacy," she said with a wink to Audrey.

A crackling campfire staved off the chill of the canyon night, as the grownups sat around it in lawn chairs solving the problems of the world. Finally, Vivian announced she was going to bed. "Those girls will have me up at the crack of dawn."

Even though Danny and MaryBeth had brought bedrolls, Son-dra insisted they sleep inside with her and Ike.

Then they were alone. Maxwell held Audrey's hand as they walked down to the river and along its bank. The night was quiet except for the sounds of rushing water and the wind whispering through the trees. Audrey stopped and turned to him.

"Do you remember the first thing you ever said to me?"

He shook his head, then smiled. "Hi, gorgeous?"

"No. You said, 'I'll fix it for you.'"

A crooked smile came to his face. "Well, didn't I?"

"Everything but the tire," she said, a smile playing on her lips.

"Well, I'll just have to fix a tire for you one of these days. We've got all the time in the world now."

Maxwell pulled her into his arms and kissed her slowly, with only the big moon and a million twinkling stars watching.

Dear Reader Friend,

Isn't this a great time to be a reader! There are so many wonderful books on the shelves now—something for every taste. Some of you, like me, can remember when the array was not so broad. I am thankful that I have so many books to choose from—and honored that you chose mine.

Of course, I'm writing another "marvelously mature" romance. I need your help. If you have a couple of extra minutes, I'd appreciate it if you would answer the survey questions below. When I read, I always form a picture of the character in my mind. I didn't describe Audrey so that you could form your own picture of her. I'd like to know what she looked like to you. Send your responses to:

Evelyn Palfrey
P.O. Box 142495
Austin, TX 78714
or evelyn@evelynpalfrey.com

If you're interested, I'll tell you what she looked like to me.

Thanks a bunch,
Evelyn

1. Did you notice the lack of physical description?
2. Did it bother you?
3. Were you able to "see" Audrey?
4. What did Audrey look like to you (coloring, height, weight, etc.)?
5. What is her dress size? (This one is for Vanessa.)
6. If you had been Audrey, would you have told MaryBeth or your children about Sam?